The Shadow

Neil M. Gunn

Whittles Publishing

Published by
Whittles Publishing Ltd.,
Dunbeath Mains Cottages,
Dunbeath,
Caithness, KW6 6EY,
Scotland, UK
www.whittlespublishing.com

Foreword © 2006 Dairmid Gunn

ISBN 1-870325-49-4

Printed by Bell & Bain Ltd., Glasgow

Foreword

Neil M Gunn, one of Scotland's most distinguished 20th century novelists, wrote over a period of thirty years, starting in the late 1920s with *The Grey Coast* and ending in 1956 with *The Atom of Delight,* a work that can be described as a spiritual autobiography. His period of creative writing spanned the Recession, the political crises of the 1930s and the Second World War and its aftermath. The word 'spiritual' is of immense importance when describing Gunn's work as his novels invariably depict two worlds—the world of here and now and that in which the meaning of life and the essence of living are explored.

Most of Gunn's novels are set and enacted in the Highlands of Scotland and the backdrop for *The Shadow*, published in 1948, is even more specific in terms of location there. The setting is undoubtedly based on that part of the Highlands where Gunn spent his most creative and productive years (1938–1949) in the hill country near the county town of Dingwall in Ross and Cromarty. Resemblances do not end with place; one of the most important characters in the novel, Aunt Phemie, is unmistakably a portrait of Gunn's wife, Daisy.

The Shadow has another significance; it is one of two novels, the other being an earlier book, *The Serpent*, in which some of Gunn's innermost feelings are indirectly revealed. During the years immediately prior to the publication of the book he was concerned and depressed by much of the literature of the time, which, in his view, concentrated too often on negative attitudes and violence, and a destructive analysis of the human spirit; it created an atmosphere of confusion and doubt. A challenge was there for Gunn to accept, and he met it in this enchanting novel through its female characters.

The Shadow is not what could be described as a 'war' book although it deals in depth with the causes and effects of war. The years preceding the war had seen the emergence of two totalitarian regimes, Soviet Russia and Nazi Germany; the latter perished with the Second World War, but the latter remained a protagonist in what was to be called 'the Cold War', and the idea of Marxism as a system still had its attraction in some circles for those who thought that it offered an opportunity to build a better world. The idea presented in a plausibly rational way by its adherents is a vital ingredient to the thought processes explored in this novel.

The Shadow reflects Gunn's fascination with antitheses, be they darkness and light, reason and emotion or destruction and creation. One of the two principal characters, Nan, a young Highland woman who had experienced the Blitz in London and been a member of an intellectual Marxist clique there, returns to her native country and her favourite aunt, Aunt Phemie, a widow and farmer, to recover from a nervous breakdown. The causes of her mental illness are progressively revealed in her erratic return to health. The names given to the three parts of the novel are related to Nan's condition. The first part,'Convalescence', takes the form of a monologue through letters written by Nan, but not necessarily sent, to her lover, Ranald, in London, a member of the clique she had deserted. The letters are both a paean to the wonders of nature and its healing effects and a searching analysis of herself including allusions to the hallucinations she is experiencing. The prose is complex, a mix of the sophisticated with literary allusions and the simple, expressed in a seemingly innocent way. The writing is clearly a form of release, a way of explaining her views and values without fear of contradiction, the inevitable contradiction that had blighted her thoughts and inner feelings in conversations in the clique. The letters are clearly affected by the unpleasant recollections of living in an amoral circle of people divorced from the traditional norms of social behaviour and obsessed by attaining through a rational approach the aim of building a new world order regardless of the suffering and cruelty that that process would necessitate; they are stimulated by the need to have a loved recipient always in mind to give shape to her thoughts for her own benefit, and for his. Her opening lines are joyous and full of thoughts of Ranald. 'I have discovered the world! Today, this very day in the hours that are past—just past, for I still hear them blowing in the wind, the softest loveliest wind with clouds coming up over the sky, and even as I write this, in the tail of my eye, just outside the small gable window, a long new branch of the climber—a white rose—not tied up, blows up and down. Oh, I wish I could tell you about it.' But there were dark clouds on the horizon, and Nan's movement towards recovery was interrupted by the news of the brutal murder of a local crofter; a shadow was cast over the landscape that had seemed to be a rural paradise. Nan was affected not only by the deed itself but also because the suspected murderer was a man suffering from a mental disorder caused by his military experiences in the First World War. Her condition was not helped by chance encounters with a local artist, Adam, whose ideas about nature differed so much from her own. There was a ruthless streak in him that revelled in the cruelties of animal life and placed man outside nature as a dominant force. Only Aunt Phemie as a beloved aunt, an educated woman of experience and a trusted confidante could provide the haven of peace she sought, but even her efforts could not prevent a serious relapse on the part of Nan.

The second part of the book, 'The Relapse', sees the appearance of Ranald, who has been asked by Aunt Phemie to visit Nan. The story is now in the third person and the focus moves from Nan to Ranald and Aunt Phemie. The dialogue between them takes up from where Nan ends her epistolary monologue and presents itself as a fencing match between the optimistic, sensitive and emotional outlook of the woman and the bleak materialism and harsh logic of the man. Ranald cannot but admire his interlocutor, who is not only a well-educated woman but also one who runs a farming business effectively and pleasantly. His blueprint for a more effectively organised world stands up weakly against her proven success in getting the best out of her farm and those who work on it. His ideas are rational, ruthless, and shown by history to lead to tyranny and unhappiness; hers are full of the warmth of a human and natural approach to life and have shown themselves to be successful in the small world of her farm. Although Aunt Phemie occasionally glimpses touches of humanity within the confident, self-assured and almost arrogant attitudes of Ranald, she finds him cold and remote and more of a personification of certain political ideas than someone fully responsive to the views and needs of his ill and distressed girl friend. A suppressed dislike is there. Ranald's departure after the beginning of Nan's recovery fills her with a sense of relief and the faint hope that Nan will perhaps abandon her intended return to London.

The final part of the book, 'The Recovery', brings the two women closely together again, and their relaxed and easy relationship is resumed. Aunt Phemie has still some investigative work to do regarding a serious fight between Ranald and the artist, Adam, which has been kept a secret by both men. In the process she gets to know Adam better and tries to understand his strange views on nature, in particular that of man's place relative to it. The idea of man's domination of an environment from which he is separated is at the heart of this thinking and dampens his ability to appreciate the subtleties of nature. When they are both looking with admiration at a beautiful view of a ravine and waterfall, she remarks, 'You can be part of this and still be yourself, only more full of intimacy, of love of it. You don't want to dominate it. That's the very mood that does *not* arise.' He is responsive to this, and there is a feeling that this is his first step back to spiritual health. Even earlier he pays her a compliment in the words, 'You have a gift of discreet silence.'

Aunt Phemie certainly has that gift and many other attributes natural to the female psyche. Her kindness, her courage and common sense—all loosely bound within the orbit of emotion—make her the anchor person in the novel. Her virtues are the antitheses of those of Ranald and Adam, who are victims of their own logic and theories. There is no doubt that Gunn had his wife, Daisy, in mind when Nan describes Aunt Phemie in her letter to Ranald, 'She is comfortably slim and though well over forty the gold in her hair hasn't faded. I suppose gold doesn't. She is a tirelessly energetic worker and yet can stand quite still.' It is little wonder that Gunn's inscription on his wife's copy of *The Shadow* should be, 'For one who chases the shadows away.'

This book, beautiful in its own right, leaves the reader with the question of whether the shadows have been truly swept away. It was written at a time when Marxism, or at least a debased form of that system, was seen as the great threat to the concept of democracy and the freedom and welfare of humanity. Today, it is terrorism, but not terrorism alone; in addition, in this era of 'post-modernism' there are distinct symptoms of a malaise at the heart of Western civilisation that takes many forms. The acquisitive nature of a society based on consumerism and individualism, the absence of a spiritual dimension in domestic affairs and the emphasis on rights without a concomitant emphasis on duty are but three of these. Allied to all this, there is a justifiable fear that the process of globalisation will denude the world of the immense contribution made by small communities to the happiness and spiritual health of mankind. *The Shadow* in this world of shadows maintains the strange relevance it had over fifty years ago and perhaps offers the reader a glimpse of hope.

DAIRMID GUNN

Part One

CONVALESCENCE

1

I have discovered the world! To-day, this very day, in the hours that are past—just past, for still I hear them blowing on the wind, the softest loveliest wind, with clouds coming up over the sky, and even as I write this, in the tail of my eye, just outside the small gable window, a long new branch of a climber—a white rose—not tied up, blows up and down. Oh, I wish I could tell you about it! I wish I could tell you, as I did tell you every step of the way. No, not every step. Oh dear, it's going, even as I write. It's going away. But it was lovely telling you. Am I incoherent? I can't help it and I don't care. Listen to me, Ranald. Oh, listen, listen! And forget all about my mental breakdown. Please. Though seeing the sly destructive ones called me neurotic, why shouldn't I be allowed some small licence in conjuring up hallucinations and all inconsequence? Anyway I'm taking it. Just as I should love to take the smile from your face as you read this, tear it off and throw it on the wind, and cry to it hurrah! as it sailed away with the storm of thistledown.

And what a storm! That's what started it. I was going up by the hollow between the two great fields. It's really a tiny ravine, with occasional elm trees growing out of it, gnarled and old. But I won't start on the trees just now. There's a thousand things I won't start on. And I hadn't much on myself. Anyway it felt as thin as the thistledown and was as white, including the legs and the canvas shoes, and the wind hardly noticed them in its way. Well, as I was saying about the thistledown. But first there was this field on my left. It's a great breast of a field and the up-slope

1

is fairly steep. Till now, I have found it very tiring. It's been a secret measure of my strength. I think the field knew this, for often I sat down on it. It's been a sort of game between us. The field never encouraged me once. But then it's an extraordinarily patient field. And it's big, not flat, but with the slow curve of the earth itself. Sometimes there are three brown horses in it, two of them young but no longer gawky, and one of the two with a grey face (whorls of grey, like thin lichen on a stone). The first time I came on them—at least they came on me—I was terribly frightened. I felt suddenly caught and they were enormous, and with their manes and their heads up, they stopped and stood there against the sky. *Wild horses*, I thought. Does that give you, far in, an uncanny feeling? For it's queer, isn't it, that if you say wild anything else—like *wild lions*—it's not the same? Wild lions would lie flat to the earth, their ears flat, their tails slowly twitching, and then spring. But in wild horses there is something *withholding*. Terrible and wild, not looking but *watching*. They are imminent, or is it immanent? I was always a little confused with these two words. Like that something which is always behind a real legend, or in it, or in a fairy story, the true fairy story—the kind that comes back. Can you remember that? Can you get a quick glimpse of a child face, a still face, listening with the eyes, but with a growing reserve, because it knows the something in the story as ominous, a wild gleam of peril? I can't see my own face like that—but I can see yours. A very good-looking child (were you?) with—already!—its hidden reserves, the certainty that it will take its own way—or have a way with it (if that's different)!

The involuntary chortle, please, made me forget what I was going to say about the horses. You always were a little surprised at the way in which I could forget the facts. You have always thought me a little bit scatter-brained. I know that. You really believe, deep inside, that I belong to the Party because you were in it before me. You're quite right, of course. Isn't it delightful? But you're not quite right, all the same. You see, you have the facts, the terrible economic facts, and you can produce them—you do—with inexorable and devastating power. (I tried these rolling adjectives on the field, but they rolled off it. It is so patient.) But I just feel it's splendid being in the Party, fighting for better things. And I know that's right. Deep in me, Ranald, I know. And I know it's glorious to be young, and fighting for what one believes, without thought of reward. The facts are absolutely necessary, all the statistics. When I have just read them and realised what they mean, they make me so angry that afterwards if I may not remember them *exactly*, I remember their gleam.

Then the young horse with the grey face came towards me, with movement of its head against an invisible bit, in pride and power, and its brown eyes shone, and its nostrils curled, and all the flesh melted on my bones and my skeleton shook at the knees. I think perhaps my skeleton rattled, for the beast stopped. As a small boy, my brother Archie had a hen's foot. He pulled a sinew in the leg and all the toes jerked. I squawked the first time it was done on me, and they roared with laughter. Well, this time the sinew was in me and something or someone pulled it, and every limb jerked, my arms flew up, and a surpassing discord proceeded from my lips. At once the wild horse threw its head aloft, reared against the sky, pivoted on its hind legs, and in a thunderous manner pounded back to its companions and once more formed into line above me, looking down from the sky.

Have you ever staggered against a roaring river? Neither have I, until then. But I reached the five-barred gate. It never occurred to me to try to open it. I just climbed over it and fell down on the other side. I won't say that I wept, and I won't say that I was nearly sick, but I will say it took a little time for the flesh to fall asleep on the bones, and for those awful heart-thumps, like thuds in an empty pump, to grow less and less and fall away into sleep, too. I had no idea the heart was so terrible and fierce an engine.

But you'll be tired of these horses (they're pets really, and Greyface eats now out of my hand) and I have forgotten what it was I was going to say about them. Probably it was a thought I had. But the awful thing about thoughts is that I am inclined to forget them, almost as if they were facts. Not that I mind. You can have no idea, for example, how interesting you are when you stop thinking. Oddly enough, when I think about it, you are interesting, too, on a soap-box, speaking facts, with the night and the dark crowd around. But perhaps also the facts then are not the most interesting thing about you. This is all so difficult that I can't work it out. And please don't ask me to—or criticise. I know all you're going to say. But I also know something else.

Didn't I tell you it was a patient field? You think I should tell a thing and be done with it. But the field doesn't think that. And it wouldn't think it if they put a dozen tractors on it at once this minute. Do you hate that sort of dumb patience? All right. I shan't speak of it any more. For of course we're in a hurry. We must go ahead at once, and man the barriers, and die fighting if need be. (Oh, Ran, how lovely life is!)

Well, there was the field, full of thick grass and myriads of thistles, and not a horse to be seen, only the wind. You could see the wind coming, like waves of the sea. Doesn't some poet make the folk dance like a wave of the sea? Yeats, wasn't it? Oh, yes, I remember—"The Fiddler of Dooney". *And dance like a wave of the sea.* But that, of course, must have been before Yeats took to Thought and became a real poet. It's me for the Fiddler of Dooney! (Oh, Ran! Ran! to dance like a wave of the sea!) I'll study poetry maybe when the dance is over. It will be a *compensation.* Isn't that the word the psychoanalysts use?

The wind came blowing across it from the west, from the mountains far away in conic sections blue against the utmost boundaries of the sky. And it came over pine forests that sometimes look black, swooping with a swish over lochs in the hollows of the low hills, and with a scurry across screes, and a rushing up glens, and here it was where the thistles grew in the old patient field. The thistles, too, were old and grey-headed. And they had been waiting for this wind—but oh, with so different a kind of patience.

Do you remember, as a little boy, how you ran out and held your hands up to the falling snow and shouted and ran, catching the flakes? Don't tell me you never did that.

The high wind caught the thistles, caught the thistledown

from the grey-heads, and from all across the field they came, thick as any snow shower, flying upon me and past me, soft round balls, eager, in a mad soundless hurry, myriads of them, filling the air. Never had I been caught in such a shower before, and it was exciting. Oh, it was the wildest, maddest fun. Somehow it never occurred to me to try to catch them. I just stood, my ears filled with the wind, and when I opened my mouth it filled, too. Have you ever been choked with a rushing warm wind when the sky is blue behind great sailing clouds? Warm, but with the tang of freshness, of fragrance, in it, that exhilarating scent of clover and the second growth of hay?

I tried to follow them—tiny balls of spun light—and at first I thought they were all being hurled into the little ravine, as indeed most of them were, but no sooner were they down than the up-eddy from the off side caught them and ho! there they were off again, off over the next field and lost to sight, each one of them hurrying to a new home of its own.

Yes, I know. It shouldn't have happened. The thistles ought all to have been cut long before to-day. This is very bad for agriculture. But they are desperately short-handed on the farm— that's the true reason—and only managed to cut a few.

But would it matter, please, if one here and there landed, say, in a ditch, or on a bit of waste land? Yes? I'm afraid some of them will, though. Oh, they will! I saw it in them, the eager lovely things, the rushing grey-white ghosts, lighter than any snowflakes, and so determined to be born.

I'm exhausted. Yet I had so much to say. For that was only the beginning of the discovery. I walked on and on. But now I can't write any more. As if all my strength—even my love—had departed with the thistledown. I'll write again tomorrow. Good-bye.

That lovely frenzy in which I wrote you yesterday is gone. Ah, it was going before I wrote. Sometimes you can make up things on the way, when you're writing, and that's delightful, but there's an experiencing of the thing itself, so swift, so inexpressible, that nothing ever can catch it and set it down.

Not ever. Oh, Ranald, it just can't. This page of paper is pale, like an empty face. All my images have pale faces. Perhaps I shouldn't have said empty. I don't know. For what happens when all is drained away?

Curious this seeing of things in images. For now, to-day, I see everything in images. They are remote a little and wait or walk quietly. Can you see their faces, with ghostly balls of thistledown for eyes? A faint smile is born somewhere at that last image, for I know it is a little literary. At least I think so. Yet I am not really sure. I wonder if there is an instinct in us to dramatise? Not only ourselves, but others and everything? And if it is really an instinct, there must be a need. And if a need— then drama is just as necessary as your economics. Do you think there may be the beginnings of a new theory somewhere there? I don't mean *quite* new, but yet with a direction to it?

Am I being awfully dull? You must forgive me. I know I overdid it yesterday. I was quite stiff this morning and two long muscles are still sore. The world inveigled me on and on. I couldn't stop. There was a frenzy in it. I wish I had that book of what's-his-name on the old Greeks. I know I'll read a certain dionysiac section of it now as never before. I have a sort of preliminary feeling of revelation!

Look, Ranald, we'll really have to have a talk about this sometime. Oh, I know how you detest the irrational, how it irritates you when people begin talking "ideals". The flash in your eyes when you turned on them and said: You drug yourselves with ideals. Ideal drug-addicts! I loved you at that moment. (And it not the only one, woe is me.)

But—that awful *but!* Please don't be in a hurry and stuff this in your pocket and say you'll read it again. Do you ever do that? You see, I am not sure.

I am not sure of anything to-day. Suddenly, in a moment, these two balls of thistledown have become eyes in a real face. I see them—and the face. Terrible! terrible!

Speak to me, Ran. All these ideas behind the slums and the loss of self-respect and wars and horrors—they are splendid. Yes, I know, they are consistent, too. They are real and scientific.

They are the truth. Not emotionalism. The only final truth on which a sane and healthy society can ever be built. Oh, I agree. It's splendid and comforting and full of hope. How I wish you were here, talking to me now. The very sound of you would drive that awful figure off and his eyes.

This is being morbid and I shouldn't be writing you at all. But I feel a bit lonely. Feelings can come quickly somehow. They get born out of nothing. And I *am* becoming stronger. I am really quite well. I feel health coming like something wonderful— almost like falling in love again!

That's better, isn't it? And, Ran! Ran! I have a sudden idea. You know how in our political philosophy everything finally is tested in practice. There can be no truth unless it stands the test of experience. Hurrah! Now what if I begin investigating this morbid condition of the individual who is left alone. You see what I mean? (Please keep your smile to cool your porridge, for if you think I'm thinking of you—I touch wood.) And when she is left alone she has morbid fancies. Now that's an experience. That's something you have never had, so I score over you there and can talk with authority thereanent.

For what is the next dialectical step? (Oh, dear, the sweat is coming out on me.) It's this. (I can't get the words! They won't form!) It's this. The individual by becoming too much the individual, by living too much for himself, loses touch with social relations and so goes morbid. The condition is unnatural and therefore unhealthy. Where individuals pursue each his (or her) individual way for his (or her) individual profit—the profit motive—then when you consider them in the group—that is, in society—they must arrive at a total condition which socially is unnatural and unhealthy. (I'm exhausted. The sweat has turned cold on my forehead and I can't find my hankie.)

Well, after all that labour I can see I have produced a very small and obvious mouse. But it's done me good. I never thought I'd enjoy playing with a mouse before. Don't you think he's rather a darling? These small dark eyes, quick and cute, and he's full of the most engaging ways. Ranald, he's stopped. He's gone quite still. He's swelling. He's turned into a rat!

There's a terrible number of rats about the farm. Thousands of them. Old Will, the first horseman, said the other day: War breeds rats. They're horrid brutes. We had a good laugh last night. A schoolboy, aged thirteen, was in, and we made him tell us the nicknames of all the teachers in the school. Will children ever change? Some of them were really amusing and one has stuck. The teacher's name is Mary McNutty. And they call her Bella Rats.

Why Bella? I asked. I don't know, he answered. For no reason in the world, I shake, but softly, with laughter.

Aren't you getting alarmed yet? Don't you think it's high time you took your four days off? Will I reassure you by saying that I am making up these images—or let me go all Freud and say my unconscious is doing it? For why? To draw you here, of course. Do you think the unconscious does things like that? Horrid of it, isn't it? I wish I knew.

Oh, Ranald, this is not the way I meant to write. I meant to take you with me the rest of that magic walk I went yesterday. But I can't to-day. Do you mind? I'm awfully tired. I feel like weeping. And a few tears have in very sooth downfallen. And I haven't my hankie. I'm sure some poet has said that tears are pearls. All the same, they're queer pearls. It would not be difficult to fall in love with them; anyway, to go to sleep with them. They're very wet. I'd like to be morbid again, but I don't want to overdo it. A woman has always got to be careful not to overdo anything. Perhaps that's why she does it so often. Overdoes the doing she shouldn't do, I mean. The tears are pearls because they are the quicksilver of life, and they run away, run down one's poor face.

I have just had, all in an instant, the smallest little twinge of malice. It entered me pop! It's this. Having grown afraid of feeling or emotion, we try to despise it. We look down our noses at it. (So many beaked noses I see! A whole forest of them in the air.) Emotion is so irrational, non-intellectual. Messy. Like an ingrowing toe-nail in a foot that could do with washing. Disgusting. It's subjective. Horrors! Sweep it away, away into the dustbin, and leave life cleansed and sweet as a schoolmaster's equation. We can then proceed to reform society, at least to get out of our present mess.

If I could draw really well, I'd put all an intellectual's intellectuality in his nose. It almost embarrasses me to add that you have a very distinguished nose. At the moment, mine (I have just had a look at it) is not very distinguished. Inward. That's what we think of emotion. But, oh, Ran! Ran! yesterday it was outward. Are you listening to me? It was outward. It raced over the moor. It raced over the sky. The clouds and the blue. Light. Sunlight. The sudden snipe from the bog. The lark. Life. It was life, pure lovely life, and the beating of the heart was the beating of wings. A beating and a singing. The passionate certainty that this was life, that we are stifling it, losing it. Oh, Ran! I told you! I cried to you!

I fall down after that effort. For I'll do anything, say anything, rather than look—at that figure. What made me use the word schoolmaster a little ago? Where has he come from? Who evoked him and gave him the right—to wait by my side with this merciless, appalling patience? He is about forty-five, tall, well-fleshed, straight. His hair is brushed flat, especially along the side of the head, past the ears. I know that, without having looked at him. My hand trembles. I can hardly write. Please, Ranald, forgive me these two blots on the paper. They prove I'm messy. I know. They don't look like pearls now. To think he is a creation of my own! From where? Where?

I'll have to look at him and get it over. For you know why I'm afraid to look. His awful eyes. I hang on to the pen. I keep on trying to move it, to make it go. I'm trying to speak quietly to you, Ranald. Each eyeball is a ball of thistledown. A grey ball of staring thistledown. I can see them, without looking. But I'll have to look. I'm going—to look—now——

In the wood there is a clearing, an open space like a fair-sized field. It is rather boggy, with tall grasses and tall wild flowers (pale purple scabious take over from rose-pink ragged robin). Also in the wood there is a mound, where the sunlight does not sleep but everywhere has its eyes open. You can't see those entrancing eyes. You see by them. The trees stand around and the bushes (juniper) squat lazily here and there. It's the quietest, loveliest place, full of goodness. Really, Ranald, it is. It's all health together and the young rabbits' ears are—I was going to say as pink as shells, but that would be silly for no shell can glow right through as these ears do. But to-day (that is, the day I got there after the storm of thistledown in the field below, for I'm still on that day. I must learn to be methodical) the wind was blowing as I told you, and the trees were dancing like waves of the sea. Throwing their arms about, tossing high their crests, and the sounds they made were the sounds of waves on a strand, but without the pounding beat. And it was warm and sheltered.

The buzzards had followed me. They were mewing, high up, one away to the right and one to the left—the parent birds. They were being ridiculously anxious about their young one. The young one had kept well behind and about midway between them. Like three far-separated kites they were, hanging on the wind. Now and then, as I approached the wood, the young one would fall away in a circle. Actually it did fall lower as it went with the wind, but immediately it came round into the wind it rose again. Once I heard it cry. I knew exactly what it was feeling and smiled. These enormous aerial spaces and the high wind were a little new to it. The mother, away on the right—I knew her by the tone of her voice—cried harshly, piercingly. But there was no need for her to be so anxious. She knew that, of course. She was teaching her offspring, warning it, pointing to the freedom of the sky. Old man father, far to the left, had a keen eye and would rather have sailed right off. But mother was full of bother, for she looked on these fields as her own, her home.

I left the mound and came down to the edge of the clearing in the wood. And then something happened that has stuck most vividly in my mind. It will sound ridiculous as I tell it to you, but you won't mind that. (I realise all in a heap how dreadful it would be if I could not tell you the silly things—the small change that buys the little extras with the groceries. But I shut my mind against that, and the bombed flat, and the awful black abyss of estrangement that opened between us, that valley of nightmare wherein I was broken. ... Ran, Ran, I keep telling myself they are no more.) I stepped out on the clearing and at once the boggy ground stung with its wetness. Drawing back, I stood as a small tree in front of the other trees, like a schoolgirl who had pushed her way through to the front of the audience. And the brightness of that open space was indeed like a stage where something was going to happen. I waited. Nothing happened—and the curtain came down in a rush! That's what happened. And it took my breath away, it was so completely realistic, the very perfection of a "quick curtain". It did take me a few moments to realise that one of the great, sailing clouds had crossed the sun! I wish you could have seen your own face laughing, as I saw it. It would have done you good. It did me a lot. Then up went the curtain just as quickly and the invisible play went on.

The brightness went with me. It ran before me on my own quick feet, while I walked slowly and—I hope—becomingly. Oh, Ran! the gift of such a moment between us, the lightness and brightness, and the swift-tumbling shadow-darkness of the curtains! For that shadow-darkness was itself as exciting and full of life as the light. Entrances and exits an' all. I do love you.

So at last I was on the moor. But I won't tell you about that. Too many things. I don't know how it is that I run on so. Things that I never noticed before—or hardly—have now a life of their own and are full of an exquisite significance. That last word is too, too heavy. Do you think it is because the final curtain so very nearly rang down on me—and so narrow a reprieve does something to the eyes? Anyway, it's done it! When you crashed— but I won't ask. I see you going through the future shadows of the world, crying *Never again!* Oh, I know why you go. I am with you. I am far from you at the moment. It is as if—I had come out on the other side. Please do not be impatient about that. For, Ran! Ran! I know—though I cannot tell you yet— what there *could* be on the other side. And I'm afraid, Ran, of those who think and *think only.* That's a foolish way to put it. We need efficiency, we need certainty, we need thought more than anything. Scientific analysis and construction. Yes, yes, yes. If only we could also keep our eyes real eyes. What happened when the schoolmaster with the thistledown eyes looked? Horror rose—and shook—and died, and what they looked on, withered.

Why had I to think of him again? Where did he come from? What does he mean? But I'm not going to be psychoanalysed. Not on your life! Simply a delusion or illusion of convalescence. You can even say I'm being hallucinated though I'd hate you if you did, not because it may not be true—what does that matter?—but because of an awful smugness in the voice of the analyst!

Now I've fought back to the moor again, to freedom. And oh, Ran!—this *will* annoy you—how awfully smug is our Party's definition of freedom as "the recognition of necessity"! But it's true? Of course! As true as true can be. But oh! with its philosophic highbrowism, how smug! Just plain smug. I know that will annoy you completely, even anger you a little, for haven't whole books, brilliant and earnest works, been written with this definition as the most marvellous all-round tin-opener of our wonder age? They have indeed. I bow—and glance through my long and, I hope, attractive lashes.

Lovely on the moor. Lovely, lovely. But I'll restrict myself, with the economy of the artist, to two pieces of attraction.

Again, I am happy to say, there was nothing in them. Entirely decorative. The first, a matter of colour and curiosity. It was what made me overdo it, for it lay beyond the moor stream, on the up-slope to the mountains. In such a waste land the colour was quite incredible. Exotic. The heather had not yet come into bloom, and upon its vast dun spaces was set down this one acre of glowing colour. You remember the tone of that yellow chartreuse when you held it against the light? That, then. So I took off my shoes and waded the stream, and on I went.

Nothing so marvellous as yellow chartreuse, of course! Only the tough hill grass burnt at the tops. Nothing more—except for the spikes, everywhere, rust-coloured rather than withered, of the golden bog asphodel. But when I took one blade of grass, what variety was there, from the fawn-coloured tip, that was the seed, through the brown, the mottled yellow and green, to the green! And I lay down flat in the midst thereof, and the wind blew.

I got back to the brook, and hung my harp on a salley bush, and did not want to go home. Some day I may tell you what a hill burn says. There are those who say that it tinkles, or even that it sings. But if you care to take it from me—it talks. Please don't think this is childish. Or—can you get this?—think of it as truly childish. Have you ever heard a child tell you a story it believes in, a strange story? Do you know that curious monotone that comes upon the voice, as if the voice itself and the eyes were far off where the story is happening—but careful, too, lest what was far comes near, and overhears, which would be terrible?

But I won't go on. We have, rightly, an awful horror of the grown-up childish. So we avoid it. I chuckle with laughter at the thought of our avoidances. I shake. And the voice of the burn isn't childish, even in the true way. But oh! it has a monotone. And where we go wrong—I suddenly saw this (it would be far truer to say it was revealed to me, for I did not try to see)—is in trying to personify what cannot be personified. If I were to say that the prehistoric mountain spoke out of this prehistoric burn in the voice of a child—how ridiculous! Saints and mystics may say something like that—that's why we don't understand them, even if, for some mysterious reason, we cannot forget them. Their real trouble, I see, is that there are no words for all this. So they make a story of it, a personification, and tell it to us, their children. Us, who know so very much more than they do, us the refugees wrinkled with an age older than the mountains!

Where are all these words coming from? Who is talking them? You know it can't be me. (There are long pauses, and such thrills somewhere, but I try to be restrained. I do my best—but it's difficult when in my vanity I see the rare glow—where? On your face? My pen, absolutely on its own, was going to underline "rare". Can this be spirit-writing? And how you spurned that! I sway.)

All the time the pool in the burn was waiting. It wasn't talking but only looking up at me, not with veiled, lidded eyes, but quite openly. Full of immense age, of course, but no satire. An immensely ancient ledge of grey rock, moor-brown pebbles, and floating foam-flecks from the throat. A pale heather-honey

brown in the water, a softness of warmth. The excitement began
to mount. I stood up, and everywhere there was nobody; far as
the eye could wander, not a soul. Off everything came. First one
foot, then another—I plunged and gasped and it's a wonder you
didn't hear me.

Such shuddering ecstasy! Then in a moment—the water was
warm. It was all about me and soft and warm. You wouldn't
believe it. Though remember it had taken all summer to make
it warm. *All summer.* (That's where you pause and the
enchantment comes.)

Not having wherewith to dry myself, I did a little dance on
the old rock, and then I sat on it.

You never sat on an old rock in a hill burn and let sun and
wind dry you?

There was a time, I think, when I lost consciousness, when
either I fell asleep or thinned away on sun and wind. Perhaps it
was only a second or two, but I have the feeling it was longer,
perhaps five minutes.

I came home hardly walking on my own feet. I must have
been terribly tired and weak. But I did not feel it that way. And
a glory came with me. It was in my skin. I smiled, it was so
friendly. My skin and the glory and all my eyes could see and
the eyes themselves and you. And something I learned will be
for ever with me. Come weal or woe, it will be there, heightening
or deepening, sunlight or shadow. Oh, Ran! I am shy suddenly
of saying outright what I want to say to you. I seem only to have
been saying it through everything in the world.

2

A terrible thing has happened. The old man who lived in the
cottage away round the shoulder of the hill has been murdered.
He lived all alone and some say he couldn't have had much
money because he was getting the Old Age Pension, but Will
here—the first horseman—who knew him said he wouldn't be
surprised if he had a good thing in his kist. His kist—a brown-
painted wooden chest—was smashed open with the axe which

still had the blood on it. I stood behind listening to Aunt Phemie
and Will going over all the details. I couldn't move. I saw the
kist and the white splinters. I tried not to see much else but it
was no use, because Will knew where the hacks and gashes were.
He put his hand up to his neck and then to his temples and
drew the gashes with a thick red-blue finger. He said it was clear
that old Farquhar had put up a bit of a fight. There was a notion,
he said, that the fellow (the murderer) must first of all have gone
in and asked Farquhar for money. Something like a smile came
to Will's face. I cannot describe it to you. He is well over sixty
and looks older and has been a farm worker all his life. The smile
that whin-roots make under the ground. In an instant I saw that
Farquhar was like that too, only older still, and for anyone to
demand money—money!—it was a joke so profound that the
smile could no more come up than the roots—or the money.
Farquhar would fairly have shown him the door then! said Will.
But I can't remember Will's words any more for they made me
see the fellow going out, the woodblock and the axe by the barn
door, the loneliness of the cottage, the quietness, the hand lifting
the axe, then back to the door. Farquhar barred the door inside.
The door is driven in by the axe. I began to see the theory, for
Will was very explicit at this point; he plays draughts with a lad
in the bothy; he was in no hurry, enjoying his moves. For why
would Farquhar have barred the door? Even if he had been in
bed he would have got up and opened it to anyone. He would
have opened to anyone at any hour, he always did, said Will.
And Farquhar must now have been expecting him, for the long
iron tongs ... Suddenly, before I could properly turn round, I
was sick. They had forgotten I was there. Aunt Phemie helped
me into the house for my legs gave under me. I got terribly cold.
When was in bed and she was leaving the room, I wanted to call
her back. I had to shut my teeth with all my strength. I longed
for everything to be blotted out. My wish grew so strong, my
teeth bit so strongly on Aunt Phemie's pillowcase, that my wish
was granted.

I am writing this to you, Ranald, quite calmly. That part of it
is past. And the horrible night I had. It was really very horrible.

There was a time when I thought I was going off my head for good. I think I must have gone off it for a bit because Aunt Phemie came in in her nightdress. I clung to her. But I was quite cunning. Isn't it extraordinary how deep the cunning root goes in us? I know I had been calling out but when I got a hold on myself as well as on Aunt Phemie I said it was a nightmare. She accepted that. Though as I write this I am not now quite so sure. For she was—well, at first she was kind but firm. Then she was firm and tender. Then somehow she was tenderness itself and I entered in there. But that is too feminine altogether to mention to you. Yet I wish I could, too, because, Ranald—oh, I haven't words for it. I entered a region. I was in that place where tenderness is. It is a country. Actually I was in Aunt Phemie's bed, and you will think that she was petting me, and for a grown woman of twenty-five solid years to be made a mother's darling again in that way is a bit too terrible if not positively indecent. I know, Ranald. Believe me, I am learning a lot—and particularly this: how awful a thing is man created in the image of the psychoanalyst. That's not said lightly. I didn't toy with Freud's great tome on *The Interpretation of Dreams* for nothing. And I am not saying anything against that or any other work of the kind, for I know how instinctively we react, try to get our own back, against what we feel is a degradation of the spirit, a defilement of the springing source or fountain of life. You see, I cannot use even these words without now being aware of their sexual symbolism. And I don't mind. I don't really, Ranald. Not any more. For there is a region in which they matter no more than (or as much as, if you like) any other old myth or legend. It's in that region I was with Aunt Phemie. I wandered there, and as she talked, telling me things out of her life, the tenderness was given form and shape as by a kind of irony which was beyond us but which we understood. I wish I could tell you how clear all this was, like an understanding of fate or destiny that was not hopeless though it was without hope—in the sense that we could never understand the meaning, the purpose, or the end. But it was there, as children are there, looked at by a woman's eyes.

But I mustn't go on like this or you'll be thinking I have

gone potty again, finally neurotic. Yet, seeing I am on the topic, I would like to mention two thoughts I had (next day, probably, when I was thinking about this, in order to keep myself from thinking about the murder). The first was that it is a pity all the psychoanalysts are men, all the famous ones. There should have been at least one famous woman pioneer. The second thought was that there shouldn't. Biologically speaking, woman is the creative partner. ("She bears the burden," said Aunt Phemie.) It is not her particular business to analyse, to tear the strands and bits apart. Once she started that, the very unnaturalness (biologically, again) of her attitude would make her a perfect demon at it. You know how Julie went with drugs.

My thought slipped there, Ranald. For I got very tired. I had a sudden awful longing to hand you the burden of myself. I am trying to be honest. I resent all this. I want the sun, the light, the light glistening on grass, on leaves; the wind that snares you with an eddy that you break out of with a laugh on your own dancing feet.

My head drooped there. I squirmed a bit. For I know how the girls of our set—the quite serious ones, too, like Winifred— would feel uncomfortable before such appalling naïvety. They would see me throwing an act. Nan's new act. Oh God, Ran, Ran, it's terrible! With the world as it is, it's terrifying.

I am writing all this in snatches, in little spurts. I may not send it to you, or not all of it. I'll see. I feel awfully lonely sometimes. Like a child. Like one that's never grown up. (And that immediately brought in Barrie. Just as a moment ago when I wrote about wanting the sun I thought of the young artist, going blind from his father's disease, crying to his mother for the sun in that play of Ibsen's. The free literary associations from our moderns! How ghastly! Will there be no end to it—until the ends of the world come upon us, soon?)

The hypersensitive condition of the convalescent! Of course. I know quite well. And if I'm going to get physically fit for London again it's high time I was sensibly busy about it. This time there wouldn't be a blitz, no excuse for breaking in bits in your hands on the spot. So as Aunt Phemie was going to the market town, five miles away, I set out for the wood and the moor and the hill burn.

I suddenly hate to worry you further with doleful thoughts (how moods change in the course of a letter!) so I shan't tell you how the wonder was gone from the grass and the leaves and even from the wild flowers. I plodded on. That murder of the old man hadn't done me any good. You know what I mean, Ranald, quite simply. I had seen dead bodies and bits of bodies in London town and helped where I could. I was sick often, but never mind. I was tough as most and it took what followed to get me down. I can only ask you to believe me when I say that this murder was for me more horrible in my imagination than what happened in London from bombs. For this was the living figure of destruction, this was the murderer, come away from the city where he had been impersonal and many-shaped, shapes flying across the sky, come at last to the country, to the quiet countryside, to prowl around on two feet and smell out a poor old man and murder him for his money.

But, Ranald, I mustn't tell you about the awful images I had of him. He was at once a real human being and, as my thought and sight whirled away like wild birds from the lines on his face, a mythical one, with stooped shoulders, moving darkly through the pattern that Farquhar's cottage made with the high land. But I mustn't tell you. I mustn't give you the detail. Be patient with me, please, Ran. I cannot tell Aunt Phemie of that inward place. I couldn't tell you face to face. Perhaps I am only telling myself out loud by writing. My brain at times works like lightning. Aunt Phemie took the pendulum off the old clock this morning. You should have heard time galloping! After that word writing—before I had got it down— I went through a sort of lifetime of experience beginning with an understanding of why a child speaks out loud to itself. And I don't mind saying that, whatever you think, because, Ranald, I also had an awful intuition of how human beings suffer *in secret.* It came upon me. I joined millions of them in all their prison camps, their inward places ...

If you're alone on a moor by a burn you can shout out quite

loud to yourself: Oh, stop it! And the very sound of your voice stops it! Good, isn't it?

It's quite a bare moor. It slowly dips down to the burn and then up to the mountains. As it goes on its way, however, it enters a gorge, wooded with birches, not very big ones. The ground on the right bank rolls slowly upward from the top of the gorge to a crest just over which stands Farquhar's cottage. It must be nearly two miles from where I stand. I have never been there, though of course now I know all about it. I wonder for a moment if the cottage is like what I imagine it to be.

It is the last place on earth I want to visit. So much so that I feel I have overcome something even in coming so far. It makes me feel stronger. I look all around and up to the mountain ridges in front. They are high but flat mountains and their lines flow along the sky. Over all the square miles there is no-one in sight. Some sheep dotted here and there like white stones, and a solitary old horse on a green patch up the burn on my left. That's all. Otherwise just space and the earth. I have the feeling I can listen a long way. I do. I look at the pool where I bathed. And the burn is still talking away; and the bubbles make themselves and float off.

I stand some time in order to get used to my conquest. It's nice to feel at home again, knowing nothing can come at you. I look with more confidence towards Farquhar's crest. It's very bare and the heather dark. My eyes fall to the birches in the gorge. I love birches. I begin to walk down the bank of the stream.

I am a little nervous so that I am not in the least tired, indeed exhilarated if anything. If I stumble sometimes it's because I keep my head too high. Everything *is* high and distant. The sun is shining and quiet. Then all at once it's in me—the secret delight. It has come, like a whiff of honeysuckle or wild roses.

Ran, Ran, don't misunderstand me or you'll break my heart. It's *not* mystical. I could shake you because of that doubt in your eyes. You're horrid. As if I could pretend at such a moment! Please do understand that I am trying to tell you of life, of something brighter than any eyes and lighter than laughter on its toes. The delicious bubbling fun of it. Why do young children race around; why do young women—I don't know about young

men—want to race with them? Don't you see the awful thing
that has happened to us, the awful curse on us? Don't you see
that I can hardly write two sentences without going all self-
conscious and wanting to explain? It brings the tears to my eyes.
It does. I am weeping like a fool. We have murdered spontaneity.
That's what we have done. The faces of analysts, everywhere,
with bits of matter on slides, and bits of mind on slides, saying:
That's all it is. And we wonder about war and horror! About
murderers … !

That was a bad break! Even if you have been saved what I
thought (where the dots are) but did not write. Right to the end
of this letter—and I warn you it's a dreadful end—I am now
simply going to tell you what happened on this day's outing.

I came near the first of the birches. Some warblers were
singing. I like trees, particularly small birches, because they bring
back my childhood, and I was happy as a child. The path was
narrow and soft to the feet and went winding on, some little
way above the burn, which was now in a hurry. The trees rose
above me and every now and then a small bird flashed and was
gone. I was fascinated and quite forgot about the murder. I came
to a point where I could see the falls, the solid pour-over of the
water that goes white and then black in the swirls of the rock
pool below. I must have been staring some time for when the
man spoke to me I got a dreadful start.

He was wearing a dark blue shirt and a light green tie. His
clothes were a peppery brown. He had no hat. His hair, straight
and dark brown, was smoothed back from a wide forehead. His
eyes were a deep brown and looked at me with that extra attention
which certain men have. It's the kind of look that many women—
perhaps all women—are immediately aware of. I refuse to
comment. There was also a moustache. He was not noticeably
tall. His bones were fine but I knew he could move instantly
and was strong.

That he was not a native was clear on the instant, apart from
his tie. Good afternoon, he said, and smiled. I said good
afternoon. I was not really afraid. I mean I never thought of the
murder. But something in me told me to back away, to get home,

and to do it with polite indifference as the surest way. Yet it was for a moment awfully difficult. We agreed it was a lovely day. I got turned round, looking about the trees in a way that excluded him. I am not without training in this business! Then sideways I gave him the cool nod of farewell and, taking the middle of the narrow path where no-one could walk beside me, I began strolling back.

He was walking behind me. I became terribly conscious of him and angry. I had to suppose there was no real reason why he should not walk behind me if he was going my way. But at least he might have kept farther from my heels. This was hardly a bus-stop. Unfortunately my physical strength wasn't enough to keep this mood and myself going. So I stopped on the inner edge of the path, looking with private interest up the hillside so that he might pass. Shall I get them for you? he asked. I did not know what he meant. Before I could look at him coldly, he climbed up and plucked some bluebells (harebells to you). This was excruciating. I walked on. He started down upon me and presented the bluebells. His brown eyes had glints in them. No thanks, I said, please keep them for yourself. And I said it in such a way as left no doubt I meant him to keep to himself. He laughed—not loudly but with a horrible sort of understanding. Men with his eyes have that sort of understanding of women. The laugh was not horrible, it was, what is so much more horrible, delicious. I went hot. I felt my face burn. I had the absurd but paralysing notion that he was going to spring on me. He was gathering himself. His right hand came up and across his breast. The seam under his shoulder was burst for three inches. As his face followed his hand I saw a red streak on his neck—a flesh wound. He stuck the bluebells in his button-hole and looked at me from under his eyebrows.

I went on, I hardly know how. It would be quite impossible to give you any idea of the state I was in. The sight of the wound had made me think of the murderer. I could not look round. Had I looked round and found him following me, I would have screamed and collapsed gibbering.

I think the worst spot was just after I got out of the wood and knew he was not following me. But I didn't run. Then the tremors and trembles so came on me that it was like being drunk and you can't keep going any more. But I kept going because to stop now, to sit down, would be to invite him, to cry to him. And the wood was still holding him, but only just.

At last I got so far that what held me to the wood snapped like an elastic and I fell. How the earth took me, like rain! To sink in—ah, Ranald, it's lovely. I wish I could tell you. Perhaps— some day.

Light in body, and light in the head too, there I was leaving the moor and coming towards our Wood (yours and mine though you've never been there). I thought of the Mound, the juniper bushes, the bank that breathes of the warm south. There I would rest. For I hadn't rested long on the moor. And now the pine trees are at hand and I am looking for the sagging place in the old wire fence that you step over. And then—one of the tree trunks moved. Buttons on a blue tunic. A body. It was a policeman. The policeman looked at me. I was staring at his eyes. I knew the eyes. They were grey like thistledown.

I can only believe I was so bereft of sense and motion that I looked merely astounded. Anyway I stood on nothing, staring at him. A curious hard glimmer came into his face, oddly self-conscious. He was like one caught playing a queer part in an unexpected place. He said good day and I didn't answer. I couldn't. And then, Ranald, he asked me: *Did you see anyone about?*

Oh I knew instantly, overwhelmingly, what he meant. It went crying through me, through the world. My brows gathered. *Anyone?* I repeated. *No.*

Before such bewildered innocence he shifted on his feet. He could not have seen me, could not have seen what happened in the trees of the gorge. He could not see the gorge from here, not until he went nearly a mile onto the moor. All that went through my head like lightning.

We are looking for someone—we have reason to believe he may be somewhere about, he said. As I had nothing to say he looked me over and added, You are staying at Greenbank with Mrs. Robertson? I said Yes. Then he asked me, Have you been far? I said I had been to the Altfey burn. The grey eyes considered me. It might be as well, he suggested, if you were more careful; he may be a bit off his head.

I had to move, but in going over the fence I stumbled badly. He at once supported me, kept me on my feet. I didn't mean to frighten you, he said.

I was trembling and he made to accompany me. I gathered all my resources, thanked him, and smiled. I went on, knowing that if I let go he would be by my side. I shut everything out of my mind except the queer discovery I had made. I hung onto that as to a rope. Remember my telling you in the letter about the thistledown how my imagination produced the face of a schoolmaster with thistledown eyes? *It was the policeman's face.* He is the policeman in the village of Elver, over two miles away. Once Aunt Phemie and I passed him there. Aunt Phemie greeted him. He had looked at me then in the way policemen do. Only that once, and I had forgotten him entirely—until I saw his grey eyes by the wood.

When I went to earth I was pretty bad, Ranald. It was a touch of hysteria. I let go only for a minute or two. I fought my best. I was desperately afraid the policeman would come on me. But I kept the bits together. And strangely enough it was not so much what I had just been through as that last spell in London—up it came again.

You would think I had had enough for one day. I was now quite damp with sweat. But when I felt for my hankie to clear my eyes I found I hadn't got it. I had lost it. The last time I could remember using it was just after I had entered the gorge. It had been warm walking in the sun. I could remember crushing it in my hand. It's a small square of linen with my initials hand-stitched in one corner. I need not tell you how I imagined its being picked up by the man in the gorge. A curious thing to find in his pocket on being searched. I felt trussed.

3

I couldn't finish that last letter. My pen wouldn't make any more writing. I can't even read it over. To muff such an opportunity of a dramatic finish, too! We were so merry this afternoon, Aunt Phemie and myself. Aunt Phemie is a darling. You'll love her. I took her in hand over some old frocks of hers. I told her she was becoming dowdy and a perfect fright. How can she expect to impress Will, I asked, if she does not appear at least once in the day as the lady of the manor. For it is really quite a decent farmhouse. All of five bedrooms and an enormous bathroom which may have been another bedroom once. I can't say I ever liked pitch pine. I think it is because when I was tiny and went to church first, the tall straight-backed pews—like stalls—and the pulpit and the steps up to it and everything except the whitewashed walls were pitch pine. Everyone was so silent and strange, too, and when—being about six—you had to say something and whispered, you were shushed by so solemn a face that for the first time you realised the awfulness of guilt and crime. Yet deep in your little heart you did not believe it and rebelled, for you knew that the crime and the guilt were outside you, like something in the air and not in you. They were in this awful large place, the church, and you looked up under your brows, and down, and you wanted to go away home and you felt the tears surging up. Before the wail could come out a sweet was put in your hand and you fought the good fight because in a vague way you realised the kind bribery of that sweet. Not that it altered anything. Yet the pitch pine is, I think, a more particular memory, because one Sunday I found that by pressing my hot little hand against the wood, I could make it stick just a little. The pew had no doubt been newly varnished. This was an interesting game during the interminable sermon and probably I sat fairly still for a long time with my own thoughts. Besides, I had on a new frock and that is something you just can't forget. You have to live up to it. With a new frock you are the little lady, you have responsibilities. Wonderful, isn't it? And then the sermon was over, I got my feet on the floor— and the frock stuck to the seat! It came away with a faint tear— and the colour of the varnished wood was brown in my mind.

The doors and the mantelpieces and the skirtings and the

cupboards are all pitch pine, but Aunt Phemie has wallpaper and carpets that tone with, it, taking away the grim bareness and giving quite an impression of warmth. And some of the bedroom doors, inside, are painted cream, with fittings to match. My bedroom has two windows, one to the south looking across the valley, and the other in the west wall through which I can see the steading and, beyond, the tops of spruce trees that are still in the grey evening and quite translated in the moonlight as if the earth had its own mute Christmas trees, and between and beyond them, very far away, a glimpse of blue mountain tops—real tops, like cones, not the great flat squatting mountains beyond the hill burn. There is so much sun in this bedroom that I love it. When I come into it I feel lifted up. I cannot tell you how real a feeling this is. Of course the room *is* lifted up in a way. I mean, you see over the valley and far away. It's like being up in the air, on a tree. Perhaps that delicious childhood feeling? If ever I have a house of my own, I should like it to be on a slope, facing south. Never on a flat. Perhaps it was just poverty that sent all the lovable philosophers to the roofs so that their thoughts could fly away past the myriads of chimney pots. Blessed poverty! And dear Ranald!

Do you mind my writing to you all this? But I'm not really asking because of course I've decided I'll only send you what I think is good for you! Aunt Phemie thinks I come up to write letters, or read, and every afternoon—she is imperative about this—to rest for an hour in bed. She thinks this treatment is doing me great good because sometimes—when happiness has come to me all in a moment from writing to you—I bolt downstairs to worry her. (I bolted after the end of the last paragraph—after writing the haunting and distinguished word Ranald.) Anyway, I always come up here to write to you. I could not do it anywhere else.

This is a room of my own. And another astonishing thing about writing you is this. Most times the writing just flows from me. Thoughts teem in my head, each one touching off a hundred others, and if I could get them down fast enough it would be a spate. This is bewildering to me at times, in a wild sort of amazing way, because I once tried to write, seriously, to make a living, as you know. Then I laboured. How I laboured! And what came was dead. I had bits, but when I got them together they were dead. I perfectly understood why editors returned the poor things. The made-up toys that won't go. Children are impatient with them—except maybe the odd child who thinks they look sad. You'll always find that odd one. Perhaps he's the saviour.

My saviour was *The Last Word*. The word the woman has—in fashion and the arts. Aunt Phemie loves the brilliant illustrations and thinks I must be very clever to hold down a job on the staff. What really astonishes her is how the affair comes out every month all new and fresh as paint. "Wizard" is no slang of yesteryear to her.

Aunt Phemie is really a remarkable woman. Let me describe her to you (for I feel well to-day and won't allow any horrid thought within arm's length). But first let me dispel a nagging notion, raised a moment ago. I agree that this isn't real writing, in any literary way. I'm not fancying myself, dear mind-piercing Ranald. Easy, facile. Very well. But if I had to write it, such as it is, as a literary composition, a creation, a work, it would make me sweat and would go dead. It's because I'm writing to you. Do you understand, Ranald dear? Must I tell you that love is the wizard? Is that perhaps the ultimate secret of all great writing? And not only love of a person. Though always at the core, whether of a tree or a mountain (or a political world theory!), what man finds—or loses—is himself. That's no new thought. But oh, how suddenly new to me!

May I now proceed, please, with Aunt Phemie? Thank you. Aunt Phemie is not the stout comfortable motherly woman upon whose bosom you can lay your tired head. Such women are the hope and mainstay of the world. When analysis and logic founder in their own despair, the motherly woman abides. From her I see myriads of little feet running down the world in a bright green morning—while you half suspect me of malice! Let me tell you something I have found out. The clever-clever ones in our set affected to despise the comfortable motherly woman as a brainless cow. Actually—they *hated* her. Think that one out.

Aunt Phemie wasn't long a mother. She is comfortably slim and though well over forty the gold in her hair hasn't faded much. I suppose gold doesn't. She is a tirelessly energetic worker and yet can stand quite still. She is over the average height for women, in fact exactly my own height, for we measured; but when I tried something of mine on her it wouldn't meet, and I'm no willow wand though a loss in weight produces the willowy sensation.

She was a school teacher. You would never think so until, perhaps, you heard her discussing farm business with the grieve. For of course the farm is hers. When her husband was killed within a year of their marriage, she did not go back to teaching. Everyone thought she would sell out and go back, but she didn't. I think she loved her husband. Not the wild first love of the poets, but the kind that grows unbeknownst, like a plant or a tree. The other day we were going over the garden and in one corner came on a young rowan, all of four feet, complete with fruit. She had never noticed it before. She was surprised that such a growth could have taken place without her noticing it. We laughed. It was a delightful moment.

Like myself, she comes of farming stock, and at the country school the boy who one day became her husband always had an eye for her. Aunt Phemie does not open her heart, but she can smile and there is a humour in her smile that makes it the most charming self-contained thing you ever saw. Boys at country schools don't wear their hearts on their sleeves. At a country school the profounder emotions are severely disciplined. To admit that you were courting someone—oh boy! There are fights enough in the usual way. A healthy healthy place. And possibly he was shy, because deep in him he was strong and sensitive.

That was the early position and Aunt Phemie was clever. Anyway she was good at her lessons, got a bursary to the secondary school, and won another from there to the university.

She has something—were it only her smile—and must with her red-gold locks have been attractive above the ordinary.

Which meant swains. She enjoyed it all. She would; and must have been devastating because she is kind. You can be either haughty or kind. Being haughty is possibly the more devastating because it upsets man's unconscious superiority! But kindness lingers. And Aunt Phemie can be kindly firm; which is not so far from being haughty, I suppose. She never actually became engaged. Don't ask me why. It goes too deep. After my parents had spent all that money on my education it would have been a nice thing for me to have gone and got married, wouldn't it? she said. I agreed. We also agreed that hard-working parents expect their daughter in such circumstances to do some repaying; otherwise the education would have been wasted. We saluted such wisdom with gratitude; we shook with mirth.

Actually farm people did very well out of the first Great War. Dan, her schoolboy admirer, was the same age as Phemie and old enough to have spent the two years from over seventeen to nineteen in actual fighting. He could have been exempted from fighting, for he was now indispensable on the farm, but instead he gave his age as eighteen. By this time he must definitely have concluded he had lost Phemie.

Does all this bore you? But what an amount of good it's doing me! I can almost think of the policeman now. And I'm waiting for him. With Aunt Phemie and Dan behind me, I gather strength where it's needed. Dan wrote her some letters. How I should love to see them! I suspect there was very little in them and certainly, I should say, no declaration. I know she has them tied away somewhere. Not that she definitely said so. A sparseness, an economy, in all this that toughens the last fibre of the heart. Bless them for evermore.

She became a schoolmistress in a southern town. She liked her work with the children and began to take an interest in the child mind and "advanced" systems of teaching. She went abroad during the summer vacation. Our Aunt Phemie was really becoming a very civilised creature. As a little girl, I was absolutely fascinated by her. Finally, it was to her that I owe the Art School and my "freedom".

The years roll on. Aunt Phemie became thirty-three. She is at home and it is summer. It is, in fact, the night before she is due to leave. It's as casual as that. She had seen Dan off and on, in the years. He ran his farm now and ran it successfully; interested in all the latest improvements and going ahead. She went out for a walk by herself, just to have a last look around the old place, for the following year she was going abroad to an educational conference. By chance, she ran into Dan. He was scything some bracken by a little wood in order to prove to himself how many cuttings of the young shoot were needed to kill that ravenous weed. He explained the idea to her; it made conversation easy. (I wish you could have seen the smile in Aunt Phemie's eyes as she explained it to me.) At last she is taking leave of him. He looks at her and does not put out his hand. His fists are gripping the handles of the scythe again anyway. When a person like that looks right into your eyes it takes the strength out of you; your wits fly away like startled pigeons. At least I must assume as much, for when he said, *You're not going back, are you?* she didn't know what on earth to answer. Then he said, *Are you Phemie?* And she heard her voice answer, *No.* I asked her what happened to the scythe. She looked startled for a moment, then she smiled saying she had no idea.

I can't go on, Ranald. However lightly I try to write about it, the tragedy of Dan's awful death comes looming upon me. And then when Aunt Phemie came out of the hospital, alone now as she had never been and within the scene of the appalling accident, how she could decide to stay on is something I can only grope towards.

She was a great comfort to me when I came home after saying *No* to the policeman. I was terribly shaken. She gave me some brandy. I felt sick inside as if my vitals were melting down. I know the trick of holding on, but oh, sometimes the stitches, the threads, keeping you together grow so thin and rotten. But when I cried, *Why did I say No to the policeman?* Aunt Phemie answered that that was perfectly natural and that she would have said the same herself. At once that awful question, which had kept crying in me down the fields, was eased of urgency—as if it had been properly answered. Of course I knew it had not been answered, but that now made no difference. Don't ask me to explain this.

The brandy helped the sense of conspiracy which grew on us and was warming. Aunt Phemie became thoughtful. I challenged her. But she said she was only trying to think who the fellow could be whom I met in the gorge. Obviously he was a visitor to the town who had followed the stream from the town into the hills. His description suggested to her that he was not the usual kind of visitor or tripper. He sounded more like an artist or musician, she thought. There was a nephew of the provost who had been studying in Rome before the war, but he couldn't be anything like thirty-five. However, it would be someone like that, and in my overwrought condition I had naturally—and so on. I could see she honestly thought this and was not now merely comforting me. To her it was absurd that the man could be the murderer.

It was then that a section of my past came back on me with a strange fatality, and I shook my head and said it wasn't absurd. I said that murderers were like that now. I said that murderers were no longer the "criminal type". Murderers were normal now. They just murdered. When you believe in nothing, why should you believe in not murdering … ?

I was saying a lot more like this, when I saw her eyes. There was in them not horror so much as a sort of horror of concern for me. I did not mind it. I felt suddenly alien and cool, with the trembling gone. I was not talking rationally so much as seeing in pictures. I was not arguing from what the radio called "the wave of crime" sweeping the country. The aftermath of war. The gas chambers. The mass butcheries. Jewish families are taking off their clothes, folding them, placing them in little heaps where they are told. They do this tidily. You can hear the whining sounds in their nostrils. Love sounds and love words and farewell. The naked family, one family and another and another, in the trenches they have dug. A young man is sitting on the edge of the trench with, a tommy gun on his knees. He is smoking a cigarette. You hear it on the radio. You get used to it. But what I see in pictures—I can't go on. Ran, Ran, do you hear me crying to you? It's not for myself I'm crying. Shall I ever be able to tell you——

4

You have no idea what the coming of the postman means once a day. It's the bright spot, the extra, and you never fear him. I was up here at my window trying to pretend I was not waiting for him. And actually, looking over some of this dreadful stuff I have written, I had forgotten him. I was vowing to myself that henceforth I should send you nothing but sunshine when the iron gate clicked. There's a short curving drive of trees. Behold him in his dark blue—admirable colour—and round hard hat with attractive peak. Up goes my temperature, suspended goes my breath. By flattening nose against glass and forehead hard against angle of window frame, I can just see him. Out goes his arm. I hear the wire in the wall before the bell in the kitchen. Nose over postal bag, he rummages among the oats. Elderly and grizzled, he snorts, for Aunt Phemie has appeared though I can't see her. Have disciplined myself now never to rush for postman. From him Aunt Phemie gets news, if any. Her daily moment. Out comes the little bundle tied with string. Deft unwinding of string and putting of same in mouth. Mumble mumble, but the hands deal the cards. My heart faints for I fancy I see something known. It vanishes towards Aunt Phemie. That's all to-day. String is winding round reduced bundle. Short news bulletin begins. It goes on. And on, Cheery farewell, and off the elderly but deft legs go. I wait in breathless suspense. *Nan!* In a moment I am there.

I hope I thank Aunt Phemie. Innocent of shame I turn to stairs. You'll burst your heart, lassie! calls Aunt Phemie. It feels like bursting. I subside on bed. The envelope has its own face, charged with character. I am positively shy of it. Totem and not taboo. Magic. I burst it open. At first it's not quite you. It's hurry and swiftness and what I find. Then it's you.

I agree I should have more sense. I wish to goodness I hadn't sent you that rigmarole about the thistledown. Yet I don't care—for you do say some nice things about it. I mean I read, between the lines, your concern, and though I love your concern, I'm sorry too. Please don't be concerned, Ranald. Believe me, that's not what I need at all! I see now how selfish and emotional I must appear. Dreadful. In view of the way I did my job and carried on, it must now seem to you that I really am going to bits. When you write "Don't give in, Nan," you wring my heart. Listen, Ranald. I must have someone whom I can tell. Yet that seems selfish, too, for why should I? Without discipline, life is impossible. I know. Who should know better? I could write you nice encouraging letters. But that—put it down to my breakdown—would seem a blight. Do smile, Ranald. For, you see, what was I wanting? I was wanting news of you and of everything you're doing. And instead of that you write about me as if I were an extra burden on your back. It makes me feel pretty hollow.

But don't think I am giving in to you. I am not. You say that I have got to watch this emotionalism with its queer images (you mean demented) or I may escape from you altogether and that would be dreadful. It would indeed! And it's lovely of you to put it like that. But I am not deceived. I know what you are hinting at. Let me tell you then that I am not escaping out of sanity: I am trying to escape into sanity. I may go quite mad in the process. But that's the way I'm going. It may be a terrible road, but I'm going. I think it may be terrible because the tears have sprung into my eyes. And lonely. But I'm going. I'll never go back.

All this talk about escapism. The talk is a horrible trick, a horrible trick of the intellect to guard its own deathly deeds. It's the talk of the prison guards. It's the young man with the machine gun on his knees and the cigarette in his mouth. Not to mention the smile, the murderer's sneer, that Nan is going all D. H. Lawrence. For ages of time I seem to have lived among it. And I know the reaction to the way I have mentioned the intellect. I see their faces. Real faces, pale and avid, or laughing like hyenas. I am now quite mad, they think. In bottomless swamps of horrible emotion. Blood and myth and stuff. But I'm not! We have to rescue the intellect from the destroyers. They have turned it into death rays, and it should be the sun, the sun on our earth, bringing the blossom from the earth——

I collapsed there and lay on the bed with your letter. These last words took an awful lot out of me, as if I had been shouting them. The door opened some time and Aunt Phemie was there quietly. I should have pretended to be asleep but I could not think in time. She asked me if there was anything wrong. She had called me for tea and wondered if I was asleep, she said. But I know what she is wondering and am dreadfully aware of my eyes, so I turn from her and put the pillow straight. I had such a lovely letter, I say to her. I hear her breathe for she understands this, quite understands that a letter could be so dear to the heart that the heart breaks in happiness over it. She smiles sensibly and goes out telling me to come when I feel like it. The elderly woman's relief at the sight of no more than a child's joy, and you love her for it.

I feel strangely quietened after my collapse and enjoy my tea. Aunt Phemie reads the newspaper which comes by post every day. She tells me something about what's happening in the world. I don't need to answer, but probably say something in reply. I quite forget to ask her if the postman had any news and presently I am up here again, re-reading your letter.

A silent world it is in which I hear the iron gate click. I stand at the window waiting. The policeman appears. He is coming to the house. I step back so that he may not see me but I keep my eye on him. I am not disturbed or nervous. He must be coming in connection with me but I really think of him as going to Aunt Phemie. It's not my concern. I may have told him a lie about being with a man and there's that handkerchief, but I do not positively think of them. I know that when I am called downstairs I shall be perfectly cool, polite but distant. Something was emptied out of me when I collapsed and I am quite well again. I am grateful for this because it will keep me from making a fool of myself. When I hear him pull the bell I go and watch as he waits for Aunt Phemie. We have no maid at the moment. He lifts a forefinger to his hat. There are some words. He enters. A door closes upon them.

Well, why not? Let them talk if they want to.

They talk a long time. The situation must be involved. But

my position is perfectly clear. Until this moment I had not realised how simple and obvious. Had I met a man of a certain description?—and I reply: Well, a man like that did say good day to me in the birch gorge. It simply had never occurred to me that the police might be interested in one so obviously a gentleman, taking a stroll. And this handkerchief? Oh, it is the handkerchief I had lost on my walk and did not miss until I had come home. I am glad it has been found. Where did you find it? Thank you very much. I can answer any question at once. The man was a complete stranger to me. I have no interest in him. Far from being upset by the policeman's eyes, I shall have pleasure in answering him with the utmost lucidity.

When I hear the door open and the policeman taking his leave, I have a distinct feeling of being let down. Somehow I don't want Aunt Phemie up here at the moment, so I open my own door and as I begin to go down she waves a white rag from the hall. Here's your hankie! she calls, laughter in her voice. What on earth's happened? I ask, grateful for the warmth that has come into my own. I hate pretending to Aunt Phemie. And soon we are deep in the policeman's news.

The policeman had finally left the Wood where we met and, going across the moor towards the hill burn, had come on the hankie in the heather. So I had not dropped it in the gorge. Aunt Phemie was able to assure him I had lost it, and my initials completed the evidence. I was genuinely glad about this. It might so easily have been otherwise. In fact we got some fun out of imagining it as a dramatic exhibit in court. The tame returning of it by the policeman was an anti-climax. No author of detective stories could live and throw away a clue that had been so naturally "planted". I did my best about this, and then Aunt Phemie went one better: the police are hunting a definite man, thin, with lank greying hair.

It's really a miserable story. A shell-shock case from the last war; a local man, who has completely disappeared since the murder. They think he is hiding in the countryside somewhere. Probably has taken to the hills and is lying up in some hole. But unless he dies there, he must come back for food, so there are night patrols. There is a terrific amount of feeling about it, at least the countryside can talk about nothing else. It's everywhere, like the stalking shadow of the man himself. Mothers get their children in early.

In the city we never seemed to come across men suffering from shell-shock (all here call it shell-shock anyway). But in the country things are different. Human beings are living individuals somehow, one apart from the other. Last winter four stacks of hay were burned one night, without rhyme or reason— out in a field where no-one could have been taking shelter— not insured, and a dead loss to the farmer, a decent man. Other more horrid things about animals—all pointing to a deranged condition of mind. In a neighbouring parish there's a somewhat similar case, though in the dark nights of last winter he became a menace through frightening women and girls on the country roads. I don't think he actually did any of them physical harm, but there were one or two bad cases of hysteria. Country folk don't like to do anything to these men. There's a feeling for them, a knowledge that they are as they are because they fought for us. I know you may think that stupid and not even fair to the men. I am not sure about it now. Yet I have a vague understanding too, as of some queer conception of guilt somewhere, and perhaps an unconscious acceptance of responsibility for the guilt, here in the country.

Anyhow, the police have found some clues at Farquhar's cottage. The policeman would not say what they are, but Aunt Phemie was given the impression that the shell-shocked man left unmistakable traces behind. His name is Gordon MacMaster. Aunt Phemie told me a lot about him, about his people, too, and it was like listening to a story in a country that was at once near yet distant, and one saw the strange river of his family blood. This hardly affected me, I saw it so clearly. To be able to see it was part of the mystery and this kept us from feeling too much. All we felt was a profound sadness for the man himself, but even that was distant, like an apprehension of fate. Now I could not leave Aunt Phemie, for if I were alone too soon a hand might touch me, something coming out from the story, and I did not want to lose my detached feeling, the calm emptiness inside me. We wondered where he could be. Aunt Phemie knows a lot about psychology, and not only as a science. She is wise. I mean while telling you about the mind she at the same time remains aware. You feel this, yet not as an intrusion. Cases of this kind, she said, have a sort of primitive cunning. With the money he got— and he must have got some—he may have left the countryside altogether. He would have had a clear two days' start. Very little whisky upset him, and as whisky is almost unobtainable here he may have set out for a city, perhaps where he used to spend a short leave in his old army days, and may be going from pub to pub when they open. If so, he should soon be found. The only alternative, said Aunt Phemie, is that he hasn't gone, and in that case he is already dead, for everyone in the countryside knew him. In a way beyond explanation we feel that he has not gone, as though in an ultimate moment of realisation he would be held, and desire to be held, by the dark matrix of his native earth. He would sink into it, or plunge. Whether we said so or not, I am not sure now. It is a little too like a dream, perhaps, and every dream, we are told, is the result of a wish-impulse. *Our* wish-impulse in this case. But we definitely did not discuss this. Though Aunt Phemie would certainly have done so had she thought it was between us. Perhaps it only came into my mind afterwards—only a moment ago, probably, for you know how old a new thought, or even a new happening, can appear sometimes.

There was one moment when I was nearly upset. I felt the dim tremor coming in the distance, but I deliberately turned from it. Aunt Phemie said: Poor man, he should have been treated somewhere. This raised the idea of an institution, and somehow I can't bear that yet. I very nearly answered with cold bitterness: I know—just shove him into an institution. But I stopped myself. I blacked out.

I couldn't have done it if I hadn't been cool. And I know quite well where this calm has come from. That time when I let go about intellectuals and escapism, it was really as if I had vomited something up. I look over the words I have written about it and see they convey little or nothing of the horrible spasm. And I know how open to misinterpretation they are. But words have little to do with an act of retching.

Of course it is finally clear to me now that I am not going to show you this. You have too much to bear as it is and its egoism would be unpardonable. I am making a story of myself to myself. This will help me. At least I think it will. Like one who suddenly finds himself at sea and is sick; after the bout—what relief! But there are many bouts—before he finds his sea legs and is well again. Isn't that a satisfactory literary figure? But it's a mysterious ship. The queer thing about it all, Ranald, is that I must write it to you. If I hadn't you, I couldn't write. Writing would be impossible, unthinkable. Oh, utterly. What would happen to me then—but I black out. I can afford to, for you are. Which is very marvellous. Also the writing to you will keep me within certain bounds. I know what they are. Also—for I must be honest or all would be mockery —I feel that I am doing this for you. And I am not just thinking selfishly of my getting well for your sake and mine. It's far deeper than that. But I cannot tell you yet. I cannot even write it. I am only hoping that I may some day.

It is after midnight. The house is very quiet and outside the quietness reigns. There should be great healing in this quietness. I wonder if I should put out my light and chance going to sleep without help? I feel I might. I hardly dare risk it. I'll take only one tablet. Good night, Ranald.

5

I had a lovely sleep. Is there anything more exquisite in the world than wakening from a perfect sleep? The light is new; it greets you. Honestly, Ranald, it does. There is a glance in it, like the glance of laughing eyes, and the sky is blue, and the old wind is wandering about fresh as clover. It's there! you think. That other world is there. It has found you with its sly mirth. It's here.

It was here all the time, of course, but when you have lost it you don't believe it's anywhere. An illusion or delusion that any psychologist can explain away without the slightest difficulty. *Nae bother,* as Hamish used to say. How is he? Did he have his picture show? Do tell me. I never could understand what he meant by *time;* I got lost in his words as in a wood. The only thing I understood was his distrust of people who could explain things slickly. When I saw that momentary sobering come to his face like a dry wind, and heard his *Ay! he's a know-all,* I never could help laughing. Then he looked and laughed himself. Roared. It was always an exhilarating moment. The trees in the wood were scattered about and the sun came in. Many thought his pictures mad. I remember when a certain one—I cannot even write his name —dismissed them with know-all expression and smile as *private phantasies,* I could have slain him. All I managed was to retort that I preferred Hamish's private phantasies to most men's public thoughts. Then, knowing I was getting at him, he looked at me, and the know-all expression and smile conveyed with insinuating silence: *So that's the way the wind is blowing? A crush on Hamish!* And he showed he enjoyed the news. It was at such a moment, Ranald—and this was before the break came—that I knew that I too wanted destruction for its own sake. That awful uprising desire to catch with your hands and tear asunder, to destroy. Remember that night, the race of the two cars? As the excitement and the hectic laughter grew—faster! faster!—what were we all racing upon but destruction? And when the excitement became intolerable and Julie screamed her mad challenge and we crossed the fatal border in our minds, what were we all rushing upon but self-destruction? We knew the craving. I saw it in a face that haunts me. The unbearable craving for the final obliterating crash.

I stopped there and went out for a walk. It angered me that I could not even begin to tell you of beautiful real things without getting messed up by such memories. I know they obsess me and I must get free of them. I could not even write these three words *beautiful real things* without a qualm, without hearing the echo of their jeering laughter, without a feeling of being detected in pulpy sentimentality. Oh, there I go again! What an extraordinary power and vitality the destructive mind has! How sickening the mere quiescence of *good* is to *evil!*

Oh, stop it !

Here I am again, up for the next round. Hullo, Ranald! How lovely—if you came walking in! I would take you out and try to show you that other world. Or would I?—could I? Perhaps I had better tell you about it first. For I feel free to-day. They do say that the unconscious mind goes on thinking its own unconscious thoughts. I believe it anyway, for otherwise how could I have the feeling that what troubled me in some obscure way about the murder has been withdrawn? The sunlight looked at me this morning, then it smiled. I knew.

What I am going to tell you is very difficult to put in words. Perhaps quite impossible. All I know is that it is very, very important. For what I want to do is to take you into that other world. It isn't, of course, another world: it's this world. But what has happened to our minds has also happened to our eyes, and we can't see it. You may think it silly of me to say that, because we see it only too well. But don't get impatient, Ranald, please. I have seen you show remarkable patience when listening to fools. And on my part I promise not to mention beauty, sunsets, love, magic, and silly words like these. All I am after, Ranald, is *health*; and if I have a sort of feeling that it is not my own health only, well, don't you feel in your political work that you too are after more than your own health? Let us call it our common delusion! Doesn't that even bring the smile? Let me shake you. Ah, you smile! Sunshine! I mock you, you big intellectual tough.

But where will I begin? For this is not a new discovery to me. It couldn't be, or it wouldn't have set up the conflict which broke me. For a nervous breakdown can only come from an unconscious conflict, what? Let it be whispered it may not always be so unconscious as all that!

I'm reluctant to begin, and indeed after the last sentence I went down and did a bit of washing-up because I spotted Aunt Phemie going over to the steading. A woman from the farm cottages comes every morning to help clean and tidy up. As I was looking out of the scullery window on the field of ripening grain, I saw the wind on the grain, a fitful wandering wind. I watched it as I stood there drying a pan. I felt that the house behind me was empty, that I was alone, and there came the old old sensation of liberation which permits you to smile to yourself and think what you like. Do you know what I mean—that curious enlargement of freedom, with a something of secrecy and gaiety about it? Talk about a vague pantheism if you like; I don't give a hoot. For my toes wanted to race my heart-beats. Suddenly I remembered long ago when the need to race came— and I couldn't move. Let me tell you about it.

I must have been about sixteen at the time (nearly a whole decade ago!). I had had 'flu—our High School had been devastated by it—and I was recovering at home. I hadn't really been very bad, for illness never troubled me much. We had a terribly strict Maths. master, too, and that wasn't my best subject by more than a bit. In fact I had rather enjoyed my illness and one day had gone for a walk up through the little birch wood. It's really a long straggly wood, the narrow path slanting up it, so that you can stop here and there and look out of it. When you're very young that's an adventurous experience. One of my earliest memories is the surprise of thus looking out of it and seeing the little valley (we called it the Hallow) down below. I saw our cattle and I saw sheep and the stone ruins, and then all at once I saw my father. He was doing something to a fencing post. I cannot tell you how strange it was for me to see my father working there and him not to know I was looking away down at him. My elder sister must have been with me I suppose, but I don't remember her at that moment. I wanted to cry to my father, but I couldn't. He was alone and somehow there was a strangeness about his being all alone. Anyway—for I mustn't go on like this—I knew that wood. Birches must grow in my blood! Behold me then at the ripe age of sixteen coming down (not going up) through this wood. It is a still February day, one of those days when the earth, having been busy with the furies and changes of the elements, takes a rest. And all at once, Ranald, I realise that spring is coming. It is at hand. The birches know and are waiting. It is in the quality of the daylight, a grey soft light. I look far up into the sky and the blue is milky. Then I become aware of the birds, chaffinches, tits, the rousing song of a wren, a thrush singing away along the wood. But I don't think of them much, because of this expectancy of the spring itself that is about me, this quiet *waiting* that the singing hardly affects. There is no-one in the Hallow. The stone ruins, grey with age and lichen, are quietly still. You don't think of them as ruins because spring, so infinitely older, is near. You are aware that everything has its own secret awakening. I am only one thing, and I had better go quietly. But oh what a gladness and (I can't find the word) gratitude is in my heart. I am bursting with this knowledge and love of each thing and yet am inwardly stilled. For I mustn't make a noise. I go down the wood and distinctly get the faint fragrance of the approaching spring. It is an earthy fragrance, with a touch of burning wood or heather in it. I am trying to be exact. But it is a fragrance—and I know a few—that nothing else ever quite equals. No other scent *quickens* like this. Bear with me—for I hesitate—if I say that it quickens in a timeless, immortal way.

As I go to the house, I see snowdrops. But I don't bend and sniff them—memory of honey in the sun-warmed white scent— as I did going out. I walk past them, tall and unbending. I don't want to talk to anyone so I avoid the back door and enter by the front. Instead of going up to my bedroom, however, I quietly turn the knob of the front sitting-room—our parlour. And then a queer thing happens—I don't close the door behind me. The impulse to leave it open is too strong. In a moment—the same instant—I know why. I mustn't shut out what has been accompanying or following me. I mean the spring. I go and sit in the big armchair. There is no fire on. The room looks chilly and deserted, unused. I am distinctly aware of this, but it doesn't matter. In fact in some strange way—as if it were a strange place —it is right. Even the smell of furniture polish. I sit there waiting, slumped in the chair. Then I begin to feel it drawing near. Panic touches me. I must get up and break what's holding me and get away before it comes to the door, but I cannot move. The expectancy and the panic increase. An ancient fear is in the panic and yet what's coming is a tallness of light. I know it can come and stand in the door and look at me. Beyond that I cannot know anything, I dare not. I try to break this tension or it will become unbearable, and I assure myself of phantasy. But I cannot move. At last I do, and see my legs and tuck them under me. They had looked as if they were not my legs. But this forced effort doesn't do any good. Perhaps I don't want it to. I cannot tell (not even now). Yet it is certain that I got up, trembling, my heart not far from my mouth, not hurrying, holding myself, and went through the open door—just in time.

What had I expected? Do you imagine that there is a symbolism in all this only too easy to understand in the case of a young girl? Sort of love phantasy? Like a dream, where the wish for fulfilment is hardly even screened? It may be so. And if so, taking the way it happened, I think it was rather lovely. I shouldn't mind its being like that, I mean. Bless you, it wouldn't need many touches to make it a classical story! Therefore if I say that it wasn't quite like that, believe me it is not because of any desire to suppress or otherwise act the cunning censor.

There was no imagined Figure of Spring. Male or female. That was not it at all. It was the something in time before the Figure; in the way, say, that primitive folk first thought a mountain had a spirit. They did not in their minds give the spirit a human shape or really any other shape. I know this quite certainly. As it were, they did not dare! They might make something or accept some odd thing they found near the mountain as a *sign* of the spirit. But it wasn't the spirit itself, and certainly not its shape. Any more than an old boot found lying about would be to us the shape of the person who had worn it. But we have seen persons. No-one has seen the spirit; not even as in a glass darkly, for we only fancy—or dread—we might glimpse it so. I have had one or two very interesting talks with Aunt Phemie about this. It fascinates me, and Aunt Phemie does her best because she thinks I am trying to clean up my unfortunate mind. She is right there (though I have a cunning idea about it all which I don't tell her). In fact I know that she has been looking up Freud on *Dreams*. The thick volume has shifted its place in the small collection of books from her teaching days. Some years ago, when here on a leave, I had gone through a lot of it. What I really wanted to find out—I had heard so much know-all talk about it—was what certain things one dreams about really mean. As far as I could see almost every natural object in a dream is a sex symbol. I remember Julie once telling a remarkable dream she had, rather like a De Quincey marvel— and later I overheard the male comment: My God, isn't she sex-ridden! So I satisfied myself that I should never tell my most innocent dreams to anyone. However, I had told a curious dream to Aunt Phemie.

But I'm not going to discuss Freud now. As it happens I did not dislike the man himself as he came through his pages— though I remember being shaken when he said that a hated enemy was as indispensable to his emotional life as an intimate friend. So let it be clear that I really know little about psychology or psychoanalysis. When in uniform, I heard a few lectures, but they were puerile. I am merely trying to be honest, and perhaps if I am honest enough I may give my horrid self away to myself!

Now for Aunt Phemie helpfully quoting Freud. She turned up the actual words in the book and read that from the analysis of dreams we are encouraged to expect a knowledge of the archaic inheritance of man, a knowledge of psychical things in him that are innate. I think that is very wonderful of Freud, and it's his use of a word like "encouraged" that sort of makes you like him! Psychical things that are *innate*. So you don't as it were have to learn them. They come to you—*as spring came to me!*

Haven't I been cunning, leading you up the garden path to that? But we're not at the top of the garden yet. Oh dear, I'm excited. I feel utterly exhausted, but with my mind going like Aunt Phemie's clock with the pendulum off... .

I relaxed—but am now at it again. I seem to have bogged everything up with all these words. But what I am trying to tell you, Ranald, is very simple. It's as simple as this: when I went out just now for a walk and looked at things about me—hedge, field of grain, trees, the light on them—a tired old skin fell softly from me and I was fresh and new. You know how after a sea bathe in summer your skin does actually feel new? Only, this is your mind itself, the psychical thing; this is suddenly you yourself; and it is delightful and infinitely natural. You walk along and all the horrid things have sloughed from you. You smile at the chaffinch as he skips upon the air. Everyone at some time in his life has experienced this. You know that. *You know it's true.* You know it's *innate.* And you know that we have conspired to murder it.

I am *not* being excessive. I am only aware all in a dreadful moment that I have failed to tell you. I suddenly feel desolated about that, and if I went out now, the earth and the growing things would not know me as I should not know them.

It's not easy to know them in this way; it's only as simple as daylight. It needs a lot of re-learning. You have got to get back, to get back into your own mind; though at once I see that that is what it is only when you *think* about it. Actually what *happens* is that you step forward into it. It's as if what is far back in your mind, like a memory, is actually forward in the happening, and you step into it *now.* That must sound terribly confused. Yet suddenly there is a glimmer, and I see Hamish's face, and I hear his sudden laughter. *Nae bother!* I wonder—I wonder—if it's something like this he means by *time!* Oh, if so, then it's revelation. Past, future, and present in the one step. In an instant I realise what art could mean for us. I don't mean art that just represents or copies things. Art that does that *stops.* I see it now. It's frozen. Oh dear, it is something in your mind that has died and is stuffed.

My hand is getting shaky but I mustn't stop. If only I could write! My head hates this awful labour. Like that endless talking that went on about the meaning of time and society and dialectics. I see Julie put her palms to her ears and scream. No wonder. The scream of one who is being murdered. O God, I see it now. She shouldn't have been there? Nimble-witted but without depth, said the horrible Know-all. But I can't say any more. I'll vomit if I do.

I'm trembling like one who has been running for dear life. Perhaps I have.

6

Ranald dear, I have a lovely private job on hand. The thought of it gives me the greatest pleasure and it's secret even from Aunt Phemie. These letters must appear dreadfully gloomy, but I'll hide them, and some day perhaps we'll be able to read them together and laugh. The thought of it keeps me going; is like a dance, a healthy country dance. Life will be like that one day. I am quite sure of it. The little letters I do send you now are like that. So they are not really a deception; just a cry to you to come up out of the city on the plain. And the thought that you may be coming soon for even four days! What fresh eggs Aunt Phemie will stuff into you! I chortle. Ran, Ran, hurry up!

Meantime I shall get on with my job, not merely by helping to clean house for you—we have your room all ready already—but also (my private job) to clean up, to brush away, the shadow from the fields and trees and all the land up to the Wood (the Dark Wood, I call it now) and on across the moor to the burn and perhaps even down to the gorge of the birches. For the murder of that poor old man did cast a shadow. It did affect me pretty much, Ranald. It's this business of hallucinations. I don't have them badly at all, in the sense that I am perfectly well aware I have them. Every normal person has them in some degree. I know deep in my own mind that I am not really neurotic, and should any psychiatrist smile at that as my private delusion, I'm not giving a hoot! But I do know that I am somehow highly sensitised. Now and then I get the dreadful frightening feeling that I may be pushed over a border line. Lest something like that should happen—it won't! I'll fight like seven cats!—I may as well tell you a little first about what these hallucinations are. Just enough to help clear up the shadow, for I want it out of my own mind, of course, just as much as off the land. I want the house and the land and myself to be ready for you. And Ranald dear, whatever happens to me, always remember that I can never tell you what you have meant to me at this time. When I say I'll fight like seven cats it's because I know I have you at my back. And it's not only myself I'll fight for. But I cannot tell you about that yet. I cannot even write it. Not yet. It's my ultimate secret.

About the hallucinations (how I do wander off! My field of associations has more trees than the Dark Wood). The simplest and most troublesome, though I have now almost perfected the trick of defeating them, are what are technically known (with thanks to Aunt Phemie) as hypnogogic hallucinations. You must have had them yourself sometimes as a little boy. They occur in the interval before going to sleep. Have you never seen frightful faces then? They form against the dark with an appalling clarity. You must have, even if you have forgotten, though you won't have, if there was *one* that kept coming back. In fact when Aunt Phemie and I were talking about it, I remembered quite a lot and advanced this notion on my own about children who are frightened of the dark and need at least a light: they either feel fear coming upon them out of the unknown—up the stairs or along the corridor or even from the air above them—a thousand times stronger than I felt the sweet panic of the spring—*or* they see a face.

However, I mustn't wander again (though all the same when you sometimes called me scatter-brain you did not know how often I was wilfully so!). All I can be sure about—apart from the spring—are my own faces. They are a little larger, I should say, than life-size. But their distinctness is absolutely overwhelming. I pick out two at random, a man and a woman. I have never seen them in life to my knowledge. The woman's face is in profile. It is tragic but drained, almost with the effect of lying over against something. The *plastic* intensity is just terrific, though there is no intensity in the expression. The man's face—I first feel it forming in the darkness and coming up; I know it's coming; then I begin to see it. Swirls of the darkness, like dark bands, obscure parts of it, moving across it, but ever clearing. It's coming right up: chin with long dark hairs, hardly a beard, the cheek bones, the whole *moulded* face, eyes—I struggle from it, open and shut my eyes, move my head, speak to myself. …

Let us forget it. And lo! suddenly I realise that what I really wanted to mention is the schoolmaster's face. Does this mean that the unconscious in me has all the time been busy on its dream-trick of getting the concealed wish through? I wouldn't put it past it!

What wish, you ask? Why, my wish that you shouldn't be worried over that first long thistledown letter. (Your implied criticism or fear has stuck!) You see, I merely happened to have had, the night before writing you, a hypnogogic hallucination of that face. The following day it was quite strong—if I cared to fix on it. I knew it was there, but that's nothing. Most of the time it wasn't. I probably dramatised it a little, just to cheer you up a bit! Do you forgive me? Let me be honest and say there was real horror in each eye being a ball of thistledown. Why, I don't know.

There is horror in it yet. That part was new, like a horrid revelation. Though again what it revealed I don't know. Anyway, that's all it was. The next point is that the face must have been suggested to my mind by the face of the policeman whom I had actually seen earlier in the village when I was there with Aunt Phemie. The policeman's face is not exactly like the one in the hallucination, but near enough to be instantly recognised. Now is all that morbid business cleared up? Splendid! I feel charged with energy, like a good housewife on a bout of cleaning. A veritable *spring*-cleaning. Hurrah! I'm off to clean up the shadow.

So I set off.

It had been misty in the morning and we wondered if the weather was breaking, but just after midday the sun won through. Marvellous its coming, white with the victory of delight, and, in a moment, intimate and friendly on the hands, warm as a kitten. A distant spot glistened reddish-gold like foxes in a stir. I wander up by the little ravine. Greyface, the young horse, comes trotting along, head up. I have nothing for him and explain how forgetful I am. I manage to give his neck a friendly clap, but his head is hard and strong. Though I no longer have any fear of him, I don't quite like him following behind. *Away you go!* Thundering he goes, and I know so well what he feels (out-racing his own mind) that—I was going to say I race with him, but that's not at all what happens. And then I saw the birch tree. I don't know how I missed it before, probably because nearly all the trees in the ravine are old elms (seen from the other side of the valley, they wander up the sloping fields like the world's legendary serpent). This birch was nearly as huge as an elm. And old, too. His silver skin was all cracked. Oddly enough, he seemed to have no symmetry; an ungainly growth, with branches pushed out like an idiot-giant's arms. But then, as I looked, the marvellous balance, the subtle self-compensating arrangements, were really very wonderful. It takes nature to do a thing like this, to produce the refinement of symmetry in the apparently asymmetrical. So I went close up and began to explore the trunk. What a world! The silver-grey skin that had burst and curled over, firm to the fingers as metal; the crumbling within the cracks, where the inner bark is already turning back to soil; the remarkable formations of lichen, here like dry blistered greenish paint, there fringed and frozen like miniature Arctic forests. Within this world, so vast on its own scale, I watch an alert spider going, with abrupt stops, about his sinister business. I slip out of myself into this new vastness. And then my hand, by accident or on its own, comes flat against the tree, and suddenly, with an effect of astonishing surprise, I find that *the trunk is warm*! No wonder, of course, because I have put my hand on the side that is towards the sun. All the same, I have had the surprise of the warmth of life—and the delight.

Things are beginning to clean up pretty well, what? (I put the question to you on the spot and laughed—for there was nobody to hear but yourself.)

Let me pass through the Dark Wood. I couldn't clean it up, but I held my own. The policeman was the immediate trouble. Anyway, it's a big job, but I have taken the measure of it. Every house has its corner which you leave to the last. I want to take particular care with the Dark Wood. I have got to clean up all round about it first, so that I shan't be surprised by anything coming in on me. Better to finish with the ceiling before you sweep the floor.

At least you can *see* over the moor; the burn I love at any time; and the mountains did not overwhelm—these monstrous but serene squatters. I realise that all the time what the dear old unconscious has been concerned about is the gorge where the small birches grow. That's the *first* place to tackle. (And I wonder just how much of childhood goes into that?) So I decide to tackle it, up and down and across, until its most hidden corners know and accept my feet.

I am just a trifle nervous as I round a last tiny bluff—and then there is a commotion in the air, a dark flash, a strike, a puff of tiny feathers, and the air is empty. I cannot move, and it takes me a little time to realise that a hawk is now standing on his prey between the first of the birches. I am assailed by a feeling of terror. Every instinct urges me to fly. I see the hawk's head. It stoops and plucks. There is something suddenly so terrible and authentic about this that I must get away, sick, my heart in my throat, terrified. But I don't. I watch. There is a surging within. I advance, uttering raucous sounds, like one rescuing her child from a lion. The hawk sees and waits. The curve of his beak, intolerant cold anger, his eye. He is up and off in a low swoop down the gully. He is gone!

Brave now, I approach, but sickened at the thought of what I shall find. A young blackbird; a patch of white skin. I stand staring down. It is lying on its side quite still. I don't want to touch it, but I must. I must see its death, how death took it. I bend, am putting out my hand, when the blackbird, as if awaking out of a dream, in visible astonishment lifts its head, looks at me (I see its eye still), and then, and instantly, simply flies away. It is the most extraordinary thing! It flies away, piebald, black and white. From one big patch every feather is missing. Half-plucked but otherwise clearly all right! It is so ludicrous that in my amazement and relief I am going to laugh—when someone laughs for me. He comes out from behind a clump of birches wearing the same light green tie. The sight of my face amuses him still more. He comes towards me—out of the wood.

He begins talking about the hawk, the laughter pressed back into his eyes. He explains that he has been watching the hawk for a long time. The hawk had been hovering, working up the gully; he had stalked it—and flushed the blackbird. The blackbird had actually done a swerve—too late. The hawk's action had been flawless. Marvellous. Didn't I think so? With a consciousness of complete unreason, I said that I didn't particularly think so; I said that I thought the whole thing was horrible. But, he answered, it happens! His voice, his manner, brought in all creation. I assured him I had seen it happen. He was, he said, aware of that, and glanced about the air as if looking for more hawks. This elaborate effect of giving me time to compose myself, as though I were an overwrought child, was particularly insulting. I am not interested in hawks, I said. He glanced at me—and laughed. I turned away.

One minute, he called, because I think you are entirely wrong; you don't understand what's happened; you are crediting the blackbird with your own emotions, your own admirable and humane reactions.

Really! I answered.

Whereas, he assured me, the blackbird felt nothing at all, or next to nothing.

Now I seemed to know this argument so well, in my bones and blood out of past talk, that I could not let it go, The new realism disposing of the old sentimentality! Not that one would mind that, of course, or something like that, if it was genuine, but it is so obviously an effort at justifying the new realism which produces death that, after world war number two, it is just too sickening, too unforgivably glib. I don't say this to him, or even clearly think it, for it chokes me. I probably say Really! again, or, So long as you know! I should have left him at that, but somehow I couldn't. Perhaps I was deeply angry, perhaps I wanted to clean him up. That he was enjoying the situation, that he wanted to exploit it and me, was positively blatant.

But you saw it yourself, you saw the whole thing happen, he argues. Why are you afraid to discuss it?

Your assumption that I am afraid to discuss it is about as valid as your capacity to identify yourself with a blackbird, I suggest.

Really! he echoes me. Can you suggest any other assumption?

One so obvious that normally one is not forced to produce it, namely, that I do not wish to discuss it with *you*.

Well, that's direct enough, he agrees with a solemn effect of restrained laughter. But wait a moment! Don't you think—shouldn't you be relieved that the blackbird is so to speak put to sleep in this happy way while he is being disposed of?

You mean devoured?

Well, all right, devoured. But isn't it, as the country folk say, a mercy?

I will give this credit to the hawk—at least he doesn't babble of mercy.

He laughs and says, You think I confuse my categories?

I assure him that I do not know anything about his categories and that his use of the word, in the circumstances, is more reminiscent of the parrot than any other bird I know.

All this was silly (though words came to me marvellously) and I reproduce it more or less to amuse you. At the moment I was anything but amused. Indeed I was profoundly angry at the something that underlay it all, and after a few more passes, when he suddenly came away with the word *ecstasy* in connection with the blackbird, I could not restrain myself and words came tearing out of me about the ecstasy of the old man when he was being hacked to death by the axe.

That strangely sobered him; his face went so still it seemed to grow smaller. He looked at me in a curious, searching way. Then he looked away. I am sorry, he murmured, if I have unduly intruded.

But he wasn't sorry. That's not what it was at all. Yet in some way his words affected me. I found I was trembling. I went back along the path a short distance and sat down. He came up and began talking again, but in a different way, like a man wanting to be understood. I was now certainly not afraid of him. There was something in him that I mistrusted, but he was in his fashion appealing to me. That's what I felt anyhow. It gave me confidence and I realised I had been behaving a trifle outrageously. Moreover all this time (don't smile, please) I was wanting to clean him up. Deep in me there was the curious notion (obsession, if you like) that I must clean him up, otherwise I could never clear the shadow away, I could never come clear myself.

Presently he was telling me about a stoat and a hare. He was

a schoolboy at the time and came on them in a corner of a field
by a wood. He was in the wood, moving quietly, searching with
his eyes for wild life, when he sees the stoat and the hare going
round in a circle, not a very big circle, just a few yards across.
They are at opposite points of the circle so that, if you didn't
know wild life, you might hardly tell whether the stoat was
following the hare or the hare the stoat. This went on for some
time, but at last he could see the moment had come when the
hare could no more break the circle. It was held by the circle;
the hare depended on the stoat. But he never saw the stoat draw
the circle into the hare's throat as a needle draws the loop of a
thread, because at that moment a shepherd appeared. Whenever
the shepherd saw the hare he stopped and, when he realised what
was happening, looked warily behind for his dog. The dog now
came up over the rise and also saw the hare. Shepherd and dog
were not a hundred yards away, yet the hare and stoat continued
to circle. The dog was actually within a few yards of the hare
before that fantastic beast could come out of its dream and break
the circle. It dodged in a sort of stupefied way, then in an instant
was into the wood and disappearing at tremendous speed. The
stoat did not rush away, on the contrary it went reluctantly, its
head moving wickedly. It looked as if it spat primeval oaths. Then
it too disappeared.

He told all this very well, very realistically. I perceive that he
has the kind of imagination which I secretly understand, and
this does anything but endear him to me at the moment. I don't
want to glimpse a stoat as a spitting heraldic beast; not, of course,
that he drew such a picture; however, I'm not going into that,
for when you have a natural pictorial aptitude, have trained it
for years, and then become hyper-sensitive—to a turn of a phrase,
a gesture—you see more than you want to see.

It is perfectly obvious that he is trying to illustrate what he
said about the blackbird, to show how the hare was getting into
that hypnotised condition where it would welcome the teeth of
the stoat in order to have the whole thing over. But I affect not
to see this and coolly let his story fade out, as though presumably
it's his peculiar way of making small talk. When he forces my

comment, I turn my head and look at him and see the needle-point gleam in his curious smile. But I do not speak. In this way I compel him to be explicit. Whereupon I say: You *know* what the blackbird feels. And at once he replies: I do, and you know that I know.

Where do you know? I ask.

What do you mean *where*?

I smile. He becomes perceptibly excited, and this suits me very well for it makes me cool. He has the sort of subtle mind that flatters itself it always knows what is going on beneath the surface or behind appearances. You know the type? Like Freddie, only Freddie has become the psychic expert, gets his thrill from revealing motive, particularly when it's discreditable, while this man (I don't know his name) has the wild in him, a wild-animal freshness, and is hanging on to it for his own mental needs. There is now something a little hungry about him, as he repeats challengingly his question; hungry and prepared to pierce me. He has been cruel to more than one woman in his time, I can see.

What do I mean *where*? I repeat; and ask blandly: Where *can* you know but in your head?

Not in my bones? not in my blood?——

And not in the blackbird, I complete his sentence for him. He laughs, and becomes more excited—and more personal. He is now concentrating on me. He is, when he uses his smile, unusually attractive. But I have made my point and get up. You're not going? he asks. But I am. Annoyance invades his dismay; an inner force comes out of him; this is nonsense and he is going to stop me. But I look at him. He pauses. His brows gather and the brown eyes shoot their fires. The silent primeval oath is heard. He hesitates, then his right hand, palm up, draws inward to his breast and he bows. Calmly I walk away.

Very silly, you'll admit; but helpful in some way, immensely helpful. For I might have been caught, bogged—I mean in that blackbird. I know there is something in what he says about the way the blackbird—or the hare—behaved, what they felt. The hypnotism, blood and myth. And when I said that he knew *in the head,* I was tricking him. His is the other aspect, the curiosity that is infernal. But the result—cruelty—is the same. Destruction, the death-throe. The shepherd robbed him (even as a boy) of the final enthralling spectacle.

I must sound incoherent. I am pushing to extremes, you will think. But I *see* it all, Ranald. With a vividness there can be no words for, I see and understand.

But this time I am not overwhelmed. I have a positive feeling of having overcome something, almost of triumph. It's that shadow, Ranald. Do you know, I almost feel at the moment that I may sweep it up. And then—Ran! Ran! what a housewife I'll be, tidying up the world for you! Heaven bless you, this night and every night. Amen.

7

It's been an extraordinary day. The Christian name of the man with the green tie is Adam. That at least is what a woman called him in a story which he told me to-day. It doesn't quite suit him, he hasn't enough weight for it, yet there is a sense in which it could hardly be more apt. I never quite realised before how descriptive names may be. Farquhar is startlingly right. Gordon MacMaster was wrong—until you learn that the folk called him Gordie. Aunt Phemie is perfect. James Critchley for the policeman is neutral. The postie is Donald Munro, but they call him Jump-the-dyke. Had he been a slow personable man they would have called him Donald. They would never have called me anything but Nan; it's like a cry. Though I don't feel like crying to anyone to-night, not even to you, utterly comprehensive as Ranald may be, with its Highland ancestry holding you in its reins.

I am merely reluctant to start writing. I look at these written words on the white page, I turn back again to the words with which I finished last night—*tidying up the world for you*—and am again quietened more than ever. It's absurd to suggest that in using these words I could have had any premonition of Adam's story. It's a haunting story, so delicate and yet so profound that it affects, in a way I cannot quite grasp, my previous conception of him. But let me tell you what happened.

After my hour in bed (I slept), I came downstairs and we had our cup of afternoon tea. We always have it early, about three o'clock. In the forenoon I had been working on one of Aunt Phemie's frocks and altogether we were in good form. Last night I told her I had met again the man with the green tie (our name for him) and we had wondered if Jump-the-dyke might know of him, but felt it would be unwise to ask lest we start a rumour, for the hunt for Gordie is still hot. Some of the rumours have a really fantastic—I can't think of a word—verisimilitude. They are as like the thing, as real, as a legend. I am aware of a new insight into the creation of legend and the extraordinary power of a story. I wish I could write about this. Anyway, it has given us—Aunt Phemie and myself—a light on the *need* which Freud experienced for the old Greek legend of King Oedipus, who slew his father and married his mother. Was that legend the sudden revelation upon which the psychoanalyst built his astonishing structure?

How I wander! Much in the way I wandered off after tea and ultimately came to the hill burn, which is called Altfey. I knew the first syllable meant *burn* and had wondered if the whole meant *the fey burn*. It would have suited one who is queer or fey enough at times! But it's merely the usual English corruption of the Gaelic, and means the burn of the deer. The deer do come down there in the winter time—and even much lower to certain crofts round on another slope where they eat the turnips. A lovely memory has come back to me. Do you mind if I tell it? I was a very little girl at the time. It is twilight, almost at that stage which we called "in the darkening". There is frost in the air and white ice on the hoof marks. The world is so still that we hear distant footsteps, and my mother stops by the corner of the house. It is Ian MacGillivray, the crofter from the Heights, a very aristocratic-looking man. He greets us in his courteous way and asks "if he is about himself". We know of course that he is referring to my father and my mother answers that he is down in the Hallow. She presses him to come in and wait but he thanks her and says he would go down to the Hallow for the darkness was at hand and he had a few things to do. Yet he does not leave at once; that is not the country way. I don't remember the talk that followed because it was grown-up, but suddenly I am aware that he is talking about deer, deer that have come down *from the hills* and eaten his turnips. They actually had "saved" the turnips, had them in a long pit, but the stags had used *their antlers* to break open the pit. He talks quietly and this somehow makes everything he says extremely clear. He is not angry with the deer, he is thoughtful and mild. My mother asks him if he has ever seen them. *Seen them? Och yes. Sometimes in the grey of the morning they will be over in the fallow field, and when they see me they run together and stand still, their heads up, watching me, as if quietly debating which road they should take.*

Why is there something necromantic in that for me? But perhaps one must have seen deer to understand.

I stand by the edge of the pool in the Burn of the Deer and wonder whether I should plunge in or not. Warm from walking, I decide yes, and, as if about to do something positively unlawful, stare about me far as the eye can travel. Short of a spyglass on the mountain top I'm safe! For you can bet I was careful to keep my eyes about me coming over the moor, with a frequent glance in the direction of the gorge for the man with the green tie. I'm not going near that place to-day; I don't need to. Oddly enough the expression of his face that lingered was that of the moment when it stilled and seemed to grow smaller at my words about the ecstasy of the old man while being killed by the axe. I see his face now as a sort of mummy face, and can't get it full of cunning life. Let it mummify, smaller and smaller, until it disappears altogether! I'm going to have a bathe! And in a pool which no human feet can reach until long after I have finished. I am out of my clothes in a minute. I put a toe in. Lace-curtain bubbles go round in a jingaring behind the boulder. I take the full gasp. Lovely! And kick and splash. Green slime fronds, softer than any silk, and clean, wave upon my legs as I lie like a trout. Then out, to dance, to sit doubled on the flat rock like an ancestor of prehistory; to dance again, for the chill makes you feel as light as a Nereid (how I love those Greek legends!). And with a readiness for the panic of the legend too, so that you dance round, with eyes for the intrusions of space, and laugh at the exquisite delight of nothing until your skin is quite dry; then—reluctantly—to dress. I select my cushion of heather and, flat on my back, spread out to the warmth of the sun. Two minutes and, like an animal, I stiffen, my eyes turn up. The man with the green tie is standing a few yards behind my head.

It was an overwhelming moment. To say that I was angry as I sat up with my back to him hardly means anything. In the instant of his appearance against the sky I knew that he had been watching from a short distance the whole of my performance in the pool and on the rock. He could not have appeared from nowhere. He had been there the whole time. It was utterly unspeakable.

But he was speaking all right; had come round nearly in front of me; was remarking that I never exactly seemed pleased to see him, with the smile in his manner and voice, the knowledge of what he had seen and the secret advantage it gave him over me. I turned my eyes farther away, but I hadn't the strength to get up.

Didn't you see me? he asked, and, when I made no answer, Are you long here? Then, as I continued to ignore him, he added: I fell asleep and was wondering how long I had slept when I saw you just now.

I looked at him. His face was completely open, quite still in its frankness. He held my look and, as it were, wondered why I looked so. I began to shiver and got up. He bent down, felt the place where I had been lying, and nodded. Don't you realise, he asked, that it is very dangerous to fall asleep in the sun even on dry ground?

It's quite dry, I remark coldly, preparing to go.

Dry? Good Heavens! Feel that moss under the lanky heather! And he sank his fingers out of sight. After walking in the sun, he explains, your pores are open and draw the damp up into them. He is full of expressive explanation and astonishment at my dangerous ignorance. You have got to be very careful with the old earth, he adds.

I thought you were asleep yourself, I say with expressionless coldness, looking right into him. I cannot lower myself to accuse him directly of spying, yet I cannot leave now until I have pierced him with my contempt.

Ah, but that's different! he answers. I *know* the old earth. You always ought to choose a spot where the soil itself is dry underneath. And even then the *sun* is dangerous. But to sleep over damp moss—any doctor will tell you you're asking for rheumatic fever or worse. I knew a convalescent woman who died from it. His manner is now really earnest. He takes out a silver cigarette case and offers: Have one—it will warm you up.

I don't smoke, thank you.

Sound judge! I am trying to rid myself of the poison by degrees. It does things to your sight—and also—I think—to your vision. Have you ever smoked?

Yes.

And stopped it? Wait a minute. Please. I am dying for a spot of intelligent talk. And look! have you ever seen the little waterfall up round the bend of the burn—just yonder? Marvellous. And by the time you get there you'll be as warm as a pie. Above it there's an old cart road—actually the old cattle drovers' road through the mountains—and you should see it for this reason. ...

Why did I go with him? I try to be honest. Had I not gone, I would have been left in an angry mess. I had got to finish with him, to know him, to let him see that I knew him, and so wipe him out of my mind. He was too closely connected with the policeman and the murder, the shadow. He had become part of what I was fighting. This must sound utterly irrational. It is. That's the trouble. But it has for me an inescapable reality—like the reality in a dream. Only, this is no dream.

He is an engaging companion. His moustache suits him, balances in some way the strong hair of his head brushed straight back, as if brushed with his palms on coming up from a dive. His brown eyes are intelligent and knowing. He is full of gleams of a refreshing animal intelligence. He knows things, the heath, the flowers, stops with an upthrust of eyebrow over a pale yellow saxifrage in a slit of rock, becomes for a moment utterly absorbed, then passes from it with a vivid quickness of eye. When he found a bit of alpine mouse-ear he, exaggeratedly calling it edelweiss, laughed with pleasure and began talking of the Alps, of the South of France. All this makes it easy for me. I find I can answer him quite impersonally, and strength begins to seep back. In fact I permit myself to wonder if he did actually see me bathing. Had he been an ordinary man, I would have said no, because I should have known from a hundred signs. But he is, I recognise, the man who could peep without feeling himself a peeping-Tom. And in some obscure way that has to do with my difficulties, this is dangerous.

But it would take too long to tell everything, the talk and the look of things seen. The waterfall is a bonny place and would be very unexpected if you did not hear it long before you rounded the rock face with the small tree growing out of its brow. The pool is round and dark with a great slab of rock thrusting up from its tail like a rudder. The water chute is only about six or eight feet high and you can easily climb up round it on rock ledges. My instant delight in it was marred a little by finding his eyes waiting for my reaction. He wants to sit by the edge of the pool, but I climb up and sit on the top rock-ledge. He begins contrasting visible colours and I know he paints. I make a contrary suggestion about rock structure and at once he says: You paint? No, I reply coolly, why, do you? No, he answers, I'm a poet. There is something exaggerated and absurd about all this and suddenly he cries, throwing his arms up: Ah, thank God you can smile! He rushes into speech, telling me he has been trying to paint the falls in the gorge. His paraphernalia is down there now. When I am choked with my own poetry, he cries, I try to get rid of it in paint. This fills him with laughter. I know this kind of madness, have the incipient feeling of revulsion but control it, for knowledge of where you are does bring confidence. I feel I can deal with this fellow, have indeed a sudden vindictive wish to take it out of him. To stave off the personal, I ask him something about his treatment of the falls, and he says, looking at me: So you do paint? I reply that I don't; I went through an Art School but that's all. And I didn't go through an Art School, he answers, and that's everything. But I have made my point. I perceive his faint mistrust, his disappointment. Folk of this same kind of feather don't love each other. They know the tricks and rigmarole of reactions too well. The situation for me is perfect! I am going to clean the gorge.

I suppose I could not keep the amusement out of my face for it is so clear that he thought I was some sort of woodland creature, innocent of poisonous knowledge, with whom he could disport. It is just too bad! Do you paint what you see, I ask him courteously, or your impression of what you see, or your apocalyptic vision of it?

He looks at me steadily and says inwardly: So you're that kind of bitch! He looks away, expression fixed as any stoat's, and says audibly and quietly: I paint what I see.

I make no comment.

I paint what I see with the utmost exactness, he says; I would measure it with an architect's tools if I could; I would have it so like the thing—if I could—that you wouldn't know the difference. He says this quietly but with an extraordinary effect of repressed force, so challenging that any comment might cause an explosion. Needless to say, I offer none. He is looking narrowly at me. I assume a deep and polite interest directed towards the whirls in the pool.

You would have thought otherwise? he probes.

The mockery drives me to my mistake, for I answer: I would have thought that you would want to paint the ecstasy rather than the blackbird.

So that's what's sticking in your gullet! he cries high above the rumble of the waterfall. So you *were* hurt! Splendid! He is vastly amused, knows he has broken down something, emits his familiarity like an animal warmth, yet does not come too near. No, he goes on, I don't *paint* ecstasy: I keep that for my poetry!

But something is cleared, a danger point of explosion is passed. Then he regards me with real questioning in his eyes, as though to plumb my deeps, and asks piercingly: Do you understand? Do you understand that a point may come when *external* reality becomes *an absolute necessity?*

The effect upon me is that of an internal light. I could have cried to him I know! I know! Perhaps something does come through my face, for his eyes are on me, but not now with cunning, searching rather through threads—as though I were seeing their darkness, their dark glisten of pain, behind a spider's web. This affects me with discomfort, but whether it is what I actually see, or some notion behind it of strangled integrity in him, I don't know. I know, however, that it is real.

I have the impression of a considerable pause. He shrugs, looking away. Odd, he says, that it should also have been a woman who drove me here; but she was over fifty. And then he told me the story.

I wish I could repeat it as he told it. But how can I? Just as I fancy that two or three of the words are not those which the crofter Ian MacGillivray used about the deer in the fallow field. Ian's own words were immemorially right.

I had been working pretty hard, he began. One of those bouts. Then I had gone out and met everyone. Oh God, talk, talk, and drink. Christ, the awful sucking of your own intestines like macaroni. You see it when you come back to it, the ego-boosting, the desire to achieve in order to be talked of, the clawing scramble through the mirth. The dope we can't do without. Lord, how I love it, and wallow in it! Never mind. There's an artist I know and his wife. He paints landscapes. Just landscapes. Isn't it divine? Cool perspectives, distance. You can walk through them. Right! I hit the trail and arrive. The house is quiet with order, cool with living, and there are chairs where you sit down. You can also walk from one room to another and look out of a window on a landscape. There is no impediment in that house. You hear the silence or Helen's feet in the kitchen. No electric light, just lamps and candles. Lamps—and candles. Extraordinary thing the naked light of a candle. I am poor enough, God knows, but you don't feel poor with a candle. When your last penny is bust you are at home with a candle. Hell, after that you have to make money again, tear it out of the gizzard of the world. But never mind. People buy David's landscapes occasionally. They buy them, thank heaven. What they really buy is the love between David and Helen, but they don't know that. Neither do the art critics. Never mind. Helen has no theories. She works, looks after David and the house, trims the lamps, puts a box of matches in your candlestick, and sees that light and life go on. Not an interesting job, you may think; too much like God's to be interesting; too full of practical business, boring. I agree. However, that's what she's like; she positively has no notion that she is being imposed upon even. It's incredible, but quite true.

In talking like this, he used gesture, continuously moved, alive, his green tie swinging loose. When he talked about Helen being imposed upon you could hardly tell whether he was being ironic or interested, amused or amazed. No doubt he was both at the same time. Some of his language presumably paid me the compliment of having so lived—in circles like his own—that I could not be shocked. He goes on to describe how in the evening David and himself went out for a stroll. It is a lonely landscape with a farm in the distance. The twilight deepens to a fathomless grey dusk and a bird flies overhead. David says it is a buzzard, but as the silent bird disappears they agree it was an owl. Their talk takes on the quietude of the landscape, its illusive distance and height. They discuss theories of art and thought, cave drawings and philosophies, searching for the artist's meaning, for what the world has lost or needs. This induces an excitement that at once has the shiver of truth and the cool fathomless distances of that landscape in the dusk. They then come home to Helen's welcoming voice, to friendly movements in and about, slippers and talk of rest, of bed. Had you a good walk and would you like something? Sure you wouldn't? When he finds himself in bed he can't sleep, listening now not to the echoes of that talk outside but to the quietude. He feels completely stilled, quiescent; bathed, cleansed, and put in a white bed. An owl hoots. The silence follows. And in this silence, just before sleep comes, he has his strange illusion. It seems to him that he is downstairs again and that they are getting ready to go to bed. David, who is stoking the kitchen stove, turns with the small black shovel in his hand, still talking. But Adam is suddenly aware of Helen. She comes carrying a handlamp with a blue glass bowl and has clearly been busy seeing that the house is all secure for the night. The full responsibility of this is hers, unconsciously as it were, and he realises that a day on earth is being brought to a close. She is folding the day up to put it away, when suddenly she remembers she has forgotten something, or could not quite trust someone (like a maid) to have seen to it. She does not want to interfere, says Adam, with our high and important talk, so turns away, murmuring to herself as she is going: *Excuse me! but I'll just go and see that the moon is properly trimmed and not smoking and that all the stars are lit.*

8

I could not write a word more after finishing that story, and all I need add now is that he did contrive to make Helen's exit absolutely natural. I showed my appreciation, but for his waiting eye it wasn't nearly enough, so I asked if he told Helen in the morning. Good God no! he said, I got an urge to beat it, borrowed money and painting gear from David, and here I am. He shrugged. And then, with a subtlety of indifference beyond any words, he said: The thought of it still gives me a faint shiver—like the clean shiver you get after bathing in a summer pool.

I compliment myself that I absolutely showed no reaction beyond mild interest. I said it was high time I was home and got up. He did not try to detain me, he just waited. He did not even acknowledge my farewell as I walked away.

I recognise mine is a curious condition in which small things are magnified in an extraordinary way. There are moments when if an unexpected leaf touched me, I'd jump out of my skin. I am far more unstable than even this writing may suggest. When a sudden sound puts my heart in my mouth, I get over it by a squirming in which more than my fingers get knotted up, that is, if nobody is seeing me. I let it go on. Squirming is a tremendous relief, from which I emerge again, freed, if exhausted a little.

The body is a very curious thing with a life of its own, and occasionally it indulges in this short rigor not because of any sudden sound or touch but because it is blacking out a thought, a memory, *before* it has actually appeared in the mind. If anyone saw me at such a moment, with my face twisted and stiff as a mask, he would certainly think I was going off my rocker.

But I am not. I am seven cats, I say to myself. Nothing like an incantation for keeping you sober. And then there is this to it, too, that all the time I am aware that the magnifying of small things is necessary, that it is the only way of truly seeing them. I mean it is the small things which we overlook that matter, and in every way, whether it is a bunch of grass, a tree, the sunlight, a bird, or the thought we have about them. To see them like that is not to magnify them at all, it is just to see them. That I should have felt it necessary to use the word magnify shows the queer condition we have got into. And it is the same for persons as for things.

I suppose I am trying to quieten myself by using all these words. If Adam did see me in the pool, I know it doesn't matter. I really do know that. It's not prudery that's worrying me. After all, says a sly humour far back in me, at least he had something to look at! But that doesn't quite let me off. I'll never forgive him for doing it, for the prying way he did it, yet I can't get him out of my mind. I don't understand him and wish I could, at least I wish I could be sure my understanding of him is right. It was a remarkable story for him to tell, about Helen, the eternal woman, and I am certain that no-one could ever make up such a story. There can be no doubt about that. So therefore he is a man who could have that profound kind of vision. Yet I don't trust him. He is capable of using anything and everything that will help him to get what he wants, like a wild beast stalking its prey. And he is stalking his prey as it were *from* Farquhar's cottage. There is all *that* behind him in my mind. Horrible, isn't it? Particularly when I have the notion that I am prey... That ecstasy of the blackbird—dear God, it's terrible and unpardonable.

No, Ranald, it's not morbid. But I cannot write about it. I cannot tell you about this, and so I cannot write at all. There are long pauses. I'll have to go on with it alone. But I must go on.

9

He was waiting for me to-day in the Dark Wood. This shocked and angered me. He is stalking nearer, as if he knew I wasn't going to the birch gorge. But after a time I must admit he was friendly, attractive, made no direct inroads, could interrupt himself to follow a bird, he was full of variety, like one searching for laughter and play. I am not deceived, but it is difficult to remain unresponsive, not to acknowledge, for example, that there is something in the neatness, the exquisite surety, of the movements of a blue tit that must at least be acknowledged by the eye. Yet I have got to be careful, for if I give him an inch he will take two. His excuse for being there was characteristically plausible. He did not in so many words apologise for having intruded too often; all the same he made it plain that if his appearance in the vicinity was a nuisance to me then he had come here to assure me that he would withdraw, permanently absent himself, and on the same breath he drew my attention to the song of an invisible chaffinch in a near tree and went on talking of the variety in the song from bird to bird, and finished up by asking if I understood. I simply said, listening on my own to the chaffinch: Your presumption of importance, your own importance, is terrific. He glanced at me and laughed. That's what I like about you, he said. As if I were playing his own game! I could have hit him. I did not stay long. He came out with me to the edge of the wood and stood there watching me go away. I could not mention the meeting to Aunt Phemie.

10

I have seen Adam again. I know this looks like blackbird fascination, the dark sex-unconscious! I can hear the laughter, see Know-all's face. But I cannot let that put me off. I dreamt of Julie last night. She was alive in a fantastic Eastern place, like a room in a palace—or was it a temple?—swaying from the hips, with the smile, the drug-glitter, in her face, and then somehow in a moment I was looking at a close-up of her face (like my hypnogogic illusion) and I saw the child in her woman's face, and it was *lost*; this affected me with an extraordinary sense of terror and with a something of pathos in the terror that I could never describe. Sometimes when I think of Julie my heart could break, and never more so than when I know of her dodges and cunning. I know them as I know the branches of a tree. The polite word we used was amoral (our complacency, or insufferable superiority, in the use of such words often now makes me squirm. O God, the bone-dry deathly rattle of them, the emptiness!). The awful thing is that I see the pattern of her behaviour with a clearness, a certainty, that no ordinary moral behaviour pattern ever possesses. Know-all said she demonstrated the irrational. Even writing that last sentence blinded me. But why go on about it, for the terrible fact is that I can foretell with an appalling logic, rationality, what Julie will do at any time. She is like the something *given* in mathematics (that strange word which haunted the subject for me in school days). Know-all is an intellectual leper.

I had to stop there for a long time. It is now getting late. I have taken the tablets and in half an hour they'll work. I am vexed that I have had to go back to the full dose, but I shan't let that get the better of me. I don't know why I have to go through with this thing, with this fellow Adam. I try to keep calm about it, but I am working through myself and must go. Not to go is to *escape*. I want to go through him, to separate him and understand. He is like myself in so many ways. He *sees* things as I do. But he goes *beyond*, and it is there I have to break him—in a dream sense to tear his chest open and separate the dark. I have got to *know*, and then I will be better, I will have conquered so much of my trouble, of what haunts me from the past. Anyone reading this would think I was quite mad. Even Ranald wouldn't see that it is the madness of the world.

I'll leave it for the morning to decide whether I'll go with Adam to that place or not.

11

The sky is grey, and a grey day in the country affects me like a childhood Sabbath. I feel nervous, too, and weak, as if I were going through with some awful ordeal. I have a premonition of something dreadful. But it may work out quite the other way, and if it does, to-morrow I'll dance, I'll be free. Oh it will he lovely! I'll weep on Greyface's neck and give him all my sweet ration. Adam wants me to go with him beyond the small waterfall, in round the back of the mountain where there is a primeval country, he says, of moss hags and lochans. The burn comes from there. We all do, he said, with at once an infectious understanding, a hideous knowledge and his engaging smile. All I know is that I am taking the seven cats with me.

I don't trust him. There is something dreadful in him as Farquhar's cottage. But I can fight him. I am going.

Part Two

RELAPSE

1

Aunt Phemie stood by the station exit watching the people come off the train. It was the busiest train of the day, having travelled through the night from London to Perth, and now in the late forenoon a frowsy pallor hung about the released bodies and stared from the faces behind the carriage windows. It was a long train and, dodging the trundling trolleys, passengers converged on the exit where the ticket collector busily held them up. Single men, city clothes, commercial travellers—any one of them, she realised with dismay, might be Ranald. A couple of men looked at her questing eyes sharply. Then she saw him (tall, dark, distinguished—Nan had said), saw his eyes on her. She went forward. "You are Ranald Surrey?"

"And you are Aunt Phemie."

He used her name with the cool ease that saved unnecessary fuss or bother. His handshake was friendly but brief.

"How is Nan?"

"Coming round, thank goodness."

"That's good."

Aunt Phemie felt flustered as if she had been preparing herself to encounter warmth and anxiety, but here was the ticket collector. Ranald gave up his half ticket and followed her out into the station square where her battered twelve-year-old car was waiting. He had no luggage beyond the blue kitbag slung over a shoulder. As they got into the car she said, "I hope you didn't mind my wiring for you, but—she was really very bad— and—well—it was difficult. She spoke about you so much."

"What happened?"

Aunt Phemie got the engine going and threaded her way through the cars and buses. "It's difficult to know exactly," she said. "She was getting on well—and then she had this relapse."

"But she is pulling round again?"

"Yes, I think so." Aunt Phemie did not normally feel nervous or excited and this worried her. She cut in before a lorry too sharply and was aware that he knew it though he showed nothing. Indeed he was looking at the church, the hotels, the street traffic, the shops, observing her county town with a sort of casual thoroughness.

"Farming mostly, I suppose?" he said:

"Yes. Quite a busy place, especially on market days."

"Do you do much of the business yourself?" He looked at her in an interested way.

She kept her eyes front. "Well, a bit. I have a very good grieve."

"The man in charge? That makes a difference. So long," he added with an understanding humour, "as he doesn't feel himself too much in charge." He observed the bills in front of the cinema.

"Oh, we manage," she replied, her tone firming. For she had had precisely that difficulty with the grieve, who was over fifty, married, with six of a family.

"I'm sure you do," he answered her at once.

"What makes you think so?"

"Just looking at you."

She felt her face grow hot, for somehow he had got the compliment over very easily.

"You'll be tired after travelling all night."

"A bit," he answered, "but I don't mind. Did you send for me on your own?"

"Yes. Nan doesn't know you're coming. I hope you don't mind?"

"She must have been pretty bad, then. Nerves?"

"Yes—with temperature complications."

"Is she in bed?"

"Yes. The doctor said I should get a nurse—we have to watch night and day—but I was afraid of that, of a white stranger, especially at night. We got a woman from the cottages whom Nan knows. She is with her now."

"The local medical?"

"Yes … Do you think we should have got a specialist?"

He thought for a moment. "Who could you get here, anyway?"

"We could always send for someone. But—just whom?"

"Uhm."

"The only one I could think of was you."

He remained thoughtful.

"I felt you must know a lot—apart from anything personal. Things must have happened which I don't understand," said Aunt Phemie in a rush. "There's something troubling her which I can't get at. At least I think there is. I don't know." And after only a momentary pause, she added, "I took it for granted you were fond of her. That's why I sent for you."

"It was difficult for me to get away, and you may be sure I wouldn't have come if I hadn't wanted to." He spoke in an easy tone without emphasis, yet with a curious assurance of strength. She knew he was no more than twenty-eight. If he was really this cool casual sort of fish (she thought abruptly), however self-reliant, it would be terrible. She did not know where she was with him, hardly knew what to do. Before turning off the main road, she stopped the car.

"We had better think this out, think what we are going to do," she said with an earnestness she tried to subdue.

"Yes. It would be better. You did not tell her I was coming because you thought it might upset her?"

"I thought it might excite her," Aunt Phemie corrected him. "It would certainly have kept her from sleeping unless we dosed her too heavily. She would have been a wreck to-day." As he did not reply at once, she asked, "Do you think you should see her now?"

"I think I might. If you like, we needn't say that you wired for me. I have in fact got some business for Newcastle pushed forward, and have come here for three days before going there. If you can have me for so long?"

"Of course!" she said. "That's fine. That will explain your appearance perfectly." She nodded, suddenly relieved. "We can go in quietly and I can go up and prepare her."

"Good."

Aunt Phemie hesitated. "She has been writing you long letters. I mean you will know all about what she's been doing or thinking here?"

"Well, she did write me one long letter, about thistledown and a man who appeared—one of her hallucinatory experiences. I suggested she should not give in to that sort of thing and it had a restraining effect. Her letters after that were more normal, like her old self. I thought she was coming along all right."

"So she was," said Aunt Phemie, "then something happened. Did she mention anything about an old man being murdered in a cottage?" She felt his eyes on her.

"Yes. But not much about it. Why?"

"Well, naturally it upset her. You know how such a thing upsets us all in the country."

"I suppose so," he said thoughtfully. "So you think that's the root cause of the relapse?"

Should she tell him of Adam? Or leave him to find out from Nan? Her mind went into a whirl. "I think so," she said, "only I don't know everything. Perhaps it would be better if you found out from Nan herself. It's so difficult to know what's real—or—not."

"You would rather I found out from Nan; say to her that you told me nothing?"

He had read her mind. "To begin with, at least, I think that might be better," she answered with an apparently thoughtful nod. "Don't you?"

"I think so," he agreed, and it was as if having concluded that bit of business they could now go on. She could not move.

"You mentioned a—a specialist. That's worried me. I have felt the responsibility. I am very fond of Nan. Did you mean some mental specialist?"

"A psychoanalyst?"

"Well—yes."

"I just wondered what you thought about it. I suppose I wondered if you thought there was anything wrong with the brain itself. I don't. And I'm glad you don't. As for the psychoanalyst——" He gave a small shrug and smiled. "She could have one of them later—but I doubt if she will."

"Don't you believe in them?"

"That's a big subject."

She was nettled now. "I know it is. But if there is something that's worrying Nan, something deep, that she can't quite get or formulate—well, from such simple knowledge of Freudian analysis as I possess, I think it at least possible that she might be helped to free her mind. Or do you not believe in Freud?"

He took out a packet of cigarettes. "Have one?"

She took one, saying she didn't smoke very often. As he was lighting his own, she saw he looked tired and very pale and was on the point of suggesting they should drive on when he blew out a chestful of smoke. The bones in his face were finely shaped, the nose almost Greek; the eyebrows finely arched, the eyes hazel behind the dark lashes.

"About Freud," he said, with the lazy air of one habitually used to speaking. "It's a big subject. He's done some marvellous analytical, clinical work. But when it comes to his theories about how the whole psyche works, then I don't quite get him. All the pretty myths he makes up about the Oedipus complex and the Id and the Censor and so on, are to me just—the old bourgeois myths, not science. Ways of explaining the mind, as the Book of Genesis explains the world." He blew a stream of smoke with a half thoughtful, half-amused expression. "He looks upon the individual as something that sort of grew miraculously— altogether apart from the social conditions which really have made him. To ignore man's social-economic environment in trying to understand him is like ignoring his stomach when his digestion goes wrong."

"And you're sure you're not being prejudiced by your own political theories—or myths?"

He laughed, quietly stretching his athletic body, and looked at her with what seemed a new interest. "That's very neat," he allowed. "It's a matter, however, of fact, of scientifically finding a cause. We would have to argue that. But about Nan." He smoked for a moment. "I'll tell you quite frankly why I encouraged her to come here. As a result of what she went through in London, she had a nervous breakdown. As a result of that, to protect herself, she went back in her mind to earlier, happier conditions. She saw visions of things from long ago, her father working in a field, the security of her mother, attractive bits of scenery, and so on. She was escaping from a world with which she could not cope—a hellish world admittedly—and going back to an earlier security. This is what Freud very properly called an infantile regression. You'll accept that?"

"Well?"

"But do you?"

"Nan insists she was not escaping."

"And you agree?" He looked at her.

"We could argue that."

"You really think it is arguable? For Nan has mentioned your work with children. I should respect your opinion."

"I am not too sure about it. Nan is herself so conscious of the accusation of escaping that ... didn't she mention it, question you?"

"She did—in no uncertain terms. But then her resistance, the very fierceness of it, surely gives her away. It's what you expect in an analysis when you touch the real or sore point. Isn't it?"

"Perhaps. But I am not satisfied. The one thing such work as I did made clear to me was the tremendous difference between children—and between grown-ups, too, for that matter. However, we could go into that again. Just now I should like to know why you thought she should come here—in the condition you believed her to be in."

Aunt Phemie's tone was at last cool and firm. She poked some strands of pale gold hair up under the brim of her brown felt hat, brushed and blew cigarette ash from her green jumper and the lapel of a faded-green tweed jacket. She threw what remained of her cigarette out of the window. A sharpening mood from her Continental travel days had come back upon her.

"I thought she should come here," Ranald explained, "because I reasoned it out that if she did find her early environment she might once again get put together; become well, and so be able to go on. Simply my own idea, for psychoanalysis is—well, an analysis, not a therapy. It doesn't help Nan much for an analyst to show her the regressive nature of her own particular solution of her trouble if at the same time he cannot provide her with a better solution. And psychoanalysis can't—at least so far as I know. That's where it lets so many down. Or perhaps you don't think so."

"I think I catch your drift," said Aunt Phemie.

He smiled and his eyes flickered on her for a moment, but she wasn't looking at him. "It is complicated, too, when the neurotic's own solution is known to the neurotic—and repudiated as a neurotic solution. That seems perhaps a bit involved," he allowed.

"You mean Nan knows the argument."

"Exactly. And she's very intelligent. So it's no good going on arguing with her. She is convinced she knows all about it—and can tell you a few things over and above! Yet the *fact* is she's ill, and the neurotic nature of her illness seems only too clear. The only thing you can do then is help her out, or try to."

"But then, by sending her here aren't you in fact confirming her in her *escape*, her infantile regression?"

"Not altogether, because we re-establish the economic aspect—the actual environment in which at one time she did find health. After all, it seems simple to me that her nerves went because of the condition of things outside her. She didn't become ill because of some internal mysterious affection of the ego. The world broke her. From that *cause*, certain mental effects followed."

"You like logic."

"It's a hobby of mine."

"Why did you send her here and not to her own home?"

"I didn't do all the sending. But I strongly supported her notion of coming here."

"Why?"

"Because she believed in you."

"There doesn't seem much left for me to say, does there?"

said Aunt Phemie with a certain sparkle in her eyes, as she pressed the starting button.

2

As they drove into the cartshed, Aunt Phemie said, "The doctor is here." She parked her car in a stall alongside two uptilted carts, opened her door and got out smartly. By the time Ranald had his kitbag slung to his shoulder, she was halfway to the entrance. At the entrance, she paused, glanced back at him and went on. When he got outside, she was already greeting the doctor who drew away from his car to meet her. Ranald went on slowly, prepared to stroll by, but she called him and introduced Dr. Baxter, an active man with a full face and dark-grey hair. His small eyes rested assessingly on Ranald for a moment even as he smiled, then he turned again to Aunt Phemie.

"Mr. Surrey is a particular friend of Nan's," she explained.

"Is that so?" acknowledged the doctor politely, glancing again at Ranald.

"How is she this morning?" Aunt Phemie's tone was quiet and searching.

"Well——" The doctor's reddish brows puckered. "There's no temperature, but there's a distinct exhaustion, depression. You'll have to watch her pretty carefully. I feel fairly sure now there is nothing—physiologically wrong."

"That's good, that's so much." Aunt Phemie nodded in a businesslike way. There was a pause. "Do you think Mr. Surrey might help to—help her?"

"Well——" The doctor straightened himself, glanced away, looked at Ranald, and then at his own hand as it pulled his waistcoat down. He was distinctly well dressed. "I was going to warn you again against any form of excitement. Too sudden or strong an excitement might be definitely dangerous; would be. I had hoped you would be able to keep her quiet, rest her thoroughly, for at least a couple of days. By the way, you'll have to get them to stop that dog howling."

"What dog?" Asked Aunt Phemie.

The doctor looked at her. "I gather a dog was howling over at the cottages during the night."

"Was there?" Aunt Phemie appeared to think a moment. "I'll talk to the grieve about it."

"It might be as well," agreed the doctor. "I rather fancy," he added cheerfully, "that it was a real dog." He looked at Ranald. "You have travelled all night?"

"Yes."

"I think a rest might do you good, too. Frankly, I would rather she was not unduly excited, not anyway until we see how she is to-morrow. You understand this is a difficult case, and all I am quite sure of is that she needs rest and quiet."

"I understand," said Ranald. "Did she have a high temperature?"

"Yes, it ran dangerously high."

"With no apparent cause?"

"You knew her in London?"

"Yes."

"Did anything of the kind occur there?"

"It did. The doctor put it down to an all-night exposure. It disappeared, without leaving any traces—except that she was shattered a bit."

The doctor nodded thoughtfully, as though inwardly now more confident. "Well, I'll have a look in to-morrow. Otherwise," and he smiled to Aunt Phemie, "keep on as you are doing." He drove off.

"We'll go in the back way," said Aunt Phemie. At the side gate she paused, her hand on the latch. "We'll go quietly into the kitchen, if you don't mind. Perhaps, on the whole, we might follow the doctor's advice. What do you think?"

"All right," agreed Ranald in his casual way. "Not that I think they know a great deal about it."

"Who—the doctor?"

"Well, he is obviously fumbling, hoping for the best."

"What else can any of us do?"

Her sharpened tone brought the smile to his face. "I am not blaming him."

He closed the gate and followed her by the foot of the vegetable garden into the kitchen. "I'll make you a cup of tea," she said quietly. "Then we'll have lunch in about an hour. Would that be all right?" The kitchen faced north and in its faint gloom the pallor of his face was very distinct.

"Absolutely," he said, "and please don't trouble about me. I'll make myself a cup if you want to see Nan. Actually I don't feel hungry."

"You didn't sleep last night?" She shoved the murmuring kettle over the fire in the range.

"The carriage was packed, including an ailing child. The proletariat travelled." His tone was light and easy.

She moved quickly and soon had tea, with bread and scones, on the kitchen table. "Help yourself—and I'll go up to relieve Mrs. Fraser. Your train was very late." She went out, closing the door noiselessly behind her.

When he had drunk all the tea in the pot, he sat in the basket chair by the fire. His head drooped before the warmth and his eyes closed. There were whispering voices by the back door, then Aunt Phemie came in. He looked up.

"Would you like to rest?" she asked.

"I am feeling a bit drowsy," he admitted.

"Your bed is all ready. Would you come now?" She looked at his feet. "Have you slippers?"

"No, but that doesn't matter. I'll take off my shoes here."

She thought for a moment. "Wait." She went out, drew aside a curtain from a wall shelf by the pantry, and, from a heap of old footwear, fished out a pair of brown leather slippers. Her dead husband's. She stood with them in her hand, looking out of the side window at an old apple tree between the vegetable garden and the drying green. The apples were small but red, and suddenly she saw them very distinctly. In the kitchen she said, "Try these." They fitted him well enough. "We'll go quietly." She led the way, indicated the bathroom with a gesture, and introduced him to his room. He nodded his thanks as she silently closed the door.

Before Nan's room, which was three doors away, she listened, then went softly down the stairs and into the kitchen, closing the door behind her as in an act of privacy. Then she breathed.

She walked slowly to the window, staring through it. Infantile regression! she thought. As cool as that! His cool attitude seemed so incredible now that she stood by the sink staring blindly across the field of grain at the elms in the shallow ravine. She felt lost, wandered. She had expected him to be anxious, full of concern, of warmth. The lover; someone she would have to deal with, restrain, but use for Nan's surprise and happiness.

She could not believe it, did not know what to do, felt queerly helpless. Turning from the window, she saw his cup and plate on the table, brought them to the sink and turned the hot tap on them. The teapot she swilled out more than once, then stood with it cupped in her hands. It was still warm. Carrying it slowly towards the fire, she placed it on the hot metal, slid the kettle over the burning coal and continued to lean on its handle, waiting for the water to come to the boil, in a dumb patience.

The hot tea revived her, lifted her head. There was colour in her face, a brightness in her eyes, a tilt to her chin, as though something had happened to her in a foreign country where she was travelling alone. She would have to deal with the situation. She listened as it were to the sound of it.

Nan wasn't strong enough to cope with him, she thought. You need intelligence to cope with a man like that. His intelligence is so colossal that he breathes its air, naturally. She had felt like a flustered Victorian hen. Twenty-eight! My God! thought Aunt Phemie, who had ceased thinking in such terms for a long time.

This is the new world, she decided. Suddenly his face came before her again, paler than it had been, strangely pale, distinguished, slightly frightening, like something created in the dusk.

I'll be going neurotic next! she thought with a touch of spirited humour and recklessly drank her too hot tea. It brought tears to her eyes, and as she wiped them away with her bare hand she thought of Nan.

He would never cure Nan, never! Nan might cling to him,

trying to shake what she hungrily needed out of him. Might as well shake a tree at midday and expect the dew to fall. Honestly! declared Aunt Phemie, aware she was going all emotional but not caring. And giving him Dan's slippers too!

She felt much better after she had wept. So many years had come and gone since she had wept—that last forsaken night in bed at the time of the lambing—that she felt a new woman, emptied and lightened. She got up briskly, put her cup and saucer in the sink, turned the tap on, swilled the teapot, and began washing the dishes. As she dried his cup, her lips twisted in humour, as though she were at last getting the measure of him. Positively ancient in his calm understanding, she mocked. With a woman of her own age—she was forty-seven—she could have enjoyed herself. One would almost think, she could have said, that he had been *married* to her for twenty-eight years!

Her hands stopped drying, the cup remained poised before her breast, the dish-cloth hanging down, while she stared across the almost ripe grain. Her mouth opened slightly, her features gathered. *They have lived together,* she thought with an extreme almost paralysing enlightenment. Her breathing stopped.

As she moved quietly about the kitchen, putting things away, wiping the sink, she paused frequently. Then she sat down. This was a new and very important fact. It put everything in a different light. It so altered Nan's problem, so reflected upon the nature of her illness, that she could not—she could not—get a hold of it. The air now, the air around them, in the house, outside, was still with this enlightenment. And everything was caught in the stillness as in an appalling inevitability.

Could she be making a mistake? Nan showed so much of the élan of the lover, the naïve freshness, the youthful impatience, that Aunt Phemie had genuinely felt that the very unfulfilment of her love, the dreadful happenings which had stopped its natural flowering, was part of her actual trouble. Get these things removed, the horrible fears dissipated, and love would bloom naturally and healingly. The neurotic problem would be solved. Deep in her mind she had been certain of this—and any old Freudian could say what he liked!

It was a different and tougher problem now.

She came to herself with a sense of shock and a quick glance at the clock. The soup pot was quietly simmering. She had got everything ready before going to the station. Perhaps she had better go up and make sure Nan was not awake and "deserted". After the doctor's visit Nan had felt drowsy, profoundly indifferent, and wanted to sleep. But she had a habit of waking out of sleep, not knowing where she was, terrified. She should have had her switched egg. Aunt Phemie glanced at the clock again, then went out and quietly upstairs. On the landing she listened to the two bedrooms, aware of the distance between them as empty and unnatural. She would let Ranald sleep on. She wouldn't go near him. Then she heard Nan's bed creak faintly. She stood absolutely still, not wanting to go in. At last, however, she tiptoed to the door, pushed it slowly open, and shoved her head in.

"Hallo, had a sleep?" she asked in soft tones.

There was no answer.

"Just a minute and I'll bring you up your switched egg." She pulled the door almost shut and went quickly and quietly down the stairs, her heart beating strongly.

3

In the afternoon, with Mrs. Fraser in Nan's room, Aunt Phemie went out about the steading and found the grieve and Will in the machine shed overhauling the binder. Harvesting lay ahead and the very sight of the slim wooden arms ("flyers" the men called them) that, revolving, would thrash down the grain over the cutting blades, touched her in an airy way so that at once she felt in another world.

"Did you see Sandy about?" she asked.

Will looked at her and then at the grieve who took a few seconds to finish what he was doing before lifting his head. "Sandy?" he repeated. "No. Did you see him?" and he looked at Will.

"I think he's gone up to the top park with the stirks," said Will. "I saw him heading up that way whatever."

"Oh it doesn't matter," she said lightly.

There was silence for a little. The grieve would not question her, not at once. Sandy was the cattleman.

"That young collie of his," she went on, looking about the shed; "was he howling last night?"

"Howling? No. I can't say I heard him."

She realised that they would never hear anything so natural as a dog howling in the night; they slept too hard. She looked at Will.

"No, I can't say he's a howler," said Will slowly. "And it's hardly likely, because he sleeps in the stick shed with the ould dog."

"It's nothing; only my niece was a bit disturbed last night and the doctor insists she needs all the rest she can get."

"He may have howled of course," said the grieve. "I'll talk to Sandy if you like."

"Well, you could mention it to him—just to make sure. How is the binder doing?" She went forward a step or two.

"Not bad," said the grieve. "We're just going to look over it. How is Miss Gordon today?"

"Coming along, thanks. She only needs attention."

"I'm glad to hear that," said the grieve. Then, after waiting a moment, he added, "I was going to see you last night about one or two things, but I didn't want to disturb the house." He left the binder and they slowly went outside.

There had been rain during the night and all morning the sky had been overcast, but now the sun was out and everything was washed and fresh. She saw the bright colours of a cock chaffinch on a willow growing out of the green bank. He was declaring himself confidently as he hopped about the twigs.

She listened to the grieve's talk of repairs, the blacksmith, the recurrent trouble over the tractor's magneto and what they said in the garage. He spoke confidently for he had arranged everything, but the accounts would come to her. When he related how he had dealt with others his manner and tone always gathered a consequential air. He was a middle-sized stocky man, who said little by way of reprimand to those under him until he could no longer keep it in, when he said too much. But he was fair, and, in illness, extraordinarily considerate. She always, at the end of their year, gave him a bonus, worked out privately by herself as a percentage. In recent years it had been quite a tidy sum. The farm was as well run as any in the district. Perhaps one hidden factor more than any other kept him now her devoted ally and that was his secret consciousness of lack of schooling. His respect for the way she filled in forms and ran the farm's accountancy was very deep. She listened to him with her businesslike air and watched the cock chaffinch. A wren came out from the roots of the willow. The physical health and strength of the world had something lovely and sure about it. She said, "That's fine!" nodding. He said, "Just let me know what he charges." "I will." "Some of them are worth the watching," he added. Then he began talking about one of the horses and she went with him to the stables. The brute was crippled on the near hind leg. He clapped a haunch strongly and cried, "Get over there!" "But isn't that swollen!" "Ay," he answered calmly, "there's a swelling there." "Have you sent for the vet?" she asked with sharp concern. "Ay," he answered casually, "I put word to him this morning." "What do you think it is?" "Who knows, for he can hardly have strained himself. He was aye a lazy brute. It may be a touch of the rheumatics. We'll see." He was now treating lightly her concern for animals. She knew this. But he had sent for the vet.

When she parted from the grieve she did not want to go back to the house so walked round to the cartshed and examined a front tyre on her car which had a mysterious slow leak. This morning it had been almost flat, but now it was hard as any of the other tyres. It certainly was an odd business, she decided, pleased, however, that the tyre was holding up. There was no one about and she went and had a look first into the small byre where the four milch cows were kept. But all cattle were out at grass; stalls and cribs were empty; yet the warm thick smell was everywhere, a healthy smell that did her good. This was the main part of the steading and its emptiness was felt, asking for a cry and an echo, but with the pleasant thought back in her mind that the beasts were in the fields. Sandy, returning from the top field, would take the four milch cows with him for the evening supply to the farm house and the cottages. No milk was sold.

At last she left the steading and, going up into the vegetable garden, pulled a plump lettuce, two or three carrots, nipped off some chives, decided she would get a knife and cut a cabbage, laid down what she had already gathered in order to pull up a strong growth of groundsel and weeded for nearly an hour. There was nothing she liked better than working in the earth with her bare hands.

By the time she had made her salad, Mrs. Fraser quietly appeared. She was a small stoutish capable woman, naturally kind and good-natured, and was now going home to prepare her husband's evening meal. The men knocked off work at half-past five and her two children would be home from school, though Teenie, at eleven, was nearly as good as a woman in the house. However, they talked for over ten minutes before Mrs. Fraser went. "You should have had a lie down to yourself," were her last words, uttered in a softly reproving voice.

Before closing the kitchen door, Aunt Phemie listened to the quietness in the house, then—for her night's sleep had been very broken—she felt not tired so much as the need to sit down. The steading was still about her, the earth, a rough shagginess of strength, and she did not want to lose its comfort. She thought of her husband; as she often did.

This strength, this thickness of living, this comfort and depth of body and hands, had kept her from going back to school teaching when her husband had been killed. Her teaching life in retrospect had seemed thin and washed and pale. Not only marriage but the working of the farm itself had been a new experience, and when Dan began to tell her how he stood with the bank, his desire for a tractor, his difficulties at a time when farming was not doing well, the amount of the mortgage on the farm (he had bought it outright), his plans, the possible switch over to a dairy farm, and all the hundred and one things and personalities involved, she had not only grasped the situation but almost at once had begun to help him. This had been something he had never foreseen, and it astonished him without end. He would look at a page of her writing and figures in her new red -bound account book with a serious air but actually for the secret delight of looking at it. No row of perfectly thatched stacks had ever given him so intimate a pleasure. When he was setting off for market, she would sometimes call him back and fix his tie, fix him up properly and he would kiss her behind the kitchen door. Once, after such a happening, he had met the grieve and demanded, "What the hell are you doing that for?" "Because the damn thing is rotten," replied the grieve, instantly flaring up. Dan gave the thing a kick. "By God, you're right!" he said and went off laughing, leaving the grieve to stare after him in utter astonishment. Then his birthday drew near and Phemie decided—she had saved a bit before she married—to present him with a tractor. He had really grown serious at that and said, "Listen to me, Phemie. That's your money and I'm never going to touch a penny piece of it. You keep it by you, lass. Then he added, for he had been deeply moved, "Who knows but you may need it yet!" "Thank goodness," she had replied, "tyrant as you are, you cannot stop me doing what I like with my own." "Can't I?" "No." "We'll see about that," he said and went off with a man's laugh. But what he actually did see, on the afternoon of his birthday as he came down from the hayfield in answer to her summons, was the tractor ticking over in front of the cartshed. Phemie herself was in the driver's seat and the delivery man was explaining to her how it worked. Once out of sight of the hayfield, he had started to run, for he had feared something had happened to her, and he was now breathless. She waved to him gaily, excited as a bairn with a new toy.

He had been killed that autumn by the visiting threshing mill. The driver of the steam-engine had been trying to manipulate the mill through a gate when it got jammed and was in danger of tearing the gate-post and corner of the stone wall away. Dan had shouted to him to back. He had backed but the ground was very soft. Dan decided to go forward and speak to him at the same moment as the driver, on his own impulse, went ahead again. The mill slid, caught Dan against the gate post, and crushed him. The sight of his body had killed the child in her and an ambulance had taken her to hospital.

Before the warmth of the kitchen fire Aunt Phemie's head drooped, but her eyes were wide open, very wide. Another memory had touched her to-day when she had wept. It now came back like something that explained in some queer fatal way why she had stayed on in the farm.

After convalescence she had returned, intending to wind up all the affairs of the farm and sell out early in the year or by the May term at the latest. It had been a fairly open winter and one January morning—the seventh, for the earliness of the date surprised her—she found that the snowdrops were through, not yet opened but white, folded white on their short green stalks like tiny spears. This had an extraordinary effect on her, piercing sweet, intensifying her loss, her sorrow, even as it pierced through it, and she felt the year opening, the coming of spring, and all the springs of the years ahead.

She had bought numberless bulbs, snowdrop, crocus—yellow and purple, and daffodil, and planted them in the grass, for the house, being built on a slope, had green banks wherever the level ground tumbled over. She was going to have a wonderful show, a transformation, a glory of the spring. And now, behold! the show was beginning, had indeed brought its opening date forward in a press of eagerness as though the given time would be short enough for the full display which the green banks had in mind.

March came in and still she had not made up her mind. She should leave the place but she could not; she was somehow not ready yet. In recent years stock-rearing had been more profitable than crop-growing, and in addition to cattle her husband had a lot of sheep on the ground. The grieve was now completely dependent on her book-keeping.

On a late March afternoon she was busy about a small rockery which she had got Dan to help her to make. Blues were now predominant: grape hyacinth, scillas, and glory of the snow, with aubretia coming along. It was still a marvel to her how fragile these early flowers were. The yellow crocus was a tuning fork out of some sunny underworld, still holding the glow of the note. The snowdrops, full grown, large, in clumps, had but contrived to emphasise their delicate green veining, their bowed heads and nun-like pallor. Marvellous to think that the mature lusty growths of summer would shrivel in weather that gave to snowdrop and crocus a lovelier grace, a deeper colour.

Ah, and here at last some flakes of white—on the cherry tree! Her heart gave a bound. Into the bright cold air of March, the cherry blossom had come! As she gazed at the blown petals, two or three more petals came blowing past them. Snow-petals. Snow! She looked into the depth of the air and saw the flurry of snowflakes, not falling, but swirling darkly in the air. Then they began to shoot past in front of her, all white; to settle on the flowers, her hands, everywhere. A ewe bleated beyond the garden fence; day-old lambs answered in their thin shivering trebles.

In the dark of the night she awoke and heard the fragile voices, crying out in the field. Forlorn they sounded and lost. These particular sheep were Border Leicesters, soft, the shepherd had said, because they were so well bred.

In the darkness the bleating of the lambs was very affecting. And there rose one thin persistent plaint that she knew instinctively to be the crying of a new-born lamb. She thought of the ewes, square market-bred ewes, soft, having their lambs out there in the snow. She wished she could do something for them. A flurry of snow against the window, blind fingers against the glass before the eddy of wind bore them away. Bore them away in a small whining anxious sound into space. Nothing conveyed the idea of space so well as the wind at night. And all the time the lambs kept bleating, and the wind carried away their bleating into the gulfs of space.

To ease this burden, she thought of herself as out in the field, going from ewe to ewe, and saw the lambs with their red birth stains in the driving snow, the mother licking them in the whirling snow, each lick making them stagger. If they weren't licked dry they might die.

The soft snow-fingers at the window went away, defeated.

She hearkened for them with a sense of loss, of guilt. She got up and pulled aside the curtain. The snow shower had passed and the sloping lands lay spectral white under the stars. Something in the whiteness of purity, of virgin austerity, touched her to frightened wonder. She dressed quickly, and in the kitchen went quietly lest she waken the servant girl. Into her long gumboots, her heavy mackintosh, tightening the belt about her waist; then to the back door which she opened carefully.

The snow was surprisingly full of light and this suited her secret purpose, for she could not have taken a lantern. She did not want to be seen. Suddenly it was as if she came alive, as if something which had been holding her had let go, and a bounding invigoration went coursing through her. Some of the beasts, with lifted faces white against their fleeces, which were dark-grey against the snow, looked at her coming and, instead of showing fear, cried to her, taking even a step or two towards her. She was moved to cry back to them.

As the bleating seemed to multiply all across the field, she got into a stir of excitement, and kept speaking brightly, encouragingly. It began to snow again and soon she was wrapped about in the whirling flakes and completely blinded so that she could not see a yard in front of her, and when the wind got into her mouth it roared there and choked her. She stood quite still, her back to the wind, leaning against it. She let her voice cry out on the wind, her spirit lifting away in a wild irrational emotion like joy. Then the wind lifted her bodily along, and she kicked into a ewe giving birth to a lamb.

Ewes should give birth later in the morning as the hill ewes did at her childhood home. But now on her knees she could half see what was happening. She spoke to the beast, sheltered her, encouraged her, eased her with a tender hand, wisely, helping her, using terms of endearment in a practical voice. And as though some of her vitality and encouragement were indeed of practical help, the ewe had an easy delivery.

"Feeling it a bit cold now!" she said to the lamb. "Don't get excited, you old fool!" she said to the ewe. She would shelter them until the shower passed, and she looked over her shoulder to see if it was clearing. Coming upon her was a smother of yellow light, swinging, growing … at hand. She rose up.

The light stopped and there was a harsh exclamation. Rising snow-white like a ghost above the crying of a newborn lamb in the whirling ebb of the shower, she might have startled a mind less sensitive than the shepherd's. "It's all right, Colin," she cried, giving him time. "It was foolish of me to have come out without a light."

He came forward and said, "I wondered what you were." He muttered it, as though suspicious of her. She realised that probably he was suspicious, was thinking in his own mind: What brought her out here?

And she could hardly explain! So she talked in an easy friendly way, evolving the half-lie that she had thought a ewe was in difficulties, the cries had wakened her and she had come out to see if she could help.

He muttered something about having been called away somewhere, but soon, under her natural friendliness, he thawed completely. He came from the north of Sutherland and Dan had had complete confidence in him. Of all the men about the place, she liked him best, liked his independence and a certain loneliness that went with him. He reminded her, too, of the son of a crofter from Western Ross whom she had known at college. His native gift for flattery had been disturbing for a while.

"There's a ewe over there I'm worried about," he said when they had at last got to the top corner of the field. She was now all glowing with warmth. The shower gone, what had been half-frightening in the still, white landscape was no longer so.

"We have been lucky," he said. "But we can hardly expect it to hold." So that when they came to the ewe that he had been worrying about she was prepared for death. He did everything he could with a strange concentration. When he spoke to her he was really speaking to himself. She realised his deep instinctive skill. The lamb was born but the ewe died under his hands. On his knees in the snow, he looked at the humped body, his hands hanging. He got up and said quietly, "I'll take the lamb to the bothy. We may have a mother for it soon enough." He was unmarried and about her own age.

"Come along to the kitchen," she said. "I'll make you a cup of tea." The kitchen, with its hot water, was often of service in the ailments of beasts.

"Don't you bother, mem," he answered. "I have the fire on and can get milk for the lamb in no time."

"Come," she said calmly. "I should like to give you a cup of tea." And she moved on.

She did not want to lose him now, did not want to lose the life that had come into her, did not want to lose sight of the lamb. He began tugging at the stiff iron catch of a cross-barred gate with one hand. "Give me the lamb," she said and took it from under his arm. He opened the gate and let her through.

As they came into the deep shadow of the house, she looked back. "Do you think it is going to be much?"

"No," he answered. "There is life in the air. But I'll see about shelter when the daylight comes in."

"The wireless forecast snow-showers and outlook unchanged."

"Did it?" he said politely, cleaning his hands with snow.

"Come in."

He scraped his boots clean. "I'll make such a mess of your floor."

Inside, the bleating of the lamb sounded startlingly loud. As he struck a match, cupping it with his hands, she saw the glow of the light on his brown skin and the glitter of it in his dark attractive eyes. He needed a haircut. Then his face cleared and opened as he tilted it up, looking for the lamp. "Here's the lamp," she said softly as if she might waken the house. Then she sent him out to the shed next the dairy where there were empty boxes and straw. "Hsh!" she crooned to the lamb, cupping its head in her hand, her fingertips at its mouth. The fragile body butted, the little bones slithering under the thin skin. She saw the discoloured skin and her own hands and wrists. He came in with the box and put it on the, floor by the kitchen range. "It's a feed he wants," he said.

She nodded. "I'll wash my hands and then put on the fire." She was no longer excited by the crying of the lamb and watched the way he took the sticks Jean had drying over the range and set about raking the embers which were still red under the ashes. He put a wisp of straw over the red, the dry sticks carefully on top, and blew. Up came the flames.

"You haven't a feeding bottle?" he asked.

She hadn't.

"I'll be back in a minute with one," he said.

By the time he came back she had the milk blood-warm and the kettle over the fire with no more water in it than would make tea for two.

They spoke in quiet tones as she spread a tea-cloth over a corner of the kitchen table and set two cups on it, bread and biscuits, bright plates, butter and knives. "Leave him now and wash your hands," she said.

She was lifting the teapot to fill his cup when a noise arrested her. The noise drew nearer. She knew it was Jean, but could not say a word, could not move the hand with the lifted teapot. They both stared at the door. It opened—and, her face half-petulant and flushed from sleep, there stood Jean, the servant girl. Her eyes widened as she gazed at Colin and then right down her neck, as she turned her face away, went a deep blush. Dark, well-built, with a clear skin, she was inclined to moods occasionally but was a capital worker. At this moment, in her twenty-fifth year, she looked disturbingly attractive.

"Come in, Jean," said her mistress quietly. She glanced at Colin. He was looking at his plate.

The emotion between them, whether it had ever been declared or not, was so obvious to their mistress that her hand shook slightly as she poured Colin's tea. "You're up very early."

"I heard the lamb and I wondered," Jean replied, her back to them, attending to the fire.

"Put some more water in the kettle, because there's hardly enough tea here for you." Then she began telling Jean about the experiences in the snow. When she had drunk her cup, she got up. "What's the time? Nearly five! I think I'll have an hour or two in bed. There's no need for you to hurry, Colin."

She left them and went up to her room.

She was feeling tired now, but when she had undressed and stretched between the sheets, still faintly warm, she experienced a sensation of ease, as though her body floated. A crush of snow, softer than the lamb's mouth, smothered itself against the window. And all at once she thought of the ewe—that she had quite forgotten—with the head thrown out and back, the neck stretched as to an invisible knife. The snow would be drifting about the body, covering it up ... .

Aunt Phemie was startled out of her reverie by the opening of the door behind her. Her heart leapt as she turned with a wild scared expression. Ranald stood there, smiling, his slippers in his hand.

4

"You gave me such a start!" explained Aunt Phemie, as she got to her feet.

"I came as quietly as I could." He had closed the door and now put on his slippers.

To have come on his socks was somehow unexpectedly thoughtful of him. "You had a good sleep?"

"Like a log."

"I didn't want to disturb you. You must be famished." She turned to the fire, got a fork and tried the potatoes. She glanced at the clock, "Dear me!" she said, then hurried to pour out what water was left in the potato pan and set the table for their meal. "Sit down. You didn't hear any sounds upstairs?"

"No. It was very quiet." He stretched himself in the chair and yawned. "That was a good sleep." The slow characteristic smile spread over his face; she turned her eyes away as though its self-assurance was still something she could not quite bear.

She had soup, a salad, cold boiled chicken, and potatoes. He got up from the chair and stood with his back to the fire, watching her arrange the table and fill his soup plate.

"You begin," she said, "and I'll go and see if Nan is ready for her tray." She closed the door quietly behind her.

When he had finished his soup, he waited for a time, then got up and began carving the chicken. Before sitting down, he went to the door, opened it and listened, closed it and went on with his meal. He ate a lot of salad with a chicken leg. The lettuce was crisp and his white teeth crunched it audibly. When at last he had finished he lit a cigarette and looked about him, leaning back.

Presently Aunt Phemie entered. She appeared agitated, scared, and, with care, did not quite close the door.

"She heard you," she whispered.

"Did she?"

She nodded and rattled the plates.

"What did she say?"

"Hsh! her door is open." She spoke no more, and in a moment went out with soup and bread on a tray. He sucked the cigarette smoke deep and blew it out slowly, his eyelids flickering in thought. When she came back she closed the door. He got up and looked at her. But beyond asking if he had had enough, she paid no attention to him.

"This can't go on," she said when she had dished herself some soup. Her tone was level but low.

"That's what I was thinking."

"She's so highly sensitised she hears things acutely. I said she couldn't have heard anyone, unless it was Mrs. Fraser going back for something she had dropped. She said it was someone coming out of Ranald's room. To prove to her it was no-one I went into your room and back."

"Did she believe you?"

She supped her soup. "That's not the difficulty."

"I see."

She looked at him. "Do you?"

"Well, if she can't believe her own senses—where is she?"

She took a couple of spoonfuls and broke some bread on her plate. "What do you think should be done?"

"I think I should go and see her."

She crumpled the bread, looking out the window. "I wish I knew," she said, with controlled distress. "She was shaking, trembling, and did not want me to touch her. She turned away, tears in her eyes, but she was not sobbing. She looked pale and alien. I was suddenly frightened."

"Alien?" he repeated.

"Yes, withdrawn into herself, into some world where I don't know—where she is alone. Away from us. I got the feeling she knew at last she was going there."

"I see," he said, almost coldly. His lids lowered. "Why don't you think I should see her?" he asked.

"Because of the effect you might have on her. I just don't know."

"But something must be done?"

"Are you sure of yourself and your effect?"

"Yes."

"Well, I'm not," said Aunt Phemic. "Not yet."

"You have to consider whether you are possibly being too emotional about it—and whether that helps."

"I assure you I have considered it. There is also the effect of an absence of emotion."

"I agree," he said reasonably, as if suddenly pleased with her capacity for direct argument.

She looked straight at him and asked, "Do you know anything about her fear of leprosy?"

His features firmed to a sustained stare as his vision travelled through her. Then he turned and after sucking a last mouthful of smoke dropped the stub of his cigarette in the fire. "So that phantasy has come back?"

"So you know about it?"

"I think I do. But—well—it was merely a fantastic exaggeration of a—of a happening."

"Don't you think I should know about it?"

"Certainly. It might take a little time to explain."

"Do you know anything about Kronos?"

"Kronos?" His brows gathered as he looked at her. "No. Money, is it?"

"I don't know—but I hardly think so."

"Who was Kronos again?"

"Kronos was the father who devoured his own sons." She got up and began separating the thin slices of chicken breast which he had cut.

"Has she some delusion about it?"

"It's hard to tell. It's a Greek myth—like the one about Oedipus."

He gave a dry appreciative smile, then asked, "How did she use it?"

"I don't know. It would doubtless be a displacement, or transference is it?"

"When she was very ill?"

"Yes."

"You mean her unconscious used the figure of Kronos—to cover up someone else—even from herself?"

"Possibly. Who can say?"

"She was as bad as that?"

Aunt Phemie put a potato on the plate and the plate on a small round tray.

"Tell me," he asked. "What *did* happen to her?"

She lifted the tray, then paused to look at him. "Should you see her now—or should we have a talk first?"

"I think you're right," he agreed. "It might be better."

He turned to the fire and she went out.

Later, when Mrs. Fraser was up with Nan, Aunt Phemie said, "We can talk now. She took some of the soup but wouldn't look at the chicken. However, she can still drink milk, thank goodness. She thinks I'm seeing the grieve. I try to interest her in what goes on about the farm. I saw her struggle to be interested, to come back from—from where she is. It's getting a bit dark in here."

"It's all right. Have a cigarette?"

"No thank you. By the way, when we do go up to bed you could come in your stockings behind me. Your door is open. You can manage to see to yourself?"

"I have slept in some queer places in my time."

"You were in the Air Force?" She sat down.

"Yes," he answered, taking the chair which she indicated.

"Nan told me. You had a nasty crash——"

"Grounded, long before the war ended, so here I am." He smiled. "They gave me an office job. It was good cover for more interesting work. That's when I really got to know Nan."

"You know her very well?"

"Naturally, or I shouldn't be here."

"Of course. I was merely thinking of knowing what she is really like. Far as I can gather, she seemed to move in a pretty fast set, and in my experience—it may not be much, but still…you don't get really to know people in such a milieu, not as a rule."

"You don't think so?"

"No. Why, do you?"

"I do. I should say it's the acid test."

Aunt Phemie was silent for a few moments. "Acid test of what?" she asked.

"Of sticking power; character, if you like."

"I don't see it like that. I may be wrong but it seems to me that every set has its own rules—of behaviour and so on—its own beliefs. To be of the set you must conform. If you don't behave as the set do, you get broken."

"But if the set doesn't suit you, you should clear out. You *would* clear out, as a matter of fact. You don't hang on anywhere unless you're getting some kick out of it."

"It all depends on the kick, I suppose. Will you give me a cigarette, please?"

When she had it lit, she smiled slightly, taking the cigarette from her mouth with a certain elegance as if it were in a holder. "This brings back some of my remote past; late nights and endless argument. I am not without some small experience. Tell me about your set."

"There's nothing really to tell. And it wasn't a set in that sense. You must understand that. Most of us worked very hard, late into the night often. I fancy Nan has exaggerated all this. In fact, I know she has. She got delusions about it—afterwards."

"After what?"

"After she broke down. She saw people in the most exaggerated way. She magnified things, gave huge mythical meanings to—to quite simple acts. It was distressing—and very difficult to counter. But we understood it."

"*We?* You mean—all of you?"

"Yes, naturally. You may forget that London was blitzed, that bombs fell, that I myself dropped bombs, that human bodies were mangled or blown to bits as the natural order of things. That's the world we lived in. A mental breakdown of one degree or another was not unknown."

"I stand corrected," said Aunt Phemie, trying to tap ash away with an awkward forefinger. "All the same I should like to know more, if you don't mind. She mentioned, for example, someone named Freddie."

"Freddie is all right. He's satirical, with a merciless eye for foibles, but he's witty. Nan liked him at first. It was only towards the end that she felt there was something disintegrating in him, that beneath his wit there was a real desire to tear people to bits."

"And there wasn't?"

"Well, we all want to tear something to bits. At least I hope so. And Freddie could work."

"What did he work at?"

"I was thinking of the work he did *after* his daily job. He limps from hip trouble so was always a civilian."

"She mentioned Julie."

"An emotional creature—purely. That sort of female is always a damned nuisance."

"In what way exactly?"

"She distracts fellows from their work, embroils them, uses up their energy. She makes scenes. You go to her rescue—as if she were of any account! And the devil of it is that in these circumstances she is the outlet for the instincts, the full libidinous charge, the irrational lure to a fellow to let rip. We're all going to die soon so what the hell? That sort of deadly stuff." It was the first time she had seen him moved in any way, not that he gesticulated or even raised his voice much, but his tone did gather a certain merciless precision.

"I rather gather that Nan felt for Julie."

"Before her breakdown, we had some words about it. I just couldn't understand Nan then over that, for Nan has brains. And she was always so sensible, so balanced, and—really—gay. Possibly there was too much drink going. Occasional outings, all-night affairs, with illicit petrol and what not. The thing somehow got worked up. Fellows were always coming on leave, chaps I knew often. Their next trip after leave might be their last. All very normal enough, taking everything into account; but I admit it did get a bit hot in the end—and particularly after the war ended."

"Did these fellows also have your—uh—revolutionary beliefs?"

"Mostly, even if only as sympathisers—at least they were not active then. So it worked in them the other way round. I mean it was a case of—this rotten old bourgeois order needs liquidating, so let's liquidate and be merry."

"Eat, drink and be merry———"

"By no means," he interrupted. "To-morrow we were going to live—and build; what was left of us, that is; but first we had to destroy. That was clear. You have to raze the old building before you build the new."

"And that extended to beliefs, behaviour, everything?"

"Yes, in so far as they were an expression of the bourgeois order; which, inevitably, meant almost altogether."

"Revolution?"

"Precisely."

"There is no other way, no gradual evolution that could avoid destruction, death, horror?"

"Your mind there, if you don't mind my saying so, is confused. We do have gradual change, in the sense, say, that a thing gradually increases in size or in temperature or in productive capacity. By blowing up a toy balloon you make it larger; but a point comes where it bursts. In everything there is that point of revolutionary change. It's not a case of whether we like it or not. It's in the nature of things. In the wintertime you will, if there's frost about, run the water off your car. Why? Because you know that though water can get colder and colder and still remain fluid water, a point comes where it has a revolutionary change into solid ice and bursts your cylinder block."

"But I do recognise that and so run the water off."

"Exactly. In that respect you are a determinist. The point is, do you recognise it in the economic relations which *determine* our social life? Are you prepared for the revolutionary change there?"

"How do I know that that kind of change is necessary?"

"War, destruction, the concentration camps—if these result from the existing order of things in our society, go on increasing like your toy balloon, should it not be evident that their cause is within the order itself, our bourgeois order? Where else can it be?"

"So you think a bloody revolution is inevitable?"

"Revolution is inevitable. Bloody is as may be."

She glanced at him. His face was pale in the gathering dusk, and emotionless. It was as if in the last words, grown indifferent before her hopeless lack of knowledge, he had turned a tap off. He lit another cigarette, remembered her, and offered his carton. She took one.

"Nan also mentioned a man—for some reason she would never use his name—Know-all, she called him."

He glanced at her, a searching glance. "Yes, he was the leprosy man," he said.

She waited. "You sound as if you were referring to the milkman."

A satiric breath came through his nostrils, a wry humour to his face. "No, he wasn't the milkman, as it happened. He was one who reckoned he had got rid of all the illusions at last, all the bourgeois repressions. He fatally attracted Nan. I mean she couldn't stand him. But by that time her emotions were getting the better of her."

"You mean she was beginning to go to bits."

"Exactly," he said, as if refreshed by such cool frankness. "Emotions work up to an awful mess. That's the trouble. You have to use emotion, of course. But once let it get out of hand—bloody awful," he concluded succinctly.

"Tell me what happened?"

"It would need a psychoanalyst," he suggested dryly, "and long sessions on a couch. However." He took a chestful of smoke and let it out in a slow hissing fullness. "The thing went on. Things have a habit of doing that—until they burst. One thing reacting on another, a dialectical process. But will folk see it? Not they! Even Fanwicke—or Know-all, if you like—although he is the ablest intellectually of the lot of us, could drive our definition of freedom to a satisfaction of his *individual* ends that he would not—or could not—perceive was in practice essentially bourgeois or anti-social. It may be—I have long suspected it— that the aggressive instincts are in him particularly powerful. He talked of liquidating institutions and politicians with a relish, that, in our off hours with drink about, was certainly infectious. He has a driving intellectual force, a certainty, a belief in himself that inspires young spirits. Quite an extraordinary thing. He makes you realise how revolutions happen."

"The need of satisfying his individual ends touched Nan?"

"It would touch anyone. Nan is a very good-looking girl with at times an extraordinarily vivid life in her, as you know. The trouble was Nan couldn't leave him alone. She always countered him. And in argument of course he flattened her. I give you no idea of a certain flair he has, a sheer brilliance."

"You imply that deep in her mind she was really attracted by him?"

"Frankly, I could not be sure. She said she hated him, hated the destructiveness in him, and so on. But when I saw that she was deliberately influencing me against him—well, I had to stop her. The emotional mess again, the personal. The awful insidious business that—— Anyhow, we quarrelled."

After a short pause, Aunt Phemie said, "I suppose relations all round were pretty free?"

"Sex relations, you mean? Reasonably free, yes. That kept a lot of frustrations out of the way and let us get on with our work—and our lives."

"And after your quarrel?"

"We remained friends, but of course I only saw her at intervals.

Remember we were all working at our jobs—some of us quite hard. If you really have some notion of a smart set in your mind, forget it. There are loathsome enough things without it."

"I think I understand. Long and even dreary spells—with outbreaks."

"That's about it, not forgetting the long spell of death and destruction. Things come in cycles. There came, as I said, a pretty hot time. The strain of the war was over. I—let out a bit myself. Nan let go. A bit of a smash-up once or twice, with some of the lads in trouble. Then I decided to call a halt; was jeered at, especially by Nan. Julie got a decent young lad into real trouble; he was damned lucky merely to be reduced to the ranks. And so on. With Fanwicke making now a dead set at Nan."

"And she wasn't responding quite right?"

"That looked like her game. And she was tough. She seemed set for anything and Fanwicke her high aim. There are beasts, aren't there—spiders or something—where the female in due course gobbles up the male? After a few drinks, the things Nan could say to Fanwicke left little to the destructive imagination. Fanwicke smiled. He reckoned he knew the symptoms of concealed love. But I need not grow lurid. Julie came gibbering for me one night. It appears there was a taxi crammed with them, pretty late. Did I mention night clubs? Anyway, Fanwicke, it seems, tried to fumble about Nan's person in the packed taxi and—her arms being pinned—she bit him badly in the neck. A hellish commotion ensued. They had to hold Nan by main force; then got her into Julie's place and doped her. Fanwicke wore sticking plaster for some time."

Aunt Phemie sat quite still. His recital of events had a conversational calm that was completely objective. His reference to spiders had been an incidental touch of macabre wit.

"Not a very pretty story," commented Aunt Phemie, subduing an involuntary skin shiver. She got hold of the poker and stirred up the fire. "Did she suffer much—after?"

"She would let no one touch her—except Julie. She had this leprosy fear; a horror of hands coming near her. I supposed it had something to do with Fanwicke's attack."

"You helped?"

"By keeping my distance, yes. I was with her quite a lot of course. It was a difficult time for a bit. She began to find her own solution by going back to early days—to put it mildly."

"Put what mildly?"

"Her hallucinated craving. However, at long last it brought her here. We were friendly again by that time."

Aunt Phemie turned from the fire. "It's getting quite dark. Would you like the lamp lit?"

"As you like. Actually I have never cared much for sitting in the dark."

"So it would seem," agreed Aunt Phemie, going towards the lamp.

He smiled. "You have a nice cool voice."

"You appreciate the absence of emotion?"

"Very much," he assured her.

5

Aunt Phemie lit the old Famos lamp and as she gave the mantle time to kindle was aware of a certain unreality about her standing body. She realised that his reference to a nice cool voice was not so much a compliment to her as a relief for himself, yet it used the channel of compliment. He just wouldn't be bothered being insincere over a small thing like that. She felt herself acting in a play whose words she had not mastered. Going to the door, she opened it quietly and listened. That, too, was part of an act.

"Mrs. Fraser is very good," she said, coming back to the fire, looking along the mantelpiece, sitting down; "comfortable—and comforting."

He nodded. "I know the type."

"Why do you use the word 'type'? She's a human being. Would you like some more coffee?"

"I would. It's good coffee."

"The right bite?"

"Not quite up to the old coffee stall in the early hours. You contrive a civilised smoothness—though doubtless the bite is concealed."

"You sound as if you had an early experience of London night life."

"I had. My views were not exactly welcomed at home, even as a college youngster. Not that having views, political or religious—or both—would really have mattered."

"No?" She stuck the aluminium coffee pot into the fire.

"No. The English are curiously sound in one respect—that's why they have lasted so long. They realise that action is the acid test of thought. Pure Marxism."

"And where do you get your Ranald from?"

"Some barbarian addition to the pure stock. A Highland grandmother it was. The family is rather inclined to blame her for having upset the genes. I take after her apparently."

"Do you? In brains?"

He smiled, switching his eyes onto her. "Brains is hardly considered a breeding point in the best circles. I'm afraid it was more a matter of looks—though doubtless, come to think of it, the looks would also cover my unfortunate aberration."

She regarded the face critically. "But you don't look particularly Highland, do you? I should say you were Greek."

Their eyes met for a moment. "Kronos, you think?"

Aunt Phemie felt exactly as though she had been invisibly stabbed. It was as if some truth, which her mind did not even entertain, which was still formless, had yet stabbed her. She caught the coffee pot handle; it was hot, if not quite hot enough to make her draw her hand away, as she did, swiftly, looking at it for the sting. He offered his handkerchief, but she persisted in finding the old singed cloth grip; then she poured him some coffee and also helped herself.

"I am taking all your cigarettes," she apologised; "I must get some."

"You were going to tell me what happened to Nan," he said, as they blew the first smoke through the silence.

"Yes." She was having difficulty with specks of tobacco sticking to her lips, got up, and taking down a jar from a top shelf surprised herself by finding a long cigarette holder among some pheasant's tail feathers. Now she looked more at ease; even her appearance was subtly changed. "Yes," she resumed, with an objective manner. "There has been some trouble. It is involved, as you will understand, not really because the man matters in any way personally but because of her condition. You appreciate that, of course."

He waited.

"I don't know much about the neuroses, not anyhow in a technical way. Nan to me isn't really or fixedly neurotic. She has certain illusions or delusions, symptoms, and is in a very dangerous condition, but she knows it and is fighting against it. So long as she keeps the strength, the balance, to fight, she'll come absolutely right, for she has a sound—foundation. When you call this foundation a sort of regression to an infantile security, I don't mind. I think the words are almost meaningless. In fact they may be, in a certain way, terribly wrong. No, 'wrong' is the wrong word. I mean terribly *blind.* But perhaps that doesn't sound very coherent."

"I get some of it, I think."

Aunt Phemie tapped her cigarette holder once or twice expertly with an extended forefinger. Her features had firmed and her eyes now had the power of veiling emotion. "We might talk of that again," and though she spoke the words conversationally, they held a suggestion of a deeper knowledge, almost a grim power. She was contemplating the fire, and Ranald's eyes travelled over her features.

They were good features, with clear evidence of the bone but not really thin. In the lamplight certain fine lines were hardly discernible. There were lines on the forehead but they gave character rather than age. It was an open face, but firm, with something attractive about the blue eyes, which yet were by themselves in no way unusual in colour or size. Her hair must at one time have been a red-gold. Now it was pale as autumn stubble in an evening light, with just that remaining glint in it. There was also that hint of glow in her fair skin. The bone of her jaw, thought Ranald, is there all right.

"For us at the moment," said Aunt Phemie, "it may be enough

if we understand about her fighting. She wants to clean up her own mind, to understand. But in spite of the cynics, a person can at the same time be doing this not only for herself but also for someone else. She might even have the notion, say, that she is doing it for *you*, in the sense that she fancies she has discovered the enormous fact that there may be more things in heaven and earth than are contained in your philosophy. Or do you think that's impossible for any human mind?"

There was a breath of laughter as Ranald stirred in his chair. "I get your point, but is not that, too, an obvious illusion? To think you are doing it for someone else is to flatter yourself the more. Isn't it?"

"So when *you* think you are going to put the world right for *everyone* else you are flattering yourself rather enormously?"

"Except for this: that I am prepared to reason the matter logically with everyone else." This kind of argument would clearly make no impression on him; he obviously liked it as a familiar intellectual exercise. The very way he stretched himself, wanting to cock his feet up on the edge of the kitchen range, indicated whole nights of talk.

"You may flatter yourself that you have a monopoly of logic. That may be your particular illusion. And more horrors are committed, I'm beginning to think, in the name of logic than in any other name."

"Even God's—remembering history?"

"Even God's," said Aunt Phemie, "and for what it's worth I took history in my degree."

"But not perhaps the materialistic interpretation of history?"

"Perhaps not," said Aunt Phemie, annoyed with herself for feeling she was actively disliking him again, his smiling cocksureness.

"We merely think that history has been taught wrongly, has been misunderstood," he said lightly, having found the right place for his heels. "Emotion has nothing to do with it."

"Emotion is the greater part of life, and to ignore it is to—is to make a mess of life." She was losing grip, couldn't get the right words now.

"I was talking scientifically, a scientific interpretation. Do you think emotion should influence the scientist in his work?"

"We didn't class history as one of the science subjects—but then of course our professors probably didn't know any better," said Aunt Phemie, sinking deeper.

He seemed to become aware for the first time that she was disturbed and studied the movement of his slipper—Dan's slipper—with a faint smile. "It's rather important to me," he said.

She made her effort at recovery: "If I said that about logic and—and God, I meant that the horrors were committed by the churchmen logically expounding their—their doctrine. It was their *logic* that drove them to the—to the Inquisition and all the rest."

"But their logic was based on false premises."

"Still, it was their logic."

"And therefore logic is to be condemned?"

"You are jumping to conclusions."

"Am I?"

His polite restraint felt to her like a superior insult. "Yes," she said flatly. "I do not condemn logic as a process. If you cannot see my distinction, I can't help you."

He remained silent.

"However," said Aunt Phemie, "I started to tell you about Nan."

He waited.

She took her time and, not looking at him, began, "She was getting on quite well, was sometimes very full of life indeed—even emotion," she added coolly. "Then this horrible murder took place in that cottage. It preyed on her mind—no doubt she felt she had left that kind of thing behind. But the war had pursued her—in this case it was the first Great War. The murder was attributed to a man who had what they call here shell-shock from that war. It cast a gloom over the place, particularly as they could not find the man. He had disappeared. They hunted for him everywhere. The police were scouring the countryside. One day Nan set out for one of her walks. As you go up the back out

105

there, you finally come on a moor. There is a burn, and down on the right a steep place with birches. It's quite a long way from here. In this place Nan met a man who seems to be an artist or poet. She was feeling a bit nervous, no doubt because the murderer was still at large. She only spoke a few words to this man and then turned for home. On the way, there is a pine plantation. The village policeman was lurking there and Nan ran into him. He asked her if she had seen anyone and she said No. That worried her."

"Why did she say No?"

Aunt Phemie remained still for a moment then looked at him. "You have no idea?"

He blew a thoughtful stream of smoke. "Well—I suppose she didn't want to get involved."

"The policeman called here," Aunt Phemie continued, "but as it turned out it was only to return a handkerchief she had dropped. And that incident blew over—at least she was getting over it."

"Why don't you tell me why she said No?" he asked.

"That was the question Nan asked me," replied Aunt Phemie. "I said I understood perfectly."

"Please go on."

She took a moment or two then went on, "She had to fight this murder shadow. I saw that and let her go ahead in her own way. She had to clear it off the land. That may sound very irrational, but at least it was real for her. I hope that's clear?"

"You needn't rub it in. I am concerned about Nan," he explained.

"She met this man, this artist fellow, once or twice again. I don't know him. But he interested her in his attitude to things. I don't think she cared much for the man himself, but the way he thought of things—of wild things and the way they behaved— fascinated her. I rather think he lay in wait for her."

"How do you mean," he asked as she paused, "that he fascinated her—if she doesn't care for him?"

She met his look for a moment. His face was pale and firm in a logical ruthless way. He was going to let nothing pass now.

"It's difficult to explain—rationally," answered Aunt Phemie without any emphasis.

"But even the irrational can be explained rationally. Do you think you can do it?"

Aunt Phemie took her time. "You told me about that fellow—Fanwicke, was it? —who fascinated her, yet she didn't like him. Or did I understand you properly?"

He thought so concentratedly that he obviously forgot her. "You said something about wild things and the way they behaved. What did you mean?"

"It's the nature of a hawk to kill a small bird. Something like that was his kind of logic."

His eyebrows gathered as he looked at her. "What are you getting at?"

"I am simply trying to explain as best I can. I never met him."

"Where does he live?"

"Somewhere in the town, I have gathered since."

"Didn't Nan know?"

"Not as far as I know."

"Not even his name?"

"She knew his first name was Adam. That's all."

"What happened then?"

"There was a final meeting. It may have been arranged, but I am not certain. She left the house immediately after lunch, instead of having her usual rest." Aunt Phemie stopped. "I want to tell you," she went on at last in a quiet earnest voice as though thinking now only of Nan, "what happened as far as I can make it out. It's difficult because she was in a very broken condition. Calm for a moment, with staring eyes, then when she spoke a word she lost control and buried her face and grabbed and tore at the bedclothes. She was upstairs when I came in. I had been over at the steading and didn't see her come in. I realised something terrible had happened. When I went near her, she started away. She shivered violently. I am trying to tell you this calmly. I can give you no idea of what she was like. More than once I thought she was completely—unhinged. It was terrifying, and I was quite helpless."

He did not speak, did not move.

"I won't try to describe the sort of night we had. Nothing would keep her quiet long. She was incoherent; would cry out in her sleep and start awake; and the paralysing thing was that what she saw in her sleep—if it was sleep—was more real than what she saw when she awoke; she still fought it—physically—stared at it in horror, cried words like 'leprosy'; you saw her being gripped, collapsing, fainting. In between times, when she was pushing away from her horror, or had a lucid moment or two, when she was taking one as an ally, someone who might help her, she said things which helped me to see a little what had actually happened. That's what I'm going to tell you."

"You did this all alone?" Curiosity and acknowledgement were in his eyes.

"Yes," she answered simply. "I could not send for the doctor. Mrs. Fraser had gone for the day; she was at this time giving me a hand in the forenoons only. And anyway," continued Aunt Phemie, "I got the feeling no-one could help me. I even knew, in a way I cannot explain, how dangerous it might be to give her too much sleeping drug. I may have been wrong. But I had a deep feeling of—of understanding. Once, for example, I knew that if only I could get my body between her and what she saw, and cry to her, so that she would know the voice, so that it would be like a cry from someone coming to relieve her—but it's no good trying to explain. All I can say is that in the desperate moment, it helped."

Aunt Phemie blew the dead stub of cigarette from her holder. Her manner was still calm, but it now concealed a quivering tension.

"You are going to tell me," he said, "that this fellow Adam attacked her—as Fanwicke did." He gathered his heels back against his chair. His words sounded harsh, satiric, but there was something in them that would not let him wait any longer.

"Yes," she answered, not now put off by him. "Only if that had been all—it might have been simple. It wasn't all."

He gave her a piercing glance.

"I told you about the man—Gordie, they called him—who

was supposed to have committed the murder of the old man in the cottage. For money, they said. They had never found him." She stopped, as if she could not go on

His eyes were fixed on her. She wasn't looking at him.

"She met this man Adam on that last day. He took her round the mountain, to a place where there are hags, little black lochs. He took her to some certain spot. It's a wild place. He tried to—he must have tried to make love to her. Remember, in her mind he was in some way part of the shadow, the murder, and he had taken her to this spot. She fought away from him—to the edge of a hag-hole—and there at their feet was the body of Gordie—drowned, bloated, horrible."

Aunt Phemie swallowed and drew a deep breath. Ranald got up. "My God!" he said.

They both stood, listening to what had been told and to the silence in the house.

"The one thing I am terribly frightened of," said Aunt Phemie as though all the time this was a secret burden she had been bearing, "is that she will find you in the house."

"I understand," he responded.

"What do you think yourself?"

"Are you uncertain in your own mind?"

"If only she could get a night's sleep. I think I could take a risk on that now—and give her an extra dose. If only she hadn't thought she heard you. If you were to walk in now ... I don't know."

"A sleep would strengthen her."

"Yes. From what you told me—from what she has just gone through—she—she mightn't want you to touch her. With a reaction of that sort—her exhaustion, from the excitement of seeing you, might be too much. I cannot help feeling that."

"I understand."

She wanted to glance at him, for there had been a suggestion, a faint recognition, of his own futility in his cool tone, and none the less so because it had been just perceptibly bitter.

"You now see my difficulty?" she asked almost gently.

"Yes."

What I have been thinking, since she heard you, was this. To-morrow, if all goes well, after the doctor's visit, I will get your telegram, saying you're coming. I'll tell her. I'll say I *wrote* you—and at once you must have wired, saying you were coming. I'll be glad about it. I'll tell her, tell her she must be getting the second sight, imagining she heard you before you came. I'll make a game of it. That would mean you would appear the day after to-morrow. If that's not too long for you?"

"No," he answered. "It's simply a question of the right action."

She nodded. All in a moment, there was no more to be said. She glanced at his face. It was pale, cold, almost intolerant, but drained.

Then she heard something. Her fingers closed on the cigarette holder; her whole forearm quivered and shook and she lowered it to her side. Going to the door, she opened it and listened. "It's Mrs. Fraser," she said on a relieved breath. "She's coming."

6

Mrs. Fraser always returned to her own home before midday to prepare her husband's meal. Ranald had gone out after breakfast to look around and wait for the doctor's visit.

Aunt Phemie was busy in the kitchen cleaning vegetables for lunch when she thought she heard a cry from Nan's room. She listened, holding her breath, and decided she must have been mistaken. Odd enough sounds often came from the steading, and the back door was wide open. But after a few moments she could not go on with her work and experienced what had now become a weakening sensation, warm and melting, for she was suffering from lack of sleep and prolonged anxiety. Last night had been at times an almost intolerable burden; horrible, she thought suddenly, blinding her inner sight.

First there had been these long talks with Ranald. The old analytic method of speech, the assumption of intellectual calm, had seemed to free her, and she was conscious of rising to meet Ranald on his own plane. She had gone right back to the old days before her marriage, to the bright give-and-take discussion on education and the child mind. She had experienced again the sense of distinguished movement, of style. This sharply stimulated intellectual interest, with its mental excitement, had been like a bright armour. She had shown Ranald to his bedroom with a decisive care, covering any noises he might make with her own pronounced movements into and out of the bathroom. At last she was approaching Nan's door, the smile on her face, the heightening of the smile in her breast, when in an instant she was aware of a new objective attitude towards Nan and her illness, an attitude in which sympathy was lessened to the same degree as her intellectual or analytic interest had been aroused. This induced a feeling of competence, as though by its subtle depreciation of Nan's importance she herself was objectively strengthened. But in the next instant it aroused a feeling of guilt, for she realised she was now undergoing a withdrawal from Nan. She suddenly perceived the whole evening had been directed to that end. In bed at last (in Nan's room), with Nan asleep, this began to worry her, and she had resurgences of pure feeling in which, picture following fugitive picture, she visualised the analytic interest as a remorseless white face, like Ranald's face (there were also certain dismissive gestures of his, slight but now startlingly significant). This white taut face watched until sympathy was slain, until emotion withered. It's the slayer's face, thought told her in silence, and she was aware of being between the thought and the face, like a soul in an experiment. Then the really horrible thing began to happen. The figure of King Kronos came alive before her, the father who, in the Greek legend, devoured his own newborn sons lest some day they usurp his power. This, she realised, was the figure Nan saw. And now she was with Nan, looking at the figure, there before her, devouring a child. As the teeth tore at a knuckle—an elbow—there was no blood, as though the child had been boiled like a fowl. The lump of pale flesh stuck in her own throat, choked her, choked down her vomit, and the horrible revolting nature of the experience shook her and blinded her, for she saw more than she could let herself see. But all this was sickeningly complicated by the knowledge that she was at last at the hidden core of Nan's innermost experience or delusion. For the crowning horror lay in the resemblance of Kronos to Ranald. A quiver of vision, of thought, and the face *was* Ranald's, and the shoulders, the stooping shoulders. Ranald was devouring his own son—Nan's son—before Nan's face.

Aunt Phemie, turning over in her bed, smashed the abominable vision out of her head, cried to herself that this was a mad delusion of her own, and that, for Nan, Kronos had not been a devouring father in the literal image, but just a slayer of sons, of young men. He was the dictator who purged and killed wherever he saw a threat to his authority. The new multiple-Kronos of the world Nan had experienced in war, in the streets. He stood for the destructiveness which in Nan's world to-day would, in order to achieve its clear rational aim, coldly ignore emotion (the emotion Nan knew profoundly in her as the very pulse and warmth of creation) and so inevitably and fatally destroy life. To achieve, he would multiply himself and kill.

There followed a still, appalling moment, wherein Aunt Phemie dwelt with the utmost cause, the last dark root, of Nan's illness: *she wanted to save Ranald from becoming Kronos.*

Mad—mad as the Oedipus legend—mad as all the legends; but, like them, absolutely haunting. Once a thing like that got a grip of you, Aunt Phemie saw, not as a theoretic or psychoanalytic formulation, but as an actuality, as an emotion, *a picture*, as something that rose undeniably out of your depths, out of what seemed the very essence of your being, you could only protect yourself by going neurotic, psychotic, and ultimately mad, lunatic.

Fear was the basis, but in Nan's case not only fear for herself, for her life instincts, but also fear for Ranald, for her love. She had had to break Fanwicke and the others—or get broken.

At this point Nan moved in her bed and instantly Aunt Phemie, as though still in the pulse of Nan's mind, experienced a sudden shift of anxiety, gripped now by an actual fear. She knew quite certainly that Nan would get up and go into Ranald's room. She would go looking for him, in a strange dream sense. From that moment, natural sleep had become impossible for Aunt Phemie.

Yet exhausted, she must have dozed, for some time during the night she came fully to herself to find Nan already standing by the small mahogany chest of drawers just inside the door. There was the creak of a top drawer. Aunt Phemie watched, knowing Nan kept her writing materials there. Outside, the moonlight must have been fairly strong, for Nan's bowed head was solid against the pale-daffodil wall. An elbow lifted; a hand moved in the drawer—paused and slowly withdrew. Slowly she shut the drawer, stood quite still for a little while, then moved to the door. As the knob was turning, Aunt Phemie called her in a low voice, at the same time getting out of bed and going towards her, but not touching her. Nan stood but never spoke. Aunt Phemie had an impulse to get over the moment, to make it easy for Nan, by asking her if she wanted to go to the bathroom. But something deeper restrained her and, instead, she suggested, "Won't you go to your bed, Nan?" And, as if acting on the suggestion in quite an automatic way, Nan went back to her bed, covered herself with the clothes, and lay quite still.

The whole night's experience was now in Aunt Phemie as she stood listening, after hearing what she thought was a cry from upstairs. But the cry was not repeated. Yet she could not go on with her kitchen work; she had to make sure.

Before Nan's room she took a deep breath, noiselessly turned the knob and put her head round the door. Nan was sitting up in bed and stared at her with a steady fixity as if watching what her visitor was going to do next.

"I was wondering if you were asleep," said Aunt Phemie, smiling, closing the door behind her. After her first look at Nan she cast her eyes about the room as though to make sure the place was tidy, then in a natural companionable way went to the south window and said cheerfully, "The sun is shining." She glanced about the fields and farther away, but Nan did not answer, did not move. Fear had touched Aunt Phemie with its sickly feather. The look on Nan's face had gone completely alien.

Turning from the window and still interested, remarking the room could do with a proper tidy-up, she now sat, as though only for a few minutes, on the foot of Nan's bed, and looked at her patient again to confirm what appeared her obvious impression that everything was going well. "And how are you, Nan?" she asked gently but cheerfully, smiling, with a frank look.

Nan held her look then removed her eyes, though it was indeed as if the eyes themselves had removed, like the eyes of a child who has grown unaccountably serious, who lives in another place and has found there what is outside time.

Aunt Phemie experienced the clutch at the mother's heart. Nan did not answer.

Aunt Phemie regarded Nan's face with an unconscious concentration. With its bright chestnut hair, in a wave-broken disorder which enriched its colour and depth, the face took on an arrested beauty that drew Aunt Phemie out of herself so that she was held in a moment of pure wonder. The eyes had grown larger, with the blue a shade lighter than Aunt Phemie's own blue, but miraculously clear, translucent, the light that no flower ever quite has, nor any sky. The face had a fragile firmness, not pale but cool. The quiet lines ran flawlessly down until they met on her chest for a moment then gathered to a deepening flow between her breasts, to disappear beneath her blue pyjama jacket which was plucked away on one side where the top button had come unfastened.

She was like a plucked flower, like a single daffodil in a vase, whose trumpet hears the quietness of the snow outside, the mysterious quietness that is known to it.

Aunt Phemie's eyes followed the arms to the hands which lay together on the light-blue satin quilt. The hands were relaxed, but then she noticed that every now and then they tremored slightly of their own accord. As she glanced up, she met Nan's full regard, which remained on her for quite a time, in a distant silence that yet had in it something of incommunicable speech.

"Tell me, Nan," said Aunt Phemie, but speaking also through her eyes from the pressure of her emotion, "is there anything worrying you?"

Nan's eyes went away to the wall behind Aunt Phemie where there hung a framed water colour of a woman sitting with bowed head, as if asleep, before the sea. But the eyes found nothing in the picture and shifted to the blank pale-daffodil distemper of the wall. Then, without movement of the head, they were on Aunt Phemie again, but only for a moment.

"Won't you tell me?" begged Aunt Phemie.

"I saw him," she said, quite suddenly and clearly.

Aunt Phemie was so completely taken aback, so instantly confused by the notion that she might have seen Ranald, that she had an impulse to bluster, to say it was quite impossible. Nan's eyes were on her like the eyes of the child who knows what it has done and is coolly curious, and yet incurious, about the effect.

"But," said Aunt Phemie, "but—how could you? You were in your bed."

Nan's eyes went back to the wall. "I wasn't," she said.

Aunt Phemie had now got control of herself. "Where were you?"

Nan did not answer.

"Won't you tell me?" asked Aunt Phemie gently. "Do tell me."

The subdued roar of a lorry as it took the brae to the steading came into the room; a lowing of moving cattle; a commotion and stamping movement; the shrill barking of Sandy's young dog; all was in that outside world, which seemed in a moment even more remote and strange than the world which Aunt Phemie was now in. The noises died away, leaving only the rumble of the engine as it idled over.

"They are moving some cattle to-day," explained Aunt Phemie, under a sudden heavy weight of reluctance to find out any more.

Nan did not speak, but she stirred slightly, lifted her hand to her breast; but the hand trembled and she laid it down again.

The hand clutched at Aunt Phemie's heart, weakening her; but more gently and sensibly than ever she asked, "Won't you tell me, Nan? You know you can tell me anything."

Nan shook her head slowly once.

Encouraged, Aunt Phemie asked, "Where did you go? Surely you can tell me that?"

"The sun," she said, staring at the wall.

"Is the sun troubling you?"

"The sun came into the room."

"Yes?"

"I went to see it."

"Did you? Where?"

"At the window."

"But you know you shouldn't be moving about. You had a high fever and that weakens you and makes you *imagine* all sorts of things. Besides you might get a dreadful relapse." Aunt Phemie was preparing for what might come next.

But Nan did not go on.

"And what did you see?" asked Aunt Phemie inexorably driven.

"I saw him."

"Who?"

"Ranald." Nan regarded Aunt Phemie with waiting eyes, watching.

"Did you?" replied Aunt Phemie, with the veiled air of knowing quite well that Nan could not have seen Ranald. "Where was he?" She was not looking at Nan, asked the question lightly but quite solemnly.

"He came in sight from the gate. Then he stood by the trees and looked at me. He stood quite still. Then he turned and went away."

All along Aunt Phemie was afraid that it *might* have been Ranald. Now she realised he could have been coming back to the house ... or perhaps been taking a look at it from an angle that would show Nan's window, not from any romantic feeling but out of the strange curiosity which at such a moment haunts the very core of human nature. Anyone in the glen, knowing what was going on behind that window, would experience an urge to steal in and have a long look. In Ranald's case, the matter was profoundly involved. Aunt Phemie could see him, standing there by the trees, and going away.

Overpoweringly she perceived the dreadfulness of her dilemma—and of Nan's. For Nan, from her whole behaviour, did not expect to be believed. Yet she knew she had seen Ranald. If now Aunt Phemie were to persist that it was impossible for Ranald to have been there in the flesh, then Nan's hallucination or illusion had at last crossed the border and become for her the reality. Nan would know this.

The idling motor suddenly stopped and the world became extraordinarily still. A cock crew in the distance, an echoing and forlorn cry that arched and fell away over the edge of the world. Then, with incredible nearness, there were footsteps on the stairs. They were steadily mounting, muffled to a choking stealth by the carpet, yet deliberate and confident, a man's footsteps. Aunt Phemie's heart turned over in her and the skin of her face ran cold. The footsteps came to the door and paused. A hand knocked quietly. Aunt Phemie could not move. The knob turned, the door opened slowly and a face came round it. It was the doctor's face, red and smiling in a sort of peep-bo expression, smiling at Aunt Phemie with an amused greeting ready, when the eyes suddenly switched to the bed and the smile vanished. Aunt Phemie turned. Nan was slipping away against the back of the bed, her face deathly pale. She had fainted.

7

With a poker, Aunt Phemie tried to hurry the heat under the kettle.

"If she really did see him, if he was there," the doctor said.

"You didn't see him at all as you were coming in?"

"No."

"Where on earth can he have gone?" Aunt Phemie's anxiety and impatience were unconcealed. "I feel something should be done at once."

"I don't know," said the doctor doubtfully. "You think that if Ranald could be *actually* produced, then Nan would be reassured, would be helped, by knowing that she was not absolutely obsessed?"

"Don't you?"

"Supposing she hasn't seen him?"

"That will make all the difference. That's why I wish he would come. You would have thought his anxiety would have kept him at the door," said Aunt Phemie in an angry rush.

"Wait a bit. We'll have to go easy. Why do you think it will make all the difference? Does an illusion, more or less, really matter now?"

"In this case, yes. It will make all the difference in the world."

"How?"

"Oh, it's difficult to explain, but I know. I don't care what any authority may say about what happens inside the mind at such a time. If Nan did *not* see Ranald, then however real and solid he may have seemed to her, yet somewhere deep in her she will know that it may not actually have been him. But if she *did* see the real Ranald, then the effect on her mind will be quite different, especially if you were to prove to her that it was an illusion."

The doctor regarded her unconsciously with his professional look. "I get your point," he said. "It's a subtle one. I can see I don't need to tell you that I don't know a great deal about this. It's psychiatric. But I couldn't help seeing a lot of it in the Middle East. I'm not so very long demobbed, as you know. It's not just always an easy business. Above all it needs patience and time."

"Time can run short," said Aunt Phemie.

"You mean there is a critical phase? No doubt. But then more than ever all depends on how you are going to deal with it. A wrong treatment—a wrong step—can tip the balance the wrong way. You saw what happened when I blundered into the bedroom. By the way, I did go first to the kitchen door—quietly, because I thought we might have a few words."

"I understand," said Aunt Phemie without relaxing her expression.

The doctor glanced at her. "I think—perhaps—you are over-emphasising the difficulty at the moment. We have got to be careful, I mean, that we don't shove our burden onto that young man's shoulders."

"You're telling me," said Aunt Phemie, with an impatient look at the fire.

The doctor smiled. "I suppose so," he said. After a moment he went on. "All the same, when you mentioned how he came into sight and stood by the trees and then went away, I got the feeling of something happening in a dream."

"You really think he wasn't there?" Aunt Phemie glanced at him quickly.

"Anyway, he isn't here yet! But I wasn't thinking of that. Supposing you had been up there, ill like Nan, and you saw a dream-like happening of that kind, would you be terribly distressed to find it hadn't been real?"

It was like a blow to Aunt Phemie. She momentarily lost grip and said in a distressed way, "Oh, I don't know. I just don't know."

"I don't think you need worry about that. In any case, I shouldn't like to see you begin to worry." He smiled quickly, giving her a flashing complimentary glance. "You have been pretty good."

The compliment did not help her. She was suddenly terrified at the amount of emotion that wanted to burst through. She felt on the verge of crying out everything to the doctor, of letting her choked anxiety have its wild way.

"It's a very difficult thing to deal with," the doctor was saying, as he shifted his stance and pulled down his waistcoat. His dark-brown suit was a perfect fit. He looked at once professional and elegant. "And the world is full of it. We just can't have wars and not expect this kind of reaction."

"I know," said Aunt Phemie automatically. She looked frozen.

"It's getting a bit too common for my taste. Even amongst children, neurotic school children. You would hardly believe it." He glanced away through the kitchen window. Aunt Phemie turned her fixed gaze on the kettle. It was singing.

"You keep on as you're doing and Nan will come round all right. It's been unfortunate that this murder affair on the hill got under her skin, but she is fundamentally sound." His voice, the movement of his feet, intimated that he was about to go. "I'll look in again to-morrow."

Before Aunt Phemie could speak the door opened. She started violently and the blood drained from her face. It was Ranald.

"Hallo," said the doctor, "we have been wondering where you were." His manner was courteous.

Ranald glanced at Aunt Phemie and then, in his casual way, said, "I have been out about the farm—talking to some of the men. I saw your car."

"There's been some trouble here over you," said the doctor. "Miss Gordon rather imagines she saw you from the window."

Ranald's face steadied. "Where?"

"Did you come into the drive, stand for a moment against the trees and look up at her window?"

"Yes," said Ranald, watching the doctor.

"You did? Oh." The doctor's brows gathered thoughtfully.

"Why? What happened?" asked Ranald.

"She fainted," said Aunt Phemie in a flat laconic voice. It sounded at once tragic and indifferent. As she lifted the kettle off the fire, both men looked at her back. She began making a pot of tea.

"The problem is this," said the doctor to Ranald in his professional manner. "Because of her condition—and too much excitement will be *very* bad for her—should we let her believe that she was deluded, which I fancy would do her no harm, or should you go up?"

"I have said all along," remarked Ranald calmly, "that I should go up."

The doctor suddenly looked nettled. "I hope you realise it's not just quite so simple as all that?"

"Well, I hope I'm not just a simpleton." There was no sarcasm in his voice; there was even a certain dry humour in his eyes.

The doctor smiled. "I hope not." But his voice did not sound as if he had been reassured. However, he had to go. "I'll have to leave it to yourself, Mrs. Robertson." He glanced at his gold wrist-watch. "I have a hospital appointment and need my time."

Aunt Phemie turned from the fire. "Very good, Doctor. And thank you for coming. I'll take up a cup of tea—and prepare her for Ranald's visit." Her voice was clear but without warmth, almost without life.

The doctor's eyes searched her face for a moment. "You think so?"

"Yes. I agree with Ronald."

"Very good," said the doctor. "But you needn't hurry the process."

"I won't," she said.

"Right. Good morning."

Aunt Phemie turned back from the door and began preparing a small tray. She did not look at Ranald, did not speak.

"How could she see me?" asked Ranald. "I thought she was in bed."

"She got up to welcome the sun," replied Aunt Phemie, "and saw you. Didn't you see her?"

"No. The light was on the window, blinding it."

At last she had two cups of tea and the biscuit box on the tray. "I'll take this up and try to get her to take something. I'll tell her I wrote you and you arrived suddenly to-day. You were coming in by the front drive—when suddenly you changed your mind and came in by the back."

"That's what happened," said Ranald.

"That's fine." She hesitated. But she didn't or couldn't say any more; she lifted the tray and went out. On the top landing she paused, out of breath. A twist of pain passed over her features. Then she went forward, opened the door quietly and entered the room. Nan was lying with her face to the wall. After the doctor had got her round, she had been bewildered and jumpy in a scrambling way, but soon, exhausted, had grown wearily composed and turned her face away from them. Her body had now turned away as well.

As Aunt Phemie was setting down the tray on the bedside table it quivered, slopping a little tea into the saucers. She stood looking at Nan, listening for her breathing. She couldn't hear it. For a moment she stood very still, then she bent over the bed and was putting a hand out when she saw the faint rise and fall of the bedclothes which Nan had pulled over her shoulder. Aunt

Phemie withdrew her hand and sat down on the chair. She felt very tired. She wanted to go to sleep. Several minutes passed and her head drooped.

But at Nan's first movement Aunt Phemie's eyes were waiting. Nan stirred slowly, then with a small start, for she could see no-one standing in the room. So clearly she must have heard Aunt Phemie come in. When she saw Aunt Phemie in the chair by the head of the bed, her head dropped back.

"I have brought you a cup of tea, Nan," said Aunt Phemie in kindly tones. She got up and drained the saucers into the cups. "I'm afraid it's getting cold. Wouldn't you like a cup?"

"No, thanks," said Nan in a remote voice.

"Won't you let me coax you? Do," pleaded Aunt Phemie.

Nan shook her head once.

"Nan," said Aunt Phemie, "I have got some news for you. I have heard from Ranald."

Nan's head turned slowly and her wide-open eyes settled on Aunt Phemie.

Aunt Phemie nodded, a restrained gladness infusing her manner. "He's coming to see you," she said with some of the archness of a mysterious conjurer.

Nan began to breathe slow heavy breaths, her eyes on Aunt Phemie's face but not penetrating the face.

Aunt Phemie nodded again and smiled into Nan's eyes. "He's coming soon."

"What?" said Nan, her breathing deepening. "When?" Her arms jerked out from under the bedclothes and she glanced away from Aunt Phemie in a wild bewildered way. But in an instant her eyes were back.

"Now don't grow excited," said Aunt Phemie like a wise schoolmistress. "You've got to be good and sensible. I wrote him and whenever he got my letter he set out. Wasn't that noble of him?"

Nan's breathing, still deep, was quickening as though she couldn't get enough air. Her hands were knotting in the quilt, the scraping of her fingernails harsh on the satin.

"He's here!" she said suddenly, not to Aunt Phemie but to

herself. Now her breathing became tumultuous, gulping fierce and fast; her body thrust and heaved, while her hands clawed like a dog's paws tearing at a hole; her eyes grew feverishly bright and terrified.

"Nan! Nan!" said Aunt Phemie, "control yourself now, take a hold!" She caught Nan's hands, which instantly gripped hers with remarkable strength. Then the hands were away, were wildly up at the chestnut hair, pushing it back, in a half-demented gesture of dressing, of preparing; but in an instant they were gone; she did not know what she was doing; she was half-rising in the bed, pushing herself up.

After a little, Aunt Phemie got her settled back, and the tumultuous breathing slackened, grew longer between breaths. "Where is he?" she asked little above a whisper.

"He's in the kitchen," answered Aunt Phemie. "What a surprise I got! He started to come up the drive—then thought he had better come in quietly at the back door. He did not know how ill you might be."

The breathing began to increase again, to quicken.

"He wants to see you, of course. But I just told him he wasn't going to be allowed up until you were quite ready for him! So there's no hurry." Aunt Phemie had the cool cheerfulness of a nurse, giving out strength, with her subtle sympathy watching.

Nan's second bout was not so bad as the first, but it left her more exhausted. The great gulps of breath made her shiver from cold; her jaw continuously quivered. Aunt Phemie saw the internal fight reach its climax in a tremoring and writhing that for one awful moment seemed about to break body and mind into bits. She continued her small movements and gestures about the bed, capably, preparing for Ranald as a nurse might prepare for the operation that would presently put everything right. The internal fight broke—and Nan was not defeated, had not screamed out the final negation in flight and collapse. Aunt Phemie smiled at her as she lay panting and with a cold damp sponge wiped her forehead and cheeks. "Yes, yes," she said, "you can," though Nan had not spoken. She sponged the corners of the mouth. "You are a very good-looking girl, my dear." She stood back regarding the face with satisfaction. "Now, I'll call Ranald, will I?" Nan's hands began to work, her head gave an indecisive nod, her breathing quickened again. Aunt Phemie went to the door and called in a loud cheerful voice, "Ranald!" Behind her there was a small suppressed cry, but she did not turn round. Ranald came up quickly. "Here he is!" said Aunt Phemie, taking him into the room.

Nan had pulled the clothes right up to her neck. She looked at Ranald, large-eyed with a strange wary brightness.

"Hallo, Nan!" said Ranald quietly, smiling from the end of the bed. "Not feeling too fit?" He might have been there yesterday and the day before.

Nan's eyes glanced away. She did not speak.

"Look now," said Aunt Phemie, "I'll leave you for a minute. He's starving, Nan; hasn't had anything to eat since yesterday. So you're not going to keep him. There will be plenty of time for talking." She went out.

Ranald sat on the bottom of the bed. "I'm sorry you've had another bout. Bad luck. But you're feeling all right again?"

She nodded.

"That's good. Though you *will* go on giving me frights!" His eyes warmed. "It's nice to see you again."

"Thank you," she said, with a breath of spirit.

"That's more like the old noise! I was beginning to miss it. Quite a few were, in fact. The idea has gone about that you were the life and soul of things."

"How's Julie?"

" Julie? Oh—she's all right."

Her eyes flashed upon his momentary hesitation, searched his face.

"Still worrying about Julie?" His mouth twisted in humour. "You did reform her—for a bit. But what could you expect?" He was teasing her. "I would much rather hear about yourself. Aren't you glad to see me, for example?"

Her eyes flashed upon each side. "You know I am." Her breathing began to quicken.

"You're tired," he said, observing the signs of distress.

She shook her head, but not at his remark.

"What's bothering you, Nan?" There was strong sympathy in his voice. "Something nasty happened?"

She could not look at him. Her distress mounted rapidly. The end of her endurance had at last been reached. Then an extraordinary thing happened. She suddenly looked at him and her features collapsed in a piteous way; she seemed to sink deeper into the bed while still looking at him; then in a wild, deathly withdrawal she brought the sheet up over her face.

He stood quite still. Aunt Phemie came in. The covered body heaved with sobs.

"It's all right, Nan," said Aunt Phemie. "I'll be back in a minute." Turning, she ushered Ranald quietly out of the room. At the foot of the stairs she paused, listening. "Why didn't you reassure her better about Julie?" she asked in a strong almost angry whisper.

"Julie is dead," he said indifferently and, in the grip of his own thought, he walked away from her out of the house.

8

Ranald got off the bus opposite the town hall and, after looking about him, continued along the main street, a tall slim figure, easy-moving as an athlete, in dark flannel trousers, a grey tweed jacket, hatless, with black hair which waved just perceptibly. His manner was unselfconscious, his eyes curious for the appearance of the buildings, the cars drawn up on one side of the street, the shops, and the people who moved about. Having bought cigarettes and chatted to the girl behind the counter for a minute, he continued his stroll, blowing smoke from his lungs. Near the railway station the main street widened and ended in a region of hotels, banks and other respectable business premises. He had so far seen only one policeman but now as he was passing a short thick queue of people at a main bus-stop he saw a constable at some little distance coming towards him. He continued on his way until they met, when he asked, "Could you tell me, please, where the police station is?"

The constable was even taller than Ranald and as straight, but much more heavily built, with a disconcertingly direct look from light-grey eyes. "The police station? ... Yes." He pointed. "Down there on the right, just round the corner." Then he considered Ranald again.

"Thanks." But Ranald hesitated. He looked at the policeman with an easy civilian frankness. "You are stationed here?"

"Why do you ask?"

"I am staying at Greenbank, with Mrs. Robertson. Arrived the other night." He hesitated again.

"I know Mrs. Robertson," said the policeman.

"Oh, do you?" Ranald regarded him with interest. "You're not, by any chance, the constable who called there about—Miss Gordon?"

"I am."

"Are you?" Ranald was pleasantly astonished at the odd coincidence. "You may think it strange of me to speak to you. But—it's more than just curiosity. Miss Gordon is not too fit." His eyebrows gathered in real concern. "You can't ask questions yet."

"Do you know Miss Gordon well?" The policeman's interest was aroused. He was a country policeman.

"Very well," answered Ranald. "I knew her in London."

"Are you a relation of Mrs. Robertson's?"

"No. I just know her through Miss Gordon."

"I see... What do you want to know?"

"I was wondering just what did happen when Adam—uh—what's his name?—discovered the body."

"Adam McAlpine. Do you know him?" The policeman's interest quickened.

"No, I haven't met him. But I know of him. I understand his home is here somewhere? I thought I might have a word with him. Where does he stay?"

"At a house on the south road: Beechpark."

"Thanks. If I could help in any way—I am anxious—and Mrs. Robertson has her hands full. Not having a man about the house makes a difference. As far as you are concerned, the whole affair is cleared up now?"

"I am not saying that. Miss Gordon is not yet fit for an interview?"

"No. Heavens, no," answered Ranald. "But if you cared to tell me—any difficult point—I would pass on to you personally any information I got." He spoke confidently, his manner that of an educated man who knew the world and a policeman's job.

"The doctor will let us know when she's well enough." But the policeman was now hesitating. He would clearly, country fashion, like to find out a lot on his own. He looked at Ranald. "Do you think she was with Mr. McAlpine when he found the body?"

"That's one of the things I should like to know," replied Ranald, showing no flicker of surprise.

"Why?"

"Because it would help us to understand her condition. But surely Adam McAlpine told you?"

"It's not for me to say what he told—or what information we have got since. But if you find out anything I'll be glad to hear it from you."

"Certainly," said Ranald. "You can understand that we are more anxious than you." He looked thoughtfully across the square. "I'll do what I can and let you know." He took out a packet of cigarettes. After a few more remarks he was able to ask in the light tone of one stating an accepted fact, "You are quite satisfied that Gordie was your man?"

"Satisfied enough—though the absence of money on the body is a difficulty." He was beginning to accept Ranald, from whom some new clue might come.

Ranald nodded, taking a moment. "That would confuse you on the question of motive."

"Yes. And everyone knows about the missing deposit receipt in particular. But apart from that, what could anyone know, as I said?" He regarded Ranald.

"And what use would a deposit receipt be to anyone anyhow?"

"Precisely." The policeman nodded thoughtfully. A bus drew up by the queue. "I'm stationed up at Elver village. You'll find

me there." Now he looked as if he might say more, but he had
to catch his bus.

Ranald walked out to the south road. He had just come from
Elver where a casual enquiry had drawn the information that
the policeman had left on the last bus for the town. Whenever
he had seen the thistledown-grey eyes, he had known his man.

The houses grew fewer, and presently he saw the name
BEECHPARK painted on the stone pillar of a main gate. As he
walked on, the upper parts of a large house came into view.
Shrubs and trees were everywhere, but through a narrow gap he
caught a glimpse of the front of the house. He went on for some
distance and came back, but still there was no-one to be seen
about the house. By the main gate he paused and lit a cigarette,
his features drawing together sharply in thought, but he
continued on his way back into town. Near the goods section of
the railway station he saw the name McALPINE in great white
letters spread across the roof of a large shed or warehouse. So
Adam was the son of big business as a county town knows it?
The notion seemed about right! Only, it was necessary to meet
him alone.

Ranald looked into two hotel lounges, went and had a beer
in a pub, and continued his walk through the town. He was
seeking a man with a green tie. But whether the man was wearing
the green tie or not, he reckoned he would know him. You cannot
be anything so odd as a poet or an artist, particularly if you have
lived in London and abroad, without its being immediately
apparent to a discerning eye. Ranald's thought was of that sharp
laconic kind. He was even aware of the glances cast on himself.
But though there were some visitors about the streets, in odd
enough garments, he was never for a moment uncertain. It takes
the young female of the species in her most unconventional or
daring holiday get-up to proclaim the real bourgeois or sub-
bourgeois origin; the touch of perversion that reveals; she was
being "free". Ranald didn't smile at his thought.

Now he was walking along a main thoroughfare with the
mountains rising in the distance; but presently his eye was caught
by what looked like wooden sheep pens on his right, against the

back of the town. As he went along the lane towards them they grew in extent in an astonishing way. A wooden gate was open and he went through it and along a passage between the pens towards a man who was sweeping up trodden manure, his broom noisy on the concrete.

"This is a big place," said Ranald.

"Ay, it's the auction mart," replied the man, pausing to lean on his broom, his knuckles under his chin.

"And how often do you have sales here?"

"Every Thursday."

"As often as that?" Ranald took out his packet of cigarettes; the man said "Thank *you,* sir," and they lit up.

"Big sales?" asked Ranald.

"Oh yes; big sales: too big for me sometimes!" His slow smile brought a humoured glint to his eye.

"Sheep and cattle from all round?"

"Ay, and from more than all round at the big sales."

"Really? And how many then would you handle in a day?"

"Well now, that's a teaser!" The man straightened himself slowly and scratched below his ear. Ranald leaned back, stretching his arms along a wooden rail. He looked genuinely interested. Within five minutes he had a fairly accurate picture of the auction mart as the centre of live-stock transactions over a wide area. From large low-ground agricultural farms like Greenbank, from crofts up on the "marginal" lands, from distant hill sheep grazings, innumerable droves of living beasts came to this great junction, to be sold and bought, to be despatched by rail great distances, for fattening, for further breeding, for the slaughter-house. He found out who owned the auction mart, how it was run, what commission the auctioneers got, and nearly—but not quite—what the man himself earned. When the man told a story about how a bull the other day helped a loud-voiced "county" woman with buck teeth over a wooden rail, Ranald tilted his head back and laughed. On his part, he described what happened in Smithfield, London, the early-morning scenes in that immense meat market, who ran it, what wages were paid, and other detail that greatly interested his listener, who took another cigarette and asked a few questions on his own, until Ranald had to tell him that he wasn't in the meat trade.

"Not exactly," said Ranald, "though I am interested."

"Ah, you have an interest in it?"

"No, not that kind of interest, not financial."

The man looked at him shrewdly. "Now if it is not a rude question, what will you be interested in yourself?" Their talk had become very friendly.

"Well," said Ranald, "by your age I should judge that you were in the first war."

"I was, in the Camerons."

"And I was in this one, in the Air Force."

"Are you telling me that? … I had a son in the Air Force. He was a gunner."

Ranald knew by the way the man's eyes steadied and stared that his son had been killed. But the man said no more. Automatically he gave a small sweep with his broom.

"It's tough," said Ranald calmly. "I crashed myself—but I got through."

"Ay. That's the way it goes." He made small sweepings, then paused and took the cigarette from his mouth.

"Some of us," said Ranald, "are getting a bit fed up with wars. We are beginning to think that unless the way in which things are run is changed we'll have wars until nobody is left at all.

"I have heard that too. I have a nephew who is a socialist. He has great talk on him whiles. But I don't know."

"What don't you know?"

"Ah well, I wonder——"

But what exactly was the profound nature of this countryman's wonder, Ranald did not find out, for just as the man was gathering his thoughts, his eyes hazing slightly as they looked into distance, his expression swiftly changed. "Here's McAlpine," he muttered more to himself than to Ranald and started sweeping.

Ranald looked up the lane and saw a dark stout figure of middle height coming towards them. He was wearing a bowler hat, and something purposeful and solid about him as he

advanced through the grey wooden maze of the empty pens held
for the moment a startling significance. Ranald had an impulse
to move away but suppressed it. The sweeper was now paying
no attention to him.

The man came right up. He had a pale fleshy face with small
quick-moving eyes; perfectly shaved, washed, solidly respectable.
He gave Ranald a quick glance and something less than a curt
nod, "James," he said, with a jerk of his head, and went on. "Yes,
sir," said James and followed him, carrying his broom.

Ranald left the pens and went back into the town. He had
half an hour to wait for his bus and found the pub he had already
been in. Sitting on the narrow wooden seat by the window, his
pint of beer before him, he lit a cigarette.

A faint smile came to his face as he thought of the
"significance" of the dark bowler-hatted man. What was the
dream significance of a maze? Something to do with the
intestines wasn't it, the guts? Not inapt. He blew a stream of
smoke and the smile faded. He rarely experienced that dream
effect in what he saw. Even now there was something of the
stuff of nightmare in the advance of the bowler-hatted man
through the grey empty pens. The grey slats and rails had the
greyness of wood on a sea shore, the weathered greyness of
spewed-up wood in peat bogs. But he did not like this kind of
vision and snapped it out by a blink of an internal eye—and
instantly the vision of Nan drawing the sheet over her face swam
before him. There was a perceptible constriction of his features
as he snapped that vision out also.

The trouble was the irrational nature of this kind of stuff. Give
in to it and no peat bog had a deep enough bottom for it. It was
childish, primitive, and so in a certain way shocking. The child's
shock; and fear. So poets and artists, under the impression that
they were "revolutionary", tried to shock the world. Good God.
Regression. The denial of the intellect. To call it revolutionary
art—good God. Ranald caught the barman's eye on him. The
barman removed his eye to look at the glass he was polishing.
Two countrymen in thick tweeds were talking huskily together,
standing, their pints in their hands, confidential. The barman

was discreetly listening or Ranald would have gone over and spoken to him. As he removed his glance, his internal eye saw the black-hatted figure again. Father of Adam, the man with the green tie. A pastel shade of light green. The internal eye saw the exact shade and the full length of the tie.

Adam wouldn't get much shrift from that parent. Probably a mother, dominated by the bowler hat, had made Adam her consolation, her darling boy. Eternal struggle of the weak mother to get cash to slip to Adam. Broke, he would come home. The internal eye saw one or two "coterie" poets who would gladly cut each other's throat, despising, spitting upon, the success they craved. There was an eternal conspiracy to deny them "achievement". When they went political, they called the conspiracy a "bourgeois" conspiracy. Ranald reckoned he knew them root and branch from college onwards. After a compulsory session of talk in their noisy midst, how refreshing, how sane, to talk to a barman. He took a pull at his pint, and his features went solemnly statuesque; like a death mask, with something uncommunicably sad about its carven intolerance; the barman was glancing at him again.

As he set his pint on the table Ranald had a sudden thought. Aunt Phemie had said nothing about there having been no money on Gordie when he was hauled out of the water hole. That had come as so complete a surprise that he had almost shown it to the policeman. Who the hell would have taken the money—assuming Gordie *had* done the foul deed? The one thing all these fellows—and his mind was back on his "coterie" friends again—wanted, would do any bloody thing to get, was money. Money! he thought, thinking of Adam and the murdered man. Christ!

The thought narrowed his eyes. Quite deliberately he decided that Adam could have done it, would have done it, had he got the chance. Ranald had never recovered from certain early pre-war experiences at college. There had been a small group of "Mythicals" who rampaged about, full of laughter and splendid unintelligibility in their verse. Finding verbal equivalents for the instinctual impulses of the unconscious or id was, they declared, a poetic necessity postulated by the irrational nature of the subject matter, and it was manifestly, scientifically indeed, impossible to body forth the irrational in rational terms. Hence their verse; which thus was truly revolutionary in that it achieved a new freedom of the spirit, a new synthesis.

Now Ranald had gone over completely to the Socialists and had quite a different notion of revolution, was rapidly becoming adept in the understanding and use of the dialectical method, and in a first notable inter-debate challenged their "synthesis" and, in particular, their concept of "freedom", which he then proceeded to take to bits as if it were a child's doll. In fact, he called them "bourgeois dolls" ... . And the description had just enough of the irrational in it to achieve a quite furious effect.

This adolescent war continued with gusto—and not without a growing bitterness, particularly in Ranald, who began to believe that "bourgeois dolls" might in fact play a sinister part in the impending collapse of capitalist society. With the strife at its height, Ranald, in a packed debate, was directly challenged on the nature and constitution of a civilised society, was being asked how he proposed to deal in his particular robotised society with the new expansionist forces in human thought and art as represented by pioneering mythicals, when, before the speaker could continue with his mounting rhetoric, he rose in his place as if a direct question had been put to him and said, "Mr. Chairman, the question presents no difficulty to me: I should kill them off." Then he sat down.

Ranald looked at his watch. Five minutes yet. He had come into town for cigarettes and was bringing back a packet for Aunt Phemie. She had insisted on paying and shown just a momentary confusion when he had raised no objection. The bed, with Nan on it, drawing the sheet up over her face, was there before his internal eye again. He had been avoiding it, refusing to look at it. The thing had seemed too obviously a death gesture. But now he looked at Nan's face, at that piteous, collapsing, indescribable expression with the eyes on him. Good God, it was pretty terrible. Then an extraordinary sensation of stillness began to advance upon him, to hold him. Hitherto he had accepted Nan's action as a symptom of her trouble. But a symptom has a cause. Now the stillness had him absolutely, extended beyond him into breathless space. As he stirred his chest slowly packed itself full of air. His reason stirred and he thought: But he couldn't have raped her—she would have fought?

"Good day, sir," called the barman, but Ranald, if he heard him, did not answer.

9

"I think I'll get out for a walk," said Ranald who had come down from Nan's room.

"Very well," agreed Aunt Phemie going with him to the back door. Mrs. Fraser was scrubbing in the kitchen. "What do you think of Nan this morning?"

"She's coming on all right." He spoke with a glance at the day, turning from her. Against the bright light he looked more haggard than ever and Aunt Phemie knew he had slept little, although at breakfast when she had asked him how he had slept he had replied "Not too bad". There was no penetrating that light dismissive manner; it shut a person up.

"Don't go too far," she said.

"Right." But he did not look back at her.

When she got to the top of the stairs she suddenly found she could not go into Nan's room and swerved away. She would do up Ranald's room first. Nan would hear her and that would be all right. From the side window of his room she saw Ranald leaving the cart road and strolling up towards the two Irishmen who were mending the drains in the thistledown field. Now he had stopped and was talking to them. He's a complete mystery to me! she thought in a fatal way and turned back from the window, for she just could not go on looking at him. Her only hope now was to wean Nan away from him after he had left. Her experiment had failed. There was something between these two that could not be broken down. His coming had in a dreadful, drastic way only emphasised it. Aunt Phemie experienced this so sharply in her nerves that she felt the whole house gripped by it.

What Nan felt she dared not let herself think. She lifted his folded pyjama suit off the bed and set to in a flurry of work.

Meantime Ranald was getting a lot of information from the ditchers. They were experts at their job and he admired the neat way in which they cut the turves and laid them beside the opening ditch, the methodical way they dug, the unhurrying sureness of the work. The drains, with their sunken red tiles, were at first like the veins of the field, then, more exactly, they were ducts drawing away the excess of water from its body. When he had grasped the whole underground design, he went on.

Talking to real workmen about what they did always took him out of himself. It had the easing effect upon him of a ritual, in which, because of his beliefs, he participated. They were his brothers and as they extended through all life, in all countries, they were all life. The all-inclusive certainty of this precluded any need for further thought; left an assurance before which doubt was just faintly amusing.

As he looked about the field and saw the countless withering thistles he decided that the farm was not being too well run. But what could you expect? He already knew the agricultural wage rate, plus milk, potatoes, coal, meal, and a free house. Some house! he thought; for he had also found out quite a lot about overcrowding in the farm cottages, with no water laid on, no sanitation. Pretty ghastly, at this time of day. Remarkable that the farm workers should have the interest they did have. And obviously they appreciated Aunt Phemie. He paused and looked about him and away over the broad valley.

It would be so simple to run the valley as a large-scale collective farm, with a real village for all the workers, water laid on and electric light. Aunt Phemie, who was no farmer, running this big farm for her own profit—well! But she would make an excellent secretary for a collective. Then she would really have something to do, something moreover that would deeply interest her, because her life would be mixed up with other lives, would have a concern for them. Her mothering would find an outlet.

It would be so simple to do, too, thought Ranald, going on. As things were, this kind of country life just bored him. Static, so that you went either mindless or emotional. He had had a hell of a night last night, what sleep there was being full of murder dreams. At one point he had borrowed from Nan's attack on Fanwicke and bitten Adam's throat out. That kind of stuff. The climbing made his heart beat with some discomfort and he stopped by an elm on the edge of the shallow ravine. There were odd growths on it, like huge warts, right up onto the branches. He examined one of them. It was full of young sprouts, as long as knitting needles, like hairs on a wart. He tried to pull a sprout off but it was flexible and tough as wire. Perhaps each of the warts had once been a bud-point on the tree. Cancerous sex growths? It looked like it. He glanced about the ground and found the same economic basis for all the trees, and the other trees were not cancerous. He smiled dryly, for the explanation would be simple enough to one who knew about trees ... and the law of causality. Up in the next field he heard a piercing cawing overhead. But the bird was too big for a crow. Another ... and then a silent third. They were like floating kites. Nan's thistledown letter came back into his mind. Buzzards! He watched them for a time and as the high airiness affected his mind he thought of Nan. He would have to do something about her. But what? As he went on, his mind left the question unanswered, left it alone; he did not want to force his mind to do anything, could not force it. He hadn't that kind of energy, not at the moment. In front now was the wood—the Dark Wood.

As he sat among the trees, he followed the interstices between their columns to a glade on which the daylight lay. Slender columns because they grew so closely, and, for the same reason, tall and straight. They were silent, very still, and when he glanced by his right shoulder, they closed their ranks as they receded. He twisted further round to look behind him, and again through interspaces saw a flat open mound, with squatting shrubs on green grass, bright as a players' stage in some antique world. Two legs moved, stealthy trousered legs. But even as he blinked, they vanished. Merely an illusion of movement set up by the turning of his head? He got up and walked onto the mound, slowly but deliberately, around the bushes, pausing to listen, looking for the man. But there was no man. He thought to himself: I could have sworn the legs moved there. Hearkening for footsteps, he heard the silence and, somehow, it mocked him. It had an invisible mocking face. Satire narrowed his own eyelids. The lack of sleep was doing things to him! He sat down on the rabbit-cropped turf; it was softer than velvet, and presently he stretched full length. He stared at the sky for a long time, then closed his eyes and drove his senses from him, but in no time they were back of their own accord, fully alert. They had the notion that the legs might belong to Adam McAlpine. He sat up abruptly and looked penetratingly about him, turning his head slowly. He arose and followed the direction which the legs had taken.

When he came to the far edge of the pine plantation, near the spot where Nan had met the policeman, he stood looking up and down the path that ran by the wood. There was no-one on it and at a little distance on either hand it dipped out of sight. In front the ground rolled upward but only slightly now, with a few stone mounds that were old croft ruins and massed clumps of whin. When he had got through this tumbled ground, he came on a sagging rusty wire fence, beyond which the heather spread far and wide over the moor. He stood for a few moments but saw no-one, then, his eyes lifting about him, continued across the moor until at last it fell away to the hill burn. By the burn he stood, his eyes steady on the distant birches in the gorge. Towards them he went.

The noise of the waterfall grew and, rounding a last corner, he saw below him a man painting the waterfall. The green of his tie was a shade darker than Ranald's inner eye had seen it. As Ranald approached, Adam looked up at him for a long moment, then turned his back and continued his work.

Ranald stopped behind the painter and glanced from the canvas to the waterfall. Not exactly a representational picture; there was a childish exaggeration of the whirls in the pool, like a childish fear of them, but still there was some resemblance to reality. Immature poet's work, he decided; a literary subject. The dark-boiling whirls in the pool were designed to suck the shocked eye down. The path had dipped to the flat ledge where they stood so that Ranald was looking back at the waterfall and up to its smooth brow; but the pool was some ten feet below him, rock-bound, with the ledge on which they stood overhanging it.

"Yes?" Adam was staring at him with a penetrative directness, his brows drawn.

"I was thinking," answered Ranald calmly, "what a waste of potential hydro-electric power."

The creases between Adam's eyebrows deepened and concentrated the light that shot from the eyes; then he turned his back. Ranald went to the edge and looked over and around. "It wouldn't be difficult," he said conversationally, "to dam this gully and get a pretty hefty head of water."

Adam, mixing paints on his palette, paid no attention.

"Don't you think so?" asked Ranald. "Or am I interrupting you?" He smiled.

"I am not an engineer," said Adam definitely closing the conversation. He did not look at Ranald.

"Neither am I," replied Ranald, "but it seemed to me the power of water had interested you—if I may say so, not unsuccessfully."

"Thanks very much," replied Adam, ready now to go on with his painting.

"Though I suppose, from an æsthetic point of view, you would rather it continued to run what is called *free*?"

Adam slowly turned his head and looked at Ranald. "Are you trying to be funny?"

"Well, no," replied Ranald, "I hadn't thought of that. I did hope it was at least a half-intelligent remark."

"Well, I don't. I think it's just bloody silly." The last two words were explicit; the eyes flashed, then Adam turned to his canvas.

"Sorry about that." Ranald's tone was still casual if now rather coolly amused. "I had wanted to have a few words with you."

Adam's head shot round.

"I am staying," said Ranald, "at Greenbank with Mrs. Robertson." His eyes considered Adam's expression. "I perceive you guessed as much."

"What the hell do you want?"

"Not much," replied Ranald. "But I had hoped we might discuss it reasonably."

"What?"

"Miss Gordon's condition is such that Mrs. Robertson and I thought it might help if we got *your* version of what actually did happen when you and Miss Gordon found the body."

"You do, do you?"

"Yes."

"Well, to hell with you! I hope that's clear?"

"Quite. Perhaps, then, you wouldn't mind telling me what happened *just before* you found the body?"

Adam's brown eyes concentrated to gleam-points. It was the restraint of one flaming mad.

"I ask," continued Ranald, watching the face as though its change of expression would tell him what otherwise he need not hope to find out, "because Miss Gordon, in her heightened mental condition, may possibly exaggerate what actually did occur. We are prepared to make allowances."

Adam's features constricted further, the jaw stiffening, shooting forward slightly, so that the mouth pursed and the whole expression gathered a rigid intensity.

Ranald studied the face. "She might even," he continued, "exaggerate an amusing love passage into something like rape."

"You bastard!" The words, flat and fierce, spat at him.

Ranald studied the face even more thoughtfully.

Palette and brush hit the ground and Adam stood before him. "Get out!" Ranald did not move. "Get out, damn you!" Adam's fist smashed into Ranald's jaw.

At the first movement of Adam's shoulder, Ranald's head had begun to duck, but the blow was sufficiently explosive to send him staggering back three yards. There he stood, looking at Adam. "I thought you were that kind of sod," said Ranald levelly, his eyes never moving from Adam's face. Then he began slowly moving in.

Adam yelled at him again to get the hell out of this and drove at his face, but the face dodged successfully this time and Adam staggered back from a full punch over the heart. Ranald followed him, not swiftly, but with the movement of one who would kill at his leisure, who knew he could kill at his leisure, but needed first to dominate the mind in front of him, to frighten it into gibbering bits.

Adam's mouth had opened, he was bent slightly from the punch and weakened, but his eyes were on fire, his expression that of the fighting wild thing which is not beaten until its last wriggle is stamped on. An excitement came into Ranald's face, whitening it.

It was a primitive scrambling fight, with Adam, after the first wild rushes, ready to use his knees, his feet, any weapon he could lay hands on, for it had become unmistakably clear that as a boxer Ranald completely dominated him. But Adam was nimble, extraordinarily nimble on his feet. When, after dodging a tree, he received a body punch that sent him spinning, he was not only instantly up again but had a piece of dead branch in his fist, was out in the open once more, with Ranald following up, watchful of the stick but forcing Adam towards the river, shepherding him towards the ledge. As Ranald stumbled over a shallow outcrop of rock the thrown stick went slashing across his face. Words now came from them thick with abnormal hatred. Blood began to blind Ranald's right eye. Yet when he got in a blow that felled Adam he waited for Adam to get up. Adam was not deceived. "You bloody swine!" he gasped, for he saw that Ranald wanted to break him, to make him whine before finishing him off.

But they could not keep up the pace, and presently, when Ranald had Adam with his back to the ledge, Adam made no effort to sidestep. Leaning forward slightly, he waited, his eyes wary as a stoat's, his panting mouth still spitting oaths. When Ranald moved to go in, Adam threw himself flat in a leg tackle and, as he brought Ranald down, tried at the same time, in the same motion, to heave him from off his back over the ledge. He very nearly succeeded, but Ranald just managed a grip on the legs. There was a fierce roll and scramble for a few seconds; then Ranald got the full thrust of a knee between the pit of his stomach and two short ribs which had been fractured in an air crash. The intense pain blinded him, loosened his hold, and Adam, breaking away, got to his knees, to his feet, stepped back a pace—and disappeared over the ledge with an expression of fantastic astonishment, his arms thrown up, his fingers wide.

Ranald lay doubled up and slowly writhing. As the stinging agony ebbed, he got on hands and knees and looked over the ledge. The dark pool boiled and swirled and then ran smoothly out of its narrow tail on the far side, got broken up by some boulders, widened and grew shallow in a short run. There was no sign of Adam McAlpine. Ranald got onto his seat and leaned forward to ease the pain, waiting for the sucking swirls and eddies to throw up the body or empty it down the tail of the pool. The pool was deep; in its depths would be continuous circling currents, hidden ledges. The body might never come up.

Ranald got carefully to his feet and straightened himself. His hands were streaked with the blood he had wiped from his eye. He could not see the whole of the pool because of this overhanging ledge which, down from where he stood, curved irregularly for a short distance with birches growing to its edge. He moved up towards the falls so that he might thus get a view under the ledge right to the foot of the pool on his own side. But he found he could not quite get a total view, though he could see the base of the rock which Adam had gone over and what he thought for a moment was a white handkerchief caught between two stones beyond the bottom of the pool and about a yard up from the water's edge, close in on his own side. It was clearly not a handkerchief, however, but an old piece of paper.

There was now a need upon him to search every corner and satisfy himself. He looked at the pool once more, saw the outward swirl from the rock that would have drawn the sinking body inevitably back towards the central downthrust from the falls, then walked along the ledge, in among the birches, and, still not completely satisfied after peering over, came out onto the path, intending to go down its short dip and walk in on the pool from below. But already a realisation of his position, a certain wariness, was in the movement of his body, and as he instinctively glanced down the long gorge he saw two men with fishing rods coming up. He saw them only for a second or two where the path curved outward above the river, then lost them in the trees. They were perhaps two hundred yards away. Ranald did not hesitate. He left the path, climbing up through the birches at a slant, away from the pool, back towards the moor. But soon he was completely blown, his heart knocking, and threw himself on his face.

The fight had certainly taken him right out of himself! He hadn't, he reckoned, enjoyed anything so much for years. God, how people indulged themselves by letting their emotions rip!

It was the measure of him, the sod, with his animal teeth and feet, his bloody knee! He extended the muscles of his stomach trying to ease the pain, which was now dull, not sharp, so perhaps the ribs hadn't gone. All the time he was listening, with a wariness in the eye, in the pallor of his face, the sharp criminal look of one who knew exactly what had happened—and would happen, if any kind of evidence should point towards him. The anglers should be at the falls by now—if they hadn't stopped to fish a pool on the way up. They might remain in the gully all day, fishing the deep pools with bait or minnow, hoping for the big trout, the cannibal monsters. They might hook something big enough to surprise them!

His brain now became extremely cunning and lucid. The painted picture would be found intact and he knew a sudden intimate satisfaction in having resisted the impulse to kick the wooden legs from under it as he had followed the nimble Adam. A lucky break! With no wreckage, no evidence of struggle, Adam must simply have fallen over. Not to mention the darker suspicion that would inevitably enter the human mind—of suicide. The whole affair couldn't have been arranged better had he deliberately framed it! Short of actually having been seen, he couldn't conceivably be connected with the event. He hadn't even met the fellow!

He glanced at his watch. It was time he was getting back, for if he weren't late for lunch, everything would be completely normal. There was this blood on his hands. And on his face, too; he could feel the sticky crust. Before he left the trees, went into the open, he must wash. He looked at his watch again and decided to give himself half an hour before he risked an approach to the burn.

He lay on his back, staring up through the small leafy trees. The high sky was hazed with cloud. Presently a warbler was overhead, amongst the leaves; visible now; song notes fell on him. Bird notes all along the wood; not songs but a few odd notes, now here, now there. Distance gave them a curious echoing quality. He thought of spring woods and Nan. This *was* Nan. He stirred restlessly; dammit, it was time he was out of this. But he forced himself to lie still. He would leave the farm to-morrow morning. A vague thought about his return ticket put his hand to his breast pocket. It was flat—empty. His pocket-book was gone.

He sat up with flashing eyes. If they found his pocket-book! His hands went over all his pockets, even those in his waistcoat; they were beginning to tremble. His anger, as he swore, gave a vicious twist to his features.

The spasm passed and he began to worm his way down through the trees. He hit the path above the falls and, after careful spying, slid down to a screening clump of salleys by the burnside. There he washed his hands and with every care douched his face. But he started a trickle of blood again. It took him five minutes to stop it, but by that time he had his complete explanation of a fall, for he realised that whatever happened here now, he would in any case require an excuse for Greenbank. The reflection of his face in the water made that clear. After spying and listening, he slipped up the hillside, then moved along it, until he was above the falls pool. The first thing he noticed was that the picture was gone.

He lay flat, watchful, trying to think this out. Anglers wouldn't have stolen a picture. That was quite certain. They would have removed it only if they had found the body. Nor would Adam have come miraculously up out of the pool and borne it away, not in his sodden condition! On hands and knees, Ranald moved along the hillside until he had commanded two more pools. There was no sight of the anglers, no human movement of any kind; he went back on his feet until he overlooked the falls pool once more. But now he was afraid to go down. The level ground to the ledge was flat-open like a trap whose jaws would spring if he stepped on it. In a blinding moment he realised the hell of a hole he had landed himself in. Actually he hadn't pushed Adam over, but who on earth would believe that now, with the evidence of the pocket-book containing his personal card not to mention a bloody and bruised face? And he had been looking for Adam—as the policeman of Elver could testify. Not to speak of the girl in the case!

The nausea he had experienced when the knee got him in the stomach came back; but he did not give way to it; his lips thinned against his teeth. To hell with them! To hell with that bloody trap too! He snaked his way down and did not go openly onto the bare ledge but slid noiselessly across the path and in among the trees above the tail of the pool. He leaned over the ledge to make sure nobody was squatting down below. There was no-one, but suddenly he realised that something was missing, and in a moment remembered the piece of old white paper. It was gone. So the anglers had been there.

This knit him together finally. He stood quite still, turning his head slowly. He felt no real pain now. The remorseless mood was on him again; it went down into his hands. He thought not of flight but of what might be met—or overtaken—and destroyed. To be trapped like a rat—over that sod! He moved to the edge of the trees and stood, his eyes flashing swiftly about the bare ground they had fought over. Then they stopped in a concentrated stare. The brown leather pocket-book was lying by the slight outcrop of weathered rock which he had tripped over before getting the stick in the face. He raised his eyes from the pocket-book and looked about him, lips apart, hardly breathing. Then he walked calmly forward, lifted the pocket-book, opened it for a reassuring glance, put it in his pocket, moved up onto the path, left the path, began climbing, quickened his pace, tore upwards, his breathing thick with gusts of laughter, of relief and triumph.

10

He was half an hour late for lunch and opened the door upon Aunt Phemie, who had just sat down to table, and—what was this?—Nan "Hullo, Nan!" he said with a surprise, a warmth, in his voice and manner which so completely overcame Aunt Phemie that she could not take her eyes from the blood clots on his face. He seemed changed, to have come surprisingly alive.

"Ranald!" breathed Nan, also staring at his face.

"Oh, this!" He touched his brow. "That's what's kept me." He was amused, swayed, gave a short laugh. "I came one cropper up in that pine wood of yours and the branch of the tree got me right across. Doesn't it look pretty?"

Aunt Phemie got up. "Dear me! What on earth were you doing?"

"I thought I'd climb a tree. Ancestral impulse."

"Reach down that box," said Aunt Phemie, pointing to the high shelf as she turned to the hot tap. Ranald brought the box to the kitchen sink and Aunt Phemie, after tearing off a strip of bandage, soaked it with disinfectant and began dabbing the clots.

"Ooh! that bites," said Ranald, screwing up his face.

"That's what it's meant to do." The nearness of his face with a lost boyishness coming through, so affected Aunt Phemie that her features concentrated and she wiped away smoothly the blood traces below the clots.

"And who brought Nan down?" he asked.

"Herself," answered Aunt Phemie, studying the clots with businesslike care. "The doctor ordered her up for a little while this afternoon." But she was not satisfied with her work. "I think I'll soak away these clots and bleed them clean."

"You'll do no such a thing," declared Ranald. "They're fine—thank you very much." He turned. "Hullo!" he said, looking at Nan. "Feeling all right?"

Nan had gone pale, was wavering like one about to pass out. "Fine, thank you." But she visibly pressed the table with elbows and trembling hands. "What next!" declared Aunt Phemie, rushing out. She came back with the brandy bottle and Nan, though she managed to take a good sip, said, "I think I'll go up."

"I should just think so!" Aunt Phemie caught her arm. "Come along. And next time you'll obey the doctor—or you'll hear about it! Coming walking in on me like that!"

"Sorry, Ranald," said Nan, throwing him a glance as she went out.

"Keep your teeth on it," he said encouragingly, following them to the foot of the stairs. Aunt Phemie now had her arm round Nan, was clearly bearing almost her full weight. "I'll be up to see you soon," called Ranald cheerfully.

Nan lay full out on her bed, eyes closed, her skin drained of blood, ghastly, but one hand held on to Aunt Phemie's fingers. Her breathing began to revive in short shallow gasps. "Oh, I feel such a fool," she muttered with the tragic weakness that couldn't even cry.

"A wee drop more brandy," suggested Aunt Phemie tenderly. But the fingers would not let go. "Don't hurry," whispered Aunt Phemie. "Take your time, my darling." She suspected that the sight of the blood and the change in Ranald had been too much for Nan.

Nan began to stir, to sniffle; tears came from under her lids, wetting the lashes, running slowly down her cheeks. "Oh-h!" she moaned, and her features crumpled like a crying child's.

"That's my girl!" said Aunt Phemie. "Now, where's your hankie? Oh, but yes, yes," she added as Nan's head moved from side to side in a sort of utter weakness and negation. Aunt Phemie found the handkerchief under the pillow and began wiping the tears away.

"You're good to me," murmured Nan. "You—you know."

"Yes, my dear. I know," whispered Aunt Phemie.

Nan's head lay still; she opened her eyes and saw Aunt Phemie wiping her own eyes.

Aunt Phemie nodded, smiling. "We're just two silly women," she said, "but we're tough!"

Nan closed her eyes again and gripped Aunt Phemie's hand hard. She was trying to stop a new outburst of tears. Presently a wavering smile came through the tears and she looked at Aunt Phemie. "I can feel the brandy hot."

Aunt Phemie nodded. "I can see it in your face."

"Can you?" She lay back completely relaxed, exhausted, but the smile left its ghostly presence in her face. She said after a little in a quiet natural way, "Death comes so near—you feel yourself—sinking back on him." Then she looked at Aunt Phemie again, with a strange almost shy expression in her eyes. "That was Ranald," she said.

"Yes," answered Aunt Phemie, "that was the real Ranald."

Nan gave a small nod and pressed Aunt Phemie's hand hard, then drew her own away.

"I'll bring you up a plate of soup in a little while; meantime compose yourself like a good girl, and no nonsense." At the door Aunt Phemie turned. Nan's eyes were on her in a shy gladness, in a veiled tribute. The unspoken was between them. Nan was very lovely when she looked like that. Aunt Phemie made a face at her and closed the door.

Ranald was waiting for her in the kitchen, drying his hands on the roller towel behind the cupboard door. "How is she?"

"She's come round. But she's desperately weak. We'll leave her to herself for a little while." She saw the brandy bottle.

"Would you like some?" She looked at his face. The brow showed a slight but definite swelling.

"I would, if you don't mind."

"Help yourself. I'll get you a glass."

He picked up Nan's glass, poured himself a stiff one, and drank it off. "I could have done with that earlier." He smiled. "You said the doctor was in?"

"Yes. Do sit down. The potatoes are ruined, I'm afraid. Yes, he was in. After fever, you've got to stay in bed for a day or two, but he now wants her up—and interested."

"Sounds sensible. He seems a reasonable chap."

"Yes, he's a good doctor. I hope you like the soup?"

"It's excellent. I always take Scotch broth in a restaurant. You feel there's body in it—though never like this." His voice and manner now had their casual air, but with an attentiveness, a natural warmth of life underneath, that subtly transformed them. She saw that he could, if he liked, be quite charming—perhaps, even, very charming.

She was still moved, too, over Nan. She felt in a completely irrational way that Nan had taken the turn, that something had happened which, as it were, had headed her off. If only—if only—she could be kept in her present mind! If only that awful wind of chance didn't suddenly blow her again onto the dark course! In her own body, Aunt Phemie had felt Nan's utter frailty. She was still automatically sending out her own strength as she spoke to Ranald, asking him what had really happened in that tree. And Ranald had his story, embroidered it even with a reference to bird-nesting in boyhood. "Infantile regression," he suggested with a humoured glance that broke into a short laugh when Aunt Phemie smiled.

"And I *was* interested in these Irishmen digging those drains. Experts—but why Irish?"

"Because the Irish are experts at that work. During the war— and right up until now—labour has been our difficulty. That field—Nan calls it the thistledown field—it got beyond us. But that was not the only kind of trouble."

"No?" He looked at her with genuine interest, even curiosity.

"No. Broken-down fences. Cart roads that only the tractor can take now. Over-cropping year after year with grain. Even the moles—didn't you notice them here and there in immense rashes, the molehills, I mean?"

"Now that you mention it, I did."

"And rats. Horrible." She was now wholly concentrated on interesting him.

"Really? You mean they swarmed about?"

"I tried to keep it from Nan. She came here at the tail-end of the last great hunt. She couldn't help seeing something of it. They were not only in and about the stealing. They were in the grain stacks. Everywhere. Burrowing in the banks like rabbits, actually using the rabbit burrows. Horrible—particularly," she added, "as a subject for lunch! Have some more potatoes?"

"Thanks. I feel hungry."

"Perhaps the country air is doing you good?"

"I believe it is."

"Pity you're going away so soon."

"I should really go to-morrow."

"Must you?"

"I should really." He ate his stew and potato.

"I'll slip up with a plate of broth for Nan now, if you'll excuse me."

When she came back, she looked cheerful, happy. "I do believe she's taken the turn. If she could just have a day or two to get some pith back into her!"

"Have a cigarette," he said. "Between us, we'll manage all right. Is that coffee? Good!"

"You're driving me into bad habits again." She stuck the cigarette in her holder.

"Not at all. One must have a burst occasionally—particularly after killing rats. By the way, how did you kill them?"

"It would take me hours to tell you. I remember one night in the wintertime, about bed time, hearing savage cries and going to the window to see lights rushing about the ploughed field out there. It looked as if some strange beast had got loose in the field and they were after it in a weird death hunt. I got frightened in an awful way. At last I couldn't bear it." She smiled. "Some young lads were after the rats with sticks and electric torches. I had told the grieve I would pay threepence a tail."

He laughed.

"Then there was the time when Donnie fell through the stack. Getting threshed early was a real problem. Anyway, it was well into the spring. The threshing mill was in place between the stacks in the field. Donnie had climbed up onto a stack to begin forking to the mill—when he suddenly disappeared. They had to tear the stack away to get at him. He was nearly suffocated."

"But how?"

"You know how a stack is built? Anyway, the rats had eaten the heart out of the stack and he had fallen down through it."

"Good God!"

Aunt Phemie nodded. "That was during the war—when

seamen were being torpedoed and drowned taking grain across the Atlantic."

"I say! You had your war too."

"We did what we could."

"But surely the Ministry of Agriculture should have done something about rats. Hang it, they should know about dealing with them scientifically I mean. It's really pretty bad."

"I don't know," said Aunt Phemie: "I suppose they had their problems too."

"That's the worst of it," declared Ranald with a restless movement. "You'll all go on excusing them. It's just damned silly. Clearly, over rats, they just had no plan at all. You make that clear. Don't you?"

"Believe me, I was angry enough," admitted Aunt Phemie. "But that doesn't help. We must try and be fair. Where would the Ministry of Agriculture—though it's the Department of Agriculture in Scotland—where would they get the men—the rat-killers—in war time to cover all the farms in the country? They just hadn't got them. In the end we got two men from the Department for ten days—just before Nan came. In bare traps they caught over seven hundred—I made them lock the heap in a shed until they were counted lest Nan might see them. They also used gas and poison. So we've got them under—for the time being anyway."

"But how were they allowed to multiply like that?"

"They weren't allowed to," said Aunt Phemie. "They just did in spite of us. Life is like that."

Ranald shook his head. "I see your point—but I am not being had. You can destroy that kind of life. You must. You must destroy the rat; or the rat will destroy you."

Aunt Phemie blew away a stream of smoke.

"You've got to make a plan, a national plan, to destroy rats and stick to it, ruthlessly. There is no other way." He leaned back. "However, I suppose you'll think that's politics!"

"I shouldn't mind that. It's when you actually come to deal with things, with life itself—it's difficult." She hesitated. "I know you'll think that's vague. But when you have got to get the real work done, the actual grain and calves and what not produced, the land ploughed, and so on, with real human beings working at it—it's not easy. You're only a human being, and the other person is a human being, and if you're going to respect him as an individual with a right to some freedom of his own—it's difficult to plan him in your way."

"But surely not—if your plan is the right plan. You may think—I don't know—that I'm interested in some brand of politics, some new party, as that sort of thing is understood—in the press, at election meetings, and so forth. I'm not. Not at all. We've got to get past all that. We've got to have some basis for our political thought. Everyone-for-himself, in the old capitalistic scramble, served its purpose in the historic process by smashing up feudalism. But now it in its turn is finished; it's gone rotten in our hands. It should be buried, or it will rot all life. We need a scientific socialism." He was in real earnest now, he was alive, not with that air of complacency which had earlier repelled Aunt Phemie but with a driving purpose in him, an obviously deep belief. The intolerant sharpening of the pale features with the dark blood clots held its own warrant. "You mentioned freedom, for example. Everyone, here and in America, and not only the big political bosses, but the writers, the parsons, everyone who thinks he has two ideas to rattle together, shouts *freedom*—we'll die for *freedom*—and yet not one of them has even attempted to define the word." He stopped abruptly and his features gave an ironic twist. "Like the old woman shouting her blessed word *Jerusalem!*" He lit another cigarette.

"Perhaps it's impossible to define?" suggested Aunt Phemie.

"No." He shook his head as he blew out smoke. "Take your rats again," and now he was talking without stress. "You reasoned about rats. You determined they were a menace. You took steps accordingly, and now you have won *freedom* from rats."

"But human beings are not rats."

"The same reasoning process applies nevertheless. Only you have to begin by asking how does a human being in fact attain a consciousness of freedom. The notion persists that man becomes more free the more he grows independent of his fellow men, of society. It's the old Rousseau gag about man being born free and yet being everywhere in chains. It's just sentimental nonsense. If you left a child in the forest to fend for itself it would, at the best, grow up an animal, a beast forever hunting its food. You know that. It would be absolutely conditioned by the necessity for grub-hunting. It would have no speech, no music, no literature, no philosophy, no religion. All these things it gets from society. You, in fact, taught children these very things. There are no schools in the jungle."

"I agree," said Aunt Phemie. "But I still don't see quite how it gets its consciousness of freedom in society, or what exactly you think freedom is."

"Let me give a definition of freedom and then we can argue from that. Freedom consists in the act of recognising necessity and taking the best steps you can to deal with it. Freedom, in short, is the *consciousness of necessity*. When you became conscious of the necessity for destroying the rats, you took the proper steps and obtained freedom from them."

"I'm afraid," said Aunt Phemie, "that we haven't altogether got free of them."

He gave her a glance and smiled. "You have got free of them to the extent to which your action went. Had it been scientifically thorough—in your case and every other—then we wouldn't have been bothered any more with rats. Just as we have got free of wolves, though it's not so very long ago since the last one was killed on your hills."

"I admit it was a weak point," said Aunt Phemie. "All the same, I am hazy a bit about your definition, about being free the more I recognise necessity. If I am always governed by necessity—well, I am governed by it, and how I can be free from necessity— from the urgent necessity, for example, of washing up these dishes—by recognising that I have got to wash them—well! I'll be free from the washing up after I have done it. But I sort of knew that before."

He leaned back, pushing against the edge of the table, obviously delighted with the way she had caught his argument.

"Good! Absolute freedom, of course, is a myth. Because we are animals who have to be fed and clothed and housed. Let us recognise that; let us recognise that *economic* necessity. Then let us take the next step and say that the greater will be our freedom from economic necessity, the more thoroughly we in common organise our productive resources and distribute the goods."

"And that's socialism."

"Yes. But don't forget that its aim—its philosophy, if you like—is freedom, freedom from economic fear, from want, from war. Not a vague Atlantic Charter notion, however, but something scientifically determined."

"We stand on the threshold of man's next great step forward," said Aunt Phemie, smiling with an attractive humour.

"We do. Even your friend Freud has become hopelessly old-fashioned."

"Really?"

"Yes. They literally shock patients now into sanity. Assault and battery by electric shocks. Cures them, too. It's the new age." His manner was now alert and friendly with a teasing gleam in his eyes.

She looked into his eyes, shrugged, still smiling, and got up.

He laughed and jumped up. "Let me help with the dishes."

"No. I'll tell you what," Aunt Phemie decided with a confidential air. "I'll go up first and see Nan. Then perhaps— for a wee while—you might go up. I never stay too long. Whenever you see you have cheered her up, say I've got something for you to do."

He glanced at her with a sly humour. "And have you?"

"Necessity demands," suggested Aunt Phemie, "that we break some sticks."

11

"Nothing but accounts," said Aunt Phemie cheerfully to the postman the following day as she glanced at the red penny stamps.

He took the string from his mouth and as he wound it round

the bundle of correspondence for the Greenbank area and stuck the bundle back in his bag he said, "It might be worse. You didn't hear about young McAlpine?"

"No."

"You would know him? He's a poet or artist or something queer like that."

"No," said Aunt Phemie. "I know Mr. McAlpine himself, of course. What's the young man's first name?"

"Adam. Adam McAlpine. And he's not so young. He's well over thirty. But he's never done much good. They say it's the mother. But you know how folk gossip. However, what I'm going to tell you is no gossip, for I had it last night from Jamie Johnston himself and he is one of the two—the other was Andie MacFarlane—the two who found the body at the falls pool on the Altfey yesterday."

Aunt Phemie did not speak.

"They had taken the day off for fishing. It's a habit of theirs, for they're clean daft on the fishing. Always was. Jamie and me have had more than one night in our time. However, yesterday they took the road and left their bikes at the shepherd's yonder below the gorge—you know, where the road ends—and began fishing up the deep pools with—with a bait they have." He glanced at Mrs. Robertson and though he realised that his subtle hesitation over the kind of bait was lost on her, yet the absolute nature of her attention flattered him. "In time they reached the falls pool, coming in on it from below, for there's a gravelly bit where they lie—well I know it!—and if you drop your bait—but never mind," he said, restraining himself, "for they didn't drop any bait there yesterday. Jamie said to me he saw the thing as he came in below the rock. At first he thought it was a dead otter, but then he saw it was no otter, it was the head of a man with nearly all the body in the water. He gave a cry to Andie. It was young McAlpine and they hauled the body up on the stones. At first they thought he was dead as a drowned pup—it's Jamie's own words, for he was always a cool hand, but then, as Jamie said, he noticed he was kind o' soft like, and he began working on him. And in time they got a movement of life into him. He had taken in a lot of water, but they got him sort of round. And then the queer thing happened and it's left folk talking and wondering, wondering indeed if it was poor Gordie who did murder old Farquhar. For you see—but I'm going through my story. As I say, Jamie and Andie always carry a gill apiece—hard as it is to come by—but, as Jamie always says, it's half the day. When they got some of the whisky down him, he came to in a queer sort o' lost glowering way, showing his teeth, even after he'd spewed, and they saw he had been attacked. He used a word or two I wouldn't care to mention to you. But Jamie has them." He paused in bright-eyed sober recollection. "There just was no doubt he'd been attacked. In fact Jamie sent Andie up on top to see if he could see the man lurking about. But all Andie saw was the picture that Adam had been painting and he brought it down with him, thinking that perhaps it was his picture Adam was wanting. But it wasn't the picture. No, faith, it wasn't the picture. He was wanting to be at the—at the so-and-so bastard, if you'll excuse me, Mistress, and, as Jamie said, he couldn't have hit a fly he was so weak with the spewing. But he was a little beside himself. They had almost to carry him to the shepherd's cottage, where they put him to bed. The shepherd himself was out, so Jamie stayed with the wife and Andie set out on his bike for the town. His bike punctured, but Andie kept going on the rim and cut his tube to ribbons though he knew, as he said, that devil the hae-penny would he get from old McAlpine for that. And he won't!" The postman wheezed. "His mother—Adam's mother—got into an awful state. She's a feckless downtrodden body right enough. But the car was sent and Adam taken home." The postman paused, looked shrewdly at Aunt Phemie out of his sharp face with its close-cut greying hair over the ears, and eased the hard official hat from his forehead.

"When did all this happen?" asked Aunt Phemie.

"In the middle of yesterday, not long after twelve o'clock. And maybe the queerest thing of all has yet to be told. Jamie, though he's ages with myself—fifty-five—has the eye of a hawk. He always had. I told you how they drew the body back from the rock up onto the stones. Well, when they were taking Adam away from where they'd stretched him on the stones, Jamie noticed a paper. The wet body had flattened it out. Jamie's eyes caught a figuring on it. He picked it up, read it, and put it in his pocket. He's a cool customer is Jamie. He gave it to the police inspector when he was telling him the whole story. Do you know what it was?"

Aunt Phemie waited.

"It was the missing deposit receipt in the name of Farquhar Farquharson for the sum of seventy-six pounds."

"Really," muttered Aunt Phemie.

The postman nodded, satisfied with her reaction. "It was."

"And did it—was it—on the body?"

"No, seemingly. For Jamie is quite clear about this; it's maybe the queerest thing of all. Jamie says he saw the bit of paper as he came up to the pool. It was caught between two stones, he said, as though fixed there by the last spate. And if Jamie said he saw it, he saw it."

"Extraordinary," murmured Aunt Phemie.

"Isn't it? For if there's one thing that's clear it is that the man who attacked Adam McAlpine thought he had done him in. Jamie is in no doubt about that. He said they fought on top of the ledge of rock and—as Jamie put it—just as surely as some man killed old Farquhar with an axe so did some man try to drown Adam McAlpine like a rat. And the point now is—was it the same man?"

Aunt Phemie put a hand against the door jamb and stared past the postman's avid face.

"Ay, it's a horrible story," he said, acknowledging the growing pallor of her skin, and went on more quietly, "the inspector and the sergeant went up with Jamie and Andie to the falls pool and they surveyed it from every angle. But beyond making sure that you couldn't have seen Adam's body from the ledge itself—which would satisfy the murderer he'd done his fell job—they didn't get much, nothing at all really. Not so far anyway."

"But—Adam?" said Aunt Phemie. "Hasn't he—didn't he tell them who—it was?"

"That's what we're all waiting for. But Adam McAlpine was

very poorly last night. I heard he wouldn't speak. It is to be hoped under God that he will live. The doctor was out and in." He added, "He may die yet."

"Dreadful," said Aunt Phemie.

"Ay, Mistress, it is. It's all that. But if it brings to justice the real criminal, it will have done something." He hitched his bag into position.

"Yes," said Aunt Phemie.

"Ay." He nodded. "It will that. Well, I must away. Good day, Mistress." He saluted soberly, and set off in a hurry to catch the time he was forever losing.

As Aunt Phemie turned into the house she heard Ranald's laugh from Nan's room. About to enter the kitchen, she paused, then went on through the back door and into the outside wash-house.

Quietly she closed the door behind her and stood very still.

There was no doubt in her mind at all that the person who attacked Adam McAlpine was Ranald. For a long time her mind could hold no other thought; it grew large and empty and witless. Automatically she upended a wooden box and sat on it, for her legs had grown weak. The newspaper and letters fell to the floor and she left them there. Ranald must believe now—in there—with Nan—that he had killed Adam. He must know that. The change in him—the excitement underneath—the smashed face… .

She stirred and a nervous hand began to pluck at the clothes over her heart. Nan—she must save Nan somehow—not let her know—if the police came. If only no-one came until the morning, until she got Ranald on the train. She got up. She was trembling all over, felt sick. She tried to be sick but only brought a cold sweat to her forehead. This is madness, she thought; I must control myself, show nothing. She went to the wash-tub and turned on a tap. She would do a washing. She rinsed her hands in the cold water. She drank from the tap. She pressed a wet hand against her forehead. She hardly knew what she was doing. She would do a washing.

Ranald's voice called, "Hullo!" from the back door. She stood quite still. She could not face him yet. They would think she was at the steading. Nan would be getting up. She closed her eyes. Presently, with anxious stealth, she saw her way clear to the steading.

An hour later she was back chopping wood. "So there you are!" called Ranald from the back door. "Doing my job!" As he came and took the hatchet from her, Nan stood in the door, frail and wondering, her eyes lifting from Aunt Phemie to the roofs of the outhouses, to the tops of the apple trees showing beyond, to the sky, to things at hand and far away, to the quiet loveliness of the world.

There was something in Nan at that moment, some essence of life or being, that Aunt Phemie knew she loved with a profound and tragic love; the eternal essence, forever sought, embodied for a timeless instant. Nan's eyes came smiling on her face.

Aunt Phemie's eyes answered; then in her natural voice, lightly, she said, "I was thinking of doing a small washing."

She kept on the move through the afternoon and evening, washing, cooking, sending Nan to bed, talking sensibly, going out to the steading, remembering this and that which had to be done, her ears growing sharper as the hours wore on, her eyes a hundred times on the road to the farm. But no-one came. When at last she got into bed, she sank back exhausted.

She was awakened during the night. A murmur of voices. She thought: it has come! Her body was gripped as by an actual nightmare. But she strove to listen, fought for soundless breath, and at last got to her feet, to the door. There she leaned against the wall, dizzy. No-one had come. Ranald had got up and gone into Nan's room. That was all.

Soundlessly she drew her door open a couple of inches. Ranald could not have closed Nan's door, for she could hear his voice, low but distinct, as though he were sitting on her bed, talking to her.

"I know," murmured Nan.

Silence.

"I miss you in London. I'll miss you more than ever now," he said, without any emotion. Then, after a moment, "I wanted to tell you that. Whatever happens to me—that's how it is."

He got up. Aunt Phemie closed her door without shutting it. She heard his voice again, as though he had walked to Nan's window, but she could not now make out what he said. She wanted to hear, to hear every word, but her hand, convulsively gripping the knob, drew the door quite shut; as she let the knob go there was a sharp click. They've heard me! she thought. There was complete silence in the house. She got back to bed, staggering a little. After two or three minutes, Nan's door was quietly closed and Ranald went softly to his own room.

For hours Aunt Phemie's mind turned and twisted, searching into every conceivable argument and impulse, now doubting, now perceiving with an utter clarity, quietening but to stir and think again, until she burned as from fever. She fell asleep—to be wakened by Nan. She was late! They must hurry! "Say good-bye to Nan," she called, after the rushed breakfast, "while I get out the car."

There he was coming, tall and pale, Nan's powder on his wounds, his kitbag over his shoulder. She drew all her resources together, tautened herself.

"Too bad troubling you," he said. "I had meant to catch the bus."

"It was I who slept in. However, I've got some business to do in town." She let in the clutch and they were off. She had an impulse to keep on talking, as though she might thus ward off everything and everyone, including the police. Once, during the night, she had thought she would test him on the way, by a chance remark, and be guided by his reaction, so that at the last moment, if he were secretly tortured about Adam's death, she might relieve him, even on the station platform; but now, in the daylight, in his actual presence, the notion was preposterous, a complication to be absolutely avoided. "I often have some business in town," she said in a brisk manner.

"I suppose so."

"Yes. There's an architect I've been meaning to see for a long time."

"Building?"

"Yes. The farm cottages. It's an old scheme of my husband's. It had to be abandoned when war broke out." What had made her think of that? she wondered.

As she went on talking, she had time to be inwardly and distantly amused at herself, as at a voice in an ironic play. She saw he was interested in the farm workers, of course! She described in detail her husband's scheme for lifting the cottage roofs and turning each dwelling into a two-storied house, with water laid on, lavatory and bath. Greenbank was going to have been a model farm. She intended to make it that yet, she said. That, in fact, was the main reason why she had stayed on. Her voice rose with the speedometer needle. She was analysing the position in the local building trade and the Government's attitude to farming when they entered the town. "We have eight minutes—plenty of time," she said, glancing at the clock in the steeple and easing off.

"All that's very interesting."

"I rather think so," she agreed. "Farming finally depends on the worker. Without a decent house, he won't stay—at least the girl won't." A policeman at a street corner waved her on. Her heart rose. Ranald said something, but she wasn't listening to him now. "Politicians don't understand that the basic person on crofts and farms is the young woman. If she refuses to stay and marry because of the house and amenities, it's all up," said Aunt Phemie. They were driving into the station square. There were no police here at all. "Well, that's that," she said finally taking her hands off the wheel and sitting quite still, as if resting.

"You needn't come out," he said.

She sat.

"And thank you very much."

But she suddenly changed her mind. "Might as well get an early paper," she decided and slammed the door neatly.

Now they were on the platform, before the bookstall. The minutes got lost among the crowd. The train was on time. Here it came!

"Well, good-bye, Ranald." She put out her hand. "I hope you have a nice journey."

"Thanks."

"It was good of you to come. So long!" She turned smartly away, out through the station, into her car. She waited, upright, until she heard the thresh of steam from the moving train; then for a few seconds she drooped over the wheel, closing her eyes. Limp, all stiffening gone, she lifted her head. Her vision played tricks with her as she fumbled for the self-starter.

Part Three

RECOVERY

1

No police came during the forenoon after Ranald's departure, and Aunt Phemie began to wonder if Adam McAlpine was really dead. Otherwise it seemed incredible that he should have withheld a description of Ranald from the police. The police, in view of all the circumstances, including the very odd appearance of the deposit receipt, were bound to cross-question him and even compel the information, simply because the whole mysterious affair linked up with old Farquhar's murder. For Adam to refuse to give information would now bring suspicion upon himself. And why should he refuse—seeing how, from Jump-the-dyke's story, he had so bitterly hated the man who had attacked him, who had so obviously thought he had done him to death?

Should she have stopped in town and tried indirectly to find out? Shand, the seedsman, with whom she ran her main account, would have begun on the story without a word from her. But she hadn't had the strength; and in any case her instinct had told her to keep absolutely clear of the whole affair. Before the police she would show complete astonishment, because Ranald had been at home that fatal day for lunch in the usual way. She couldn't stop them from getting on to Ranald in London—but she could keep the news from Nan.

Adam must either be dead—or too ill to be coherent. And then a new thought struck her: Adam might have had no idea who Ranald was or where he stayed. Apart from that trip to town for cigarettes, Ranald had never left the farm. Adam might have tried to describe Ranald, but his description would be—could be—only that of a mysterious stranger.

There might be a breathing space at least. And if Adam was dead, then, in the absence of any witness, Ranald could never be convicted on the capital charge.

After returning from the station she had gone upstairs to Nan's room, smiling, saying that was Ranald off, cheerfully amused at Nan's bright-eyed interest, but not lingering because, as she said, the grieve was lying in wait for her.

Nan had wanted to talk about Ranald. There was nothing else she wanted to talk about. It was so obvious that it was like a state of mesmerised suspense, could be felt without even a glance at her. From the moment Ranald had come into the kitchen with the blood clots on his face and that new subtle friendly excitement in his manner, Nan had changed. From that moment her real recovery had started. This was more certain to Aunt Phemie than anything that ever could be explained. When Nan had said "That was Ranald" she had actually meant: That was the real Ranald, the Ranald she loved. Her shy bright eyes had said silently: Now you understand? And Aunt Phemie had understood.

The *real* Ranald! Whenever Aunt Phemie thought of it, a bleakness, as from a grey wind, withered her breast. She would have to get through this talk with Nan, this endless intimate talk about Ranald. It frightened her. The pulse in her temples was beginning to throb and spread. She needed sleep to bring back calm and cunning.

When handing Nan her milk pudding at lunch, she said, "I feel a horrid headache coming on. I think I'll have an aspirin and lie down for a little. Do you mind?"

"I'm sorry," said Nan, her eyes darkening with sympathy as if she were to blame.

"Not at all," said Aunt Phemie, smiling, but incapable of hiding a sudden dryness. "A short rest and I'll be perfectly all right."

Nan was silent for a moment. "Do," she said gently. "I'm fine."

"That's good. We have plenty of time for talking!" Aunt Phemie exhibited an ironic briskness. "Now, have you everything? You're sure you're all right?"

"Yes."

Then Aunt Phemie brought her eyes to Nan's face, nodded, smiled and went out. Her heart was beating painfully. Nan's softness, her sympathy, her gentleness, had suddenly irritated her. Oh, she was getting sick of emotion! And as she went downstairs she knew a certain wild kinship to Ranald, to his destructive mood. She had eaten no lunch. She was literally feeling sick. This sudden change in her own mood dazed her, shook her with an unaccountable bitterness. She rested for a while in the kitchen, but when she stared out through the window, nature took on a new aspect, inimical in its heavy stillness. And all at once, and quietly, behind what had been happening, behind Nan and Ranald and the moods and actions of their desperate world to-day, there rose before her, dark and dead, like the pattern of a sombre landscape, her own past tragedy. She thought of Dan, and his movement in her mind was the movement of a slow figure of death. She filled a glass with water and went up with it to her bedroom. She drank down two aspirins, took off her skirt, and got under the eiderdown. Within a couple of minutes she was in a deep sleep.

Nan woke her, tapping gently on the door, bringing a cup of tea, a biscuit in the saucer.

"Goodness gracious me!" cried Aunt Phemie, "where—what time is it?"

"It's getting on for five."

"Five!"

"Yes. No-one has run away with the house."

"No-one been at all?"

"No."

Aunt Phemie relaxed, stretched herself. "I had such a lovely sleep...! This is kind of you, Nan. How are you really feeling?"

"Grand. A bit trembly, you know." She suddenly sat down on the bed, trembled, and laughed.

"My dear, you shouldn't——"

"Now don't boss me," Nan interrupted her. "Even if you see me going about on all fours. I'm up!"

Aunt Phemie looked at her with a tender humour. "You're the nearest thing to a daffodil in the snow I've seen for a long time."

"Do you know," said Nan with an air of conspiracy, letting Aunt Phemie in on the astonishing secret, "that's just how I feel!" And she added, as if listening, "Hsh-sh!"

Aunt Phemie laughed and drank her tea.

"I have a confession to make," said Nan. "I was up on the washing green."

"Nan!" It was a note of reproof, for Aunt Phemie was only now realising what might have happened had the police inspector, with his cold water-blue detecting eyes, come to the house and found Nan alone.

Nan nodded. "It's the loveliest washing green," she said mysteriously. "What a size the dockens are! And there are some nettles growing right in under the apple tree. And plantains with immense leaves. Some starlings were on the big ash beyond the hedge. Do you remember the collective nouns: a murmuration of starlings, wasn't it? It's a lovely word, but it's not right." She shook her head.

"No?"

"No," said Nan. "It should be a yatter of starlings. They were having the loveliest yatter you ever heard. Then they flew off—just for no reason in the world. Wonderful, wasn't it?"

"Quite marvellous," declared Aunt Phemie.

"Then," said Nan, "then—I heard her."

"Who?"

"The buzzard. She was far far away—up over the Dark Wood. There was something disturbing her up there. I saw the wood quite clearly in my mind, and a black collie dog came out of it and slunk along the edge of it, but then he ran down through the field. Then I heard Sandy's whistle, up in the top field. So you see I was right. But I knew the buzzard would follow. I was watching a blue opening in the grey sky, the blue of paradise. I never saw so lovely a blue. It had a quiet smile, listening—though

hardly listening either—to singing I couldn't hear. Then the
buzzard swam out upon the blue——" Nan, who had, with
restraint, been miming her story, now raised her arms, described
an arc in the air, over-balanced and fell on Aunt Phemie's legs.
She gripped one leg and tried to bite it through the eiderdown.

"Nan, you witch!"

Nan raised herself, her eyes wet and bright with love, looked
confused, got up and went out.

Aunt Phemie finished her tea in a gulp, with a reckless feeling
that life was at her door, had come into her house. She did not
care how or why. She was not going to care. She was going to
keep it alive. Strength flooded through her. To have had such a
perfect sleep—and nothing to have happened! Now and then,
with a slowness, a naturalness beyond understanding, the fates
behaved like this. The daffodil came up out of the snow. A feeling
of hunger, of miserliness, swept through, Aunt Phemie. With
the uneaten biscuit in the saucer, she went downstairs, into the
kitchen where Nan was standing at the window, glanced at the
clock, exclaimed, said she was famishing, and set about preparing
the evening meal. She would not let Nan help, in fact drove her
up to her room to rest for a little. And Nan went. When Aunt
Phemie thought of her at her bedroom window, she stole up
into the vegetable garden where she could command the farm
road and a fair stretch of the public highway beyond. For over a
minute her eyes anxiously followed a figure on a bicycle. When
she saw it was a woman, she turned her back to hide her relief,
looked at the leeks and carrots, began pulling the last of the peas
and presently had a small heap of them on a cabbage leaf.

After supper, with the dimness of early evening in the kitchen,
Aunt Phemie said, "Now, Nan, I'm going to light the lamp for
you——"

"I don't want it lit, thank you."

"You're going to bed. The first thing you have got to do, my
girl, is get strong."

"You know fine you're talking nonsense. If you were as sick
of that bed as I am!"

"If you think you can get round me——"

"Boo-hoo!"

"Look, Nan dear. Isn't it lovely that you are getting well again ——"

"That's right. Preach at me. Have you ever thought how fond Scots people are of preaching? There's a good touch of it in Ranald. I used to mock him for his grandmother."

"You would!"

"I did!" She gave a small chortle. "You heard us last night? Were you shocked?"

"I was. Wakening me out of my good sleep."

"Now that I think of it, he was preaching a little last night. But not much. He was very serious."

"I'm glad to hear it."

"He had to tell me that he would give everything up, including me, for his political work. Wasn't that sweet of him?"

"I'm glad to hear he's so sensible'"

"Yes, there are times when you would really think he's Scotch, poor fellow."

"Nan, you're a witch and a demon and I'm sorry to have to say it."

"Ay, it's sad … Aunt Phemie?"

"Yes?"

"What do you think of Ranald?"

"Think of him?" said Aunt Phemie, getting up. "I think he's a handsome fellow, with a mind of his own, and clever."

"Is that all?"

"It's not bad to be going on with." She found her long cigarette holder. "He was rapidly perverting me even in that short time—as you can see."

Nan exclaimed with delight as Aunt Phemie lit her cigarette. "Now you come back to me again. As a little girl, I used to think you the most distinguished person in the world. You can have no idea how I hung on your movements. I can still get the smell of your clothes when you mentioned Paris."

"Smell?" Aunt Phemie raised her eyebrows.

"That's it!" cried Nan, acknowledging the slight gesture. "A fragrance of silks and lovely things and wonder."

"And now the cows and the byre. How the glory has departed!" declared Aunt Phemie, blowing smoke with an amused expression.

"You know it hasn't," said Nan quietly.

"But, my dear, you know it has. We grow up. We cannot go on being sentimental. And to tell the truth, when the dairy-woman was off for two months in the early summer, I did all her work, the milking and dividing out and so on, and thoroughly enjoyed it. If you were brought up with it you never quite lose that pleasant something in the smell of cow dung. Quite fascinating, I assure you."

Nan laughed. "You would give style to a broken wheelbarrow."

"I might undertake to mend it too. And that's maybe more to the point."

"You think so?"

"Well, don't you?"

Nan's eyes turned to the fire. Aunt Phemie saw there was no avoiding the talk about Ranald. She would hold it, however, to this practical level; at all costs keep it from degenerating into that softness of sentiment which would soften the very tissues. Hold Nan for the moment as it were in the balance; then as the days went on, head her off Ranald or at least get her to that point where she was capable of judgement.

"I don't know," answered Nan. "Style is a queer thing. I cannot tell you how much *I* was affected, because I knew *you* would be affected by that cool casual way Ranald has. It was like that at first now, wasn't it? Confess!"

"I think I see what you mean."

"It was all right the way things happened—your writing to him, I mean. I couldn't help that. To have wired for him, as if he had a bourgeois responsibility, that would have been—pretty bad!" She smiled.

"I don't see that," said Aunt Phemie.

"No?" Nan's eyebrows arched. "I bet you do …! Wiring for my young man!" She laughed deliciously.

"Well, and what's wrong with that?" asked Aunt Phemie with an apparent obtuseness that made Nan sway in her laughter.

Nan stopped laughing abruptly. "That would have been terrible!" The solemn thought of it set her laughing again.

"Why? Isn't it natural that a girl should have a young man?" asked Aunt Phemie as she tapped ash from her cigarette with an elegant gesture. "Or were you grown beyond all that?"

"We were," said Nan, wiping the weakness of laughter from her. "We just were."

"Well, it didn't look like it."

"Please, Aunt Phemie, don't start me off again," begged Nan. "You know quite well what I mean. A girl cannot become a responsibility to a man, not in that way. It's not done. That old bourgeois clinging stuff has gone bye-bye for good."

"Really!" said Aunt Phemie. "I don't mind betting that the word bourgeois will soon be a slang term that will set all your precious teeth on edge. It will go bye-bye with a vengeance."

Nan looked at her. "You reminded me of someone just now— I can't remember who."

"Echoes," said Aunt Phemie. "You bring a lot of them back to myself. That's all."

"No," said Nan. "It's not all."

"No?"

Nan shook her head. "Oh no. This is not slang. Not now. Not any longer. It's life—or death. And—it's mostly death."

Aunt Phemie remained thoughtfully silent. There had been a lot of death.

"You see," said Nan, "it's because of what we have lived through. And yet," she tried to correct herself, "it's not so much that as what we have lost. I, too, was brought up with cow dung. Well you know it! But these early warm rich comforts—they have gone. All our early beliefs have gone. That's—that's how I could never somehow be at home with them in London, why I kept on struggling." She looked at Aunt Phemie, who nodded. "It's lovely talking to you," Nan added in a quiet charmed voice.

"What sort of beliefs?" asked Aunt Phemie reflectively.

Nan was thoughtful for a little while. "Every kind. It was as if all our beliefs had let us down, had betrayed us. Take God. It's not just that we knew there was no God. The scientists—and especially your friend Freud—had made that quite clear. We saw how the idea came into man's mind long ago. So that was all right. But it couldn't be left there. That was the real trouble. You couldn't forget it, because of the Church. I mean it was still there like a menace. Do you understand?"

"A sort of superstition that the Church—every Church—kept on reviving, and that was a danger because it wouldn't let man get free of its primitive evils."

"Yes!" said Nan. "You put it just like Ranald! And you see," she went on eagerly, "unless we got free of it, we could never get beyond it, into the new world that Ranald wanted —and not only Ranald of course—but the scientists, the new political thinkers, who would build this new world and do away with awful things like war. And oh! there are some fine men among them, who work and are selfless—sometimes, you know, I think—like Christ."

"The old belief comes back," said Aunt Phemie.

"No," said Nan thoughtfully. "That's not what troubled me. It's awfully difficult for me to explain. I wish I could. It's—it's what happened next. You see, among the usual crowd it meant that you didn't just ignore religion, you laughed at it. You made jokes about it, witty blasphemous jokes."

"And you couldn't do that?"

"They used to tease me about it at first. I didn't really mind. Maybe I posed a bit as the Scotch Presbyterian—and held my end up too! But it's not that I mean either. A fellow like—like Know-all—he watched me and would laugh. He hated religion. Deep down in him he loathed it. It was that loathing. And when you fought back—you saw that loathing in more than Know-all."

"Do you mean, Nan," asked Aunt Phemie, "that still, deep in you, you believed?"

"No, no, it's not that," said Nan, with a touch of distress. "It's the *loathing*. Sometimes it made me feel sick in my stomach."

"I see," said Aunt Phemie quietly.

"It put me all wrong. I didn't mind whether religion was right or wrong. But this loathing——"

"It curdled the milk in you, like rennet."

"Yes," said Nan, flashing her eyes gratefully on Aunt Phemie. "And I grew afraid. And you see it was not only about religion, but about other things. You not only laughed at sentimentalism or convention or bourgeois morality, you got a sort of horror of them. There was a certain Indian, for example. He may have been bogus; I don't know. But the word mystic—you hooted with laughter. That was all right. But when he used the word 'humility'—there was only one final thing you could do—just spit. You rocked with laughter—and spat, metaphorically or otherwise."

"And you aren't by nature a good spitter. I can see it was difficult for you."

"No, Aunt Phemie. I can't let myself off like that. It's—terribly difficult. There was Ranald. The people who just spit, they don't matter. Not ultimately. I could see that. They are the people you have to work with and use. I was seeing it—from Ranald's point."

"He had to go beyond them. And you were afraid of the bleakness beyond."

"Yes. Only I mustn't be vague. Where so much depends on it, vagueness is a crime. I understood Ranald in that. He had to be hard and clear-headed. Otherwise—everything would sink back."

Aunt Phemie nodded. "We talked, you know, a lot about it, Ranald and myself. I see what you mean about the need for being hard and clear-headed. We had better be quite frank about this, Nan. I can understand that you would be a bit sick at the loathing and the horror. Your stomach is made like that. Or we can say, if you like, that your erotic group of instincts are stronger than your aggressive or destructive group. You prefer love and creation to destruction and death. But when you went beyond that emotional reaction to where Ranald was—you grew *afraid,* not in your body now so much as in your mind."

Nan looked at Aunt Phemie. "Yes," she said.

"It's easy to analyse like this nowadays," said Aunt Phemie lightly. "In fact we did—quite a long time ago. But now, I agree with you, things have happened to give the analysis a new terrible reality. I quite understand, my dear. You feel that Ranald—has gone bleak—and may have to be—deadly."

Nan nodded.

"Tell me," said Aunt Phemie. "Ranald wasn't always so—sure of himself?"

Nan shook her head. "I told you how we met first—at that country house. It was a spring weekend and we all fetched and carried. It wasn't boring or arty. Ranald and I walked. At first he thought I was a bit enthusiastic about the flowers in the woods. You know how some girls can be. Then I think he saw that I really was. I told him things about the North. He told me about a pony he used to ride as a boy. It became exciting, particularly when I kept him at his distance—I mean, when he saw that these things were real to me, the woods and the sky and everything. That seemed to relieve him, so that he became quite himself. And we walked and walked. It was all as simple as that—but somehow terribly genuine—behind all the talk and so on. I felt he was real. I have a memory that we walked awfully fast and laughed a lot."

There was silence for a little while.

"And only later you saw that there was the other side to him?" Aunt Phemie said.

"Yes. I saw it growing."

"But it must have been there somewhere all the time."

"Oh yes. It was like a strength in him, He came to depend on it. He had to. For others depended on it too."

"And finally it got control?"

"Yes. But it was the control of one who now *had* control."

"One who has at last come fully into his faith and will let nothing divert him? I have met it. It's really religious, I suppose."

"Once a clever man said that to Ranald. I have never known Ranald more ruthless. He gets pale at such a time and logical in a remorseless way. He deliberately tore the man's mind into small bits—and showed him the bits."

"He would," said Aunt Phemie. "I wonder," she continued after a moment, "what happens to that early thing you found in him, when you were walking in the spring woods?"

"It's there! I know it's there!" said Nan, her voice rising. "It's just—it's just suppressed."

Aunt Phemie did not answer.

"Don't you think so?" asked Nan with eager concern, her eyes full on Aunt Phemie.

"I suppose so," answered Aunt Phemie quietly. "Yet I sometimes wondered if the talk about suppression and regression was always right. I don't know, but I wondered sometimes if what was suppressed mightn't, to some extent anyway, just wither away."

"You don't believe that?" asked Nan in a low voice.

"I don't know," said Aunt Phemie thoughtfully. "But perhaps I'm wrong. Yes, I think I am," she added. "The real deep impulses, the instincts—they cannot be destroyed. But they can find unusual outlets. Perhaps that's it."

"Aunt Phemie—why don't you say what's in your mind?"

"I am trying," said Aunt Phemie quietly. "And you mustn't get upset, my dear. Tell me this. Would it mean an awful lot to you—if you couldn't find again in Ranald—what you first found in the spring woods?"

Nan's head fell back against the chair and her eyes closed. "Oh yes," she said on a deep expulsion of breath. She looked utterly exhausted. Her head moved from side to side and tears came from under the lashes. In the dim light her face was drained and tragic.

Aunt Phemie got up. "You'll come to your bed," she said gently. "It's just the weakness in you, and we shouldn't have been talking so much."

But Nan turned her body away and wept. Aunt Phemie waited for a little while, then took her arm. At her bedroom door, Nan threw her arms round Aunt Phemie's neck and sobbed again. "I found it again in—in Ranald," she said in a broken voice, "when he came in from—from the Dark Wood."

"Yes, yes," murmured Aunt Phemie. "I saw it too."

2

Aunt Phemie called at a garage and at Shand's, then she drove out the south road. Some little distance beyond Beechpark she stopped, turned the car, and stopped again. When any vehicle passed she lowered her head as if preparing to start up. After about twenty minutes, she saw a man come out of Beechpark and walk towards the town. At once she set off and, drawing up alongside the footpath, waited for him.

"Excuse me," she said through the lowered window, "are you Mr. Adam McAlpine?" and she smiled in her most engaging way.

"Yes," said Adam.

"I hope you'll forgive me," said Aunt Phemie, "but I am Mrs. Robertson from Greenbank farm and I have long been anxious to meet you. Do you mind? Perhaps I can give you a lift?"

He considered her with a direct steady piercing look, then he said, "Thanks, I don't mind."

When he was seated, she said, "To be quite frank, I have been sitting along the road there, wondering if I should call. I didn't want to trouble anyone, but I am concerned about my niece Nan Gordon. She told me she had met you. She has been very ill." She left the engine idling.

"Has she?" He spoke in a flat voice.

"Yes. But she is getting on now. Perhaps you didn't know that she had been recovering from an illness?"

"No."

"Well, she had," said Aunt Phemie. "As a matter of fact, it was a mental breakdown. That was the real difficulty. In a condition like that one is inclined to get—to have—delusions of one kind or another."

In the pause he asked coolly, "What do you want to find out from me?"

"I was wondering," asked Aunt Phemie, "if you could let me know just what did happen."

"When?"

"When you and she were together—that last time."

"Didn't she tell you?"

"That's the trouble. She was so terribly upset that—I don't know how far she imagined things."

"Why do you want to know this?"

"Because," Aunt Phemie replied, "she is now getting well enough for a police interview. I don't know whether the police will come or not. But I am afraid, because of the effect such a visit will have on her. And I don't know what you told the police or really what did happen. My only concern is that Nan should not have a set-back. If you cared to help me in this, I should be very grateful."

He looked away through the windscreen, his expression closed. "I see," he said in the same cool voice. He obviously did not want to talk. "There's nothing much to tell. I reported finding the body to the police. I did not think it necessary to say that Miss Gordon was with me. It seems we were seen, however. The police came back to me, and I said that I had in fact met Miss Gordon by the Altfey burn but did not see any point in dragging her name in, as she had nothing to do with the actual discovery. They seemed to be satisfied with that."

"Thank you very much. That was very good of you."

He said no more.

"Just in case they do come," she added, "for they seem to like investigating, did you tell them that Nan saw the body?"

"Well, yes," he replied, his features gathering in an irritated way. "I had to tell how we were resting at a certain spot and how I, seeing something in the peat hag, went forward to have a look. I suspected, I said, that Miss Gordon had got a glimpse, though I tried to shield her from it and hurry her away." As he took out a silver cigarette case, he added in the same tone, "They did not ask me for a chart of the terrain."

So unexpected was the last stroke that Aunt Phemie laughed in nervous relief. He turned his brown eyes on her and searched her face now in an interested thoughtful way. There was a curious wild-animal restraint about him. She did not actively dislike it though it troubled her. Anything absurd or crooked coming from her would be hit away with a sudden paw.

"That makes everything clear," she said, "and I am very grateful to you."

He turned the cigarette case between his finger-tips, looked away through the windscreen, and said nothing. The engine was still running. After the first glance at him she had not dared stop it. The least assumption or presumption on her part would, she instinctively knew, have set up an instant reaction. Had she given the slightest indication of settling down comfortably for a sensible talk he would probably at once have shut up and gone away. Even what he would do with the cigarette case was exclusively his affair. She could not ask him to smoke. His eyes dropped to it and he put it back in his pocket. Her hand caught the knob of the gear lever. "Can I run you into town—any particular place?"

He did not respond for a moment, then he turned bodily round and looked at her. "Is that all?" he asked.

She felt the heat coming up into her face. So far, what she had said to him had in some measure been rehearsed. At least she had known that her anxiety about possible police action would seem real and authentic—for indeed it was. But how to go on from that to find out what really did happen by the falls pool she had had no idea, though she had hoped that the conversation would of itself provide a way; for this, of course, was the information she really wanted. After all, if questioned by the police, Nan would have to give her own story in simple truth about the finding of the dead body irrespective of what anyone else may have said. To have Adam's version would be reassuring—nothing more. When she had put her hand on the gear lever she had realised the impossibility of even hinting at the information she wanted; indeed, with some sense of relief, was prepared to drive away. And suddenly, in a flash, she was cornered, with reddening face and restless glance.

"Well," she replied, smiling awkwardly, "if you—if you have anything else to tell me—I should be very glad to hear it." She was aware of his brown eyes on her face like feelers.

"That's what you really wanted to know?"

Involuntarily she nearly asked: What do you mean? but

repressed it in time. Then she brought her eyes to meet his. "Yes," she said.

He smiled slowly and showed that he rather liked her face. Speculatively he asked, withdrawing his eyes, "How much do you know?"

"Nothing," she answered.

His eyes flashed on her instantly, and after a moment he said, "So that's the way?" This seemed to amuse him in a dawning way that ran deep. He stirred. "This is a noisy contraption," he said.

"Yes, it's an old engine. If you like———"

"Are you in a hurry?"

"No. I have done my business in town."

"When they brought me in from the shepherd's house they left my painting gear behind."

"It would be very simple for me to run out for it now. Shall we?" She caught the gear lever.

"All right."

They set off. The police inspector was standing at the corner of the street where they turned right towards the mountains.

"He made sure he saw us," observed Adam.

"You think this will complicate matters still further?" remarked Aunt Phemie almost solemnly.

He glanced at her with appreciation and lines of laughter deepened silently. "They just don't know what to make of me. Damn them, you would think a man mustn't have a mind of his own!" He added, "They pry."

"They do," she said, assailed by a wild impulse to laugh.

"I was tired, muddled. I said to that police inspector: 'Aw, get to hell out of this.' I don't think he appreciated it." Laughter came out of him in one or two barks.

Sobered, she felt like a young girl who wasn't too sure yet where she was. She was beginning to understand Nan's perverse interest in Adam. He seemed so abnormally natural that he could be, she thought, terrifying. They were now driving through open rising country with farm steadings near the road and croft houses up on the slopes. They crossed and recrossed the Altfey, and presently were leaving the cultivated land behind. He was completely absorbed in the lie and look of things. "I like this spot," he said.

"You would know it as a boy?"

"Yes." And then, as though belatedly appreciating her remark, turned his head. "You run pretty deep, I'm thinking."

"Me?"

"Yes, you. If he didn't tell you anything—how did you find out?"

"Find out what?"

His brows instantly gathered. "Don't tear it," he said, warningly.

She had known instantly she had made a mistake; she must be completely frank or shut up. This was disturbingly refreshing, even exciting in its strange bewilderment. "All I know," she said, "I learned from the postman the following day. That's all I know."

"He said nothing?"

"No."

He studied her face for a moment. "How then did you learn he was the one?"

"I didn't learn."

"You just knew?"

"Well—yes."

He laughed. "Good!" he said. "It's the kind of knowledge I like." He looked around the countryside. The road was deteriorating rapidly to grass and ruts. She saw the shepherd's cottage up on the slope to the left and then had to stop for a gate.

He made no effort to get out. "I just couldn't stand the bastard and hit him. What was in his mind was sticking out a mile. It came at me—Hell, I just suddenly couldn't bear it." He brought a fist in across his stomach.

She took a couple of breaths. "Did you know who he was?"

"Yes. I knew at once. He had been nosing about the town. He asked a policeman where I stayed. But it wasn't that. That he might be out to get me—well, all right! Fine! But God, that way of coming, that theoretic questioning deadly way—that almighty logical—aw to hell! And all the time, by God, behind it all—the cold death instinct. Don't tell me! I've seen enough of it."

Aunt Phemie sat still.

He glanced sideways at her after the sharpness of his emotion had subsided. "You think I exaggerate?" he suggested with the ironic humour in which there is no smile.

"Yes," she replied simply.

"Of course!" He threw up a hand. "I'm only telling you how it happened. I thought you wanted to know." He saw the gate and got out. "You can turn in there on the green and I'll go up to the house." He opened the gate and walked away.

Aunt Phemie turned the car, stopped the engine, and let her hands fall dead in her lap. "Well!" she said. Thought would not focus. Her head turned to follow his figure through the back window of the car. Her body twisted round so that she could keep on following it. He reached the door. A woman appeared. He went into the house.

Aunt Phemie faced round again. He was alive like something charged with electricity. He was like a spoiled child that had come through its fears and frustrations, through its angers and selfishness, to an amazing condition of wilfulness which would not tolerate anything but a vivid real state of being. Once his hands had moved in front of him in a sort of swimming gesture, as if clearing things away, films and obstructions, webs. And towards the end he had grown inwardly excited; the breath swelled his chest, and his brown skin had caught underneath a coldness of rime. She needed no more words to explain what had happened at the falls pool. His apperception of Ranald had been flawless and devastating. What was she to think? to do? What about Nan? But she could not think and was staring through the windscreen when the movement of his figure made her jump. He opened a rear door and dropped his gear on the floor, then he got in beside her.

"Everything all right?" she asked.

"No," he answered laconically. "The wet paint got smudged. I have lost a couple of tubes of paint too."

"Would you like to have a look for them?"

"Aw," he said, pursing his lips, "it doesn't matter."

"It's no trouble as far as I'm concerned," she assured him in a matter-of-fact voice.

"Well——" He still hesitated. Something seemed to have annoyed him. "All right. It's half-a-mile up."

"I'll come with you, if you like."

As they set off, she said sensibly, "I have never actually seen the falls, so it's an outing for me."

"They're worth seeing," he said, "though I couldn't tell you why."

She remained silent.

"I can't paint. Though something may come out of it," he concluded. After a few seconds, he added, "You have a gift of discreet silence."

"Sometimes it may be necessary."

He laughed and Aunt Phemie said no more. Suddenly he stopped. "That's pretty good, isn't it?"

Aunt Phemie looked up the gorge, with its outlines, birches, and glimpses of tumbling water. "Yes." She nodded. "For me it is not too big to lose its intimacy."

He turned his face and considered her. "I believe that's what it is."

"In Switzerland or the Tyrol," said Aunt Phemie calmly, "you get bulk and picturesqueness. It may be thrilling and all that, but somehow you can't enter into it."

"You can't have it under your feet?"

"Perhaps," said Aunt Phemie doubtfully.

"To feel free, man must dominate?"

"No," answered Aunt Phemie at once and positively. "You can become part of this and still be yourself, only more full of— intimacy, of love of it. You don't want to dominate it. That's the very mood that does *not* arise." Her cheek bones got whipped with colour.

They came to the falls pool and he searched about the cleared ground but found nothing. "That's where I went over." He looked over the ledge and studied the pool. "I was so astonished that I took in water—and I'm quite a good swimmer. I was so flummoxed that I remember clawing at the rock like a silly animal. I don't remember how I did the last yard or two. Like the hen that runs round when you have drawn its neck." He glanced sideways at her.

"Where was Ranald?" she asked.

"Lying there. I got my knee in his stomach."

"He pushed you over?"

"No. I was so pleased at having doubled him up that I forgot where I was and stepped back—and over—by mistake."

"So he didn't——" She stared at him.

"No. He tried his damnedest to punch me over, but failed." There was a real if withering humour in his face, a satisfaction.

"He left you to drown?"

"Well——" He shrugged. "He meant to drown me—as I meant to drown him. Looking from the ledge there I should say he thought I was well and truly sunk."

She turned away from him and began walking back. Presently she sat down.

"Feeling a bit sick?" he asked.

"Yes," she said coldly.

He left her, going back towards the pool. She lay over against the hillside. Deeper than her sudden feeling of nausea was an utter hopeless despair. It had little to do with any individual in particular; something was swimming in below and choking life itself. Vile, awful, terrible. This wasn't the awfulness of despair she had known once. This was vile. It spread over all life, crawling, choking everything, every thought and hope, everything.

Presently she got some control of this mood which had so blindly assailed her and sat up. Then she arose and began walking down the path. As she rounded a bend, she saw him standing away in front, his head over his shoulder, watching her approach. How he had got there she had no idea, for he hadn't passed her on the path. There was something startling about this, but she was too weary to let it trouble her. He turned his face away and strolled slowly on so that she might overtake him.

She tried not to look at his body, but saw it, the legs, the length of his jacket, his hair and his neck. He stood to one side, his head slightly tilted, a smile on his face, in his eyes.

"I got one of the tubes," he said. He held it out on his palm.

She acknowledged it in an indifferent way.

He glanced quickly at her and went on, stepping sometimes off the path in order to give her plenty of room. "I have told you now all I know," he said. "More than I told the inspector." That amused him but in an attractive way, as though he were being delicately thoughtful, prepared now to give her every consideration. It was quite plain that he had come to a decision about her, that in fact he liked her.

This did not interest her. She now just did not care about him at all. Weariness had washed her body and left it spent.

"I agree with you, of course, about the intimacy," he said. "Only it's not so easy when you want to—get at it."

"No?" she said, keeping going, but up through the indifference had come a subtle inflection of scorn.

"There was I trying to get the sucking whirls of the pool as if the whole glen was sucked in there to its own peculiar death. But all the time I was aware of—the intimacy. I knew it didn't get sucked in. At least … I know now."

She offered no comment.

"Farmers' wives are not usually so perceptive," he suggested.

"You seem to know," she said, lifting her eyes in search of the shepherd's cottage.

"I'm afraid I have offended you." He glanced at her, his eyes bright with a mirth in which there was an extraordinary tentative quality like shyness.

"No," she answered coldly. "You haven't offended me. You have merely shown me something utterly beastly."

He did not take this amiss. On the contrary, he looked now more than ever as if he would like to propitiate her. He even remained silent. They walked towards the car. He stepped forward quickly and opened the door for her, shut it and stepped round the car; by the time he got in beside her the engine was running and the gear lever waiting.

They drove in silence. In the mirror near the top of the windscreen she glimpsed his face looking slyly round at her. It not only contained a suppressed humour but also something else more alive. She realised that, given half a chance, he would make advances to her. Age did not matter. It was an intimacy, an understanding, the hidden movement of the spirit that delighted him, that was the sort of air in which he could breathe and live. He wanted this. Yet because the moment was genuine, he would not intrude. The speed of the car increased.

She was aware that he knew why the speed increased better than she did. An anger began to grow in her. She deliberately looked at the farmsteadings which they passed. Within ten minutes they were in town. A policeman seemed to be, somewhat indefinitely, on point duty. "I'll get out here," Adam said all at once as if he had seen someone. She immediately drew up. "I should like," he said, before closing his door, "to see you again."

She bowed, her eyes on the policeman. The door slammed and she stuck out an arm; the policeman waved her round the corner. Only as she was approaching her own farm road did it strike her that his gear was in behind. She drew up. Yes, it was there. Ignoring it, she sat and tried to think.

She did not care how she had behaved coming back to the town. That did not worry her. She tried to think but was merely irritated, angry, that his gear was still in her car. She had a good mind to drive right back to his home and dump it there. Why not? She gripped the wheel. But the grip slackened. Then suddenly what could no longer be denied came before her and she saw Ranald's brightness when he came in with the bloody face; saw Nan's quickening love at the new movement of his spirit. Oh God, it was terrifying! Her eyes closed; she hung her head.

3

Men have gone mad, she thought, as she drove on up to the steading. They have gone mad. Their madness stalked about her mind; stalked all over the world. She saw men as beings different from women, saw that they had gone mad. Hard and upright, stalking about, bright from eating the roots of their own logic, full of theories and purpose, aims; bright and hard and deadly; looking with their eyes for figures to pursue and break. Christ! she silently cried as she swung the car round the corner at the steading, swung it too far, and rocked it as she straightened up. When men exclaimed by Christ it had always affected her as a steel probe on a living nerve; her being quivered for an instant, darkening as in pain. She swung the car into the cart shed, backed, and drove on into the stall between the iron pillars. There was no-one there; the place was empty and silent; no beasts beyond the sliding doors in the wall; all animal sounds were out at pasture. She sat for a little while quite still, then got out, shut the door, and, without giving herself time to think, opened the door into the back of the car. She would have to do something with his gear, hide it somewhere. Her brows gathered as she peered down into the dimness. She leaned forward and lifted the picture onto the seat as though it were something wounded she hated to touch but must. One had to handle and bury things. It leaned back against the brown leather, looking at her. The waterfall, the whirls; the blue-black features of the pool boiling and swirling to central holes that sucked down the light—smeared by the brush of a body. Drunkenly the features leered at her. Her chest hardened as from the inward pressure of a suffocating growth. She lifted the palette. Smeared with its own clots, including a livid repulsive olive. A narrow cloth bundle, with the tip of a brush showing. She did not touch it. She was overwhelmed by a nightmarish apprehension of creation broken in the creator's hands. Design and blood, a fantastic experiment, toys drunken-still and strewn about, from a Creator who had turned away. She put the small picture and palette back on the floor of the car and closed the door, stood a moment, thoughtful and listening, then went and took the three keys from the engine switch and locked up the whole car. As this was something she rarely did, she moved away from the locked car with the air of one who has hidden her secret, stood for a moment in the entrance glancing along the walls of the building, then walked towards the house.

As it rose on her sight with its windows, she smoothed her face. She would have to deal with Nan, with that living sentient creature whose eyes would take in the page of her face in a glance. She swallowed and stiffened her mouth. She would say she had been upset at the garage. "Nothing can beat the old German Bosch magneto," the wiry mechanic with the greying hair had said, a certain twinkle in his eye at this tribute to the recent enemy, "and we haven't got one." Say something about the magneto to Nan, adding the usual war growl at tradesmen.

There was no-one in the kitchen. She hearkened to the house and knew it to be empty. Nan would be out, adventuring up the fields, back once more at her game of clearing up the shadow.

In the wandering movement of Nan's figure over the fields there was suddenly for Aunt Phemie a childlike, an intense pathos, so that she could have sat and wept, and buried her head. Actually she kept on hearkening, then went along the passage and up the stairs. Nan's door was standing half open. "Are you there, Nan?" she called in a controlled voice. There was no answer and she went quietly into the room, looking around as if Nan might still be there. The room was clean and tidy, with an impress on the bed where Nan had sat—where her invisible presence still sat by the writing pad. She had been writing Ranald, Aunt Phemie thought, and went slowly towards the pad. She had to twist her body above the bed in order to read the written words at the top of the page without touching the pad. *Aunt Phemie has gone to town on business and I am all alone and I hear the world outside. I am going out, Ranald. I wish I could find you there. I think I will.* Two pages had been turned over and under the pad. Aunt Phemie had no desire to read them, even if she could have touched the paper. She stared out of a window then looked about the room and saw that the top right-hand drawer of the chest was pulled out a few inches. It was the drawer Nan had looked into that moonlit midnight when in her queer somnambulistic state she seemed about to go to Ranald's room. Aunt Phemie went to the drawer and glimpsed a thick wad of written sheets. They were the long letters which Nan had not sent to Ranald. She pulled the drawer full out and began to read the top page.

She lifted the top page and went on to the next. Another page; her fingers lifted two or three. For fifteen minutes she read here and there down through the wad, then she straightened the pages, pushed the drawer back to its original position, and went into her own room where she sat on the bed staring at nothing.

The child, wandering up through the daylit fields, trying to clean the shadow from its world. Emerging from the terrors of darkness, crying for love. The thistledown, the soft eager balls, seeds on the wing—changing into the grey steady eyes, the searching eyes, of the policeman. Changing, in his turn, into the youth with the tommy gun on his knees and the cigarette in his mouth, while love in its naked family waited in the trench; he mowed them down as a pernicious corn.

Men had gone mad. Aunt Phemie saw quite clearly that men had gone mad. Her vision went all over the earth and saw then in the logical movements of their madness, stalking here and there, into council chambers and out of them, into railway stations and air ports, across fields, all the fields of the world, intent and certain, fulfilling the high and urgent law of necessity. Whose necessity? cried her anguished spirit with an obliterating mockery. She flung herself on the bed, face down, and through her smothered mouth cried aloud "Christ! Christ!" but hardly thinking of Christ for her vision had been too much for her, too terrible to bear.

4

The following morning Aunt Phemie carefully wrapped up the picture and painting materials and stitched the lot together in a piece of canvas sacking which she addressed to Mr. Adam McAlpine and left at Shand's shop. At the same time she posted Adam a note telling what she had done, and returned home with a sense of relief. For she had realised last night that the only thing which mattered now was Nan's recovery; and that Nan was at last firmly on the path to recovery she had felt with a peculiar certainty. It was something in the air, her manner, an assurance, slowness, as though she could now pause in her appreciation of the beauty of the world, pause and reflect, with a simple gratitude and wonder. Tears had brightened her eyes because she was still physically weak and abnormally sensitive to the beauty she found, but now they were like rain, with light in them. Aunt Phemie could see that Nan's secret and profound sufferings had run their course, had burnt themselves out, leaving behind some fine essence which would be forever part of her character. It was an extraordinarily delicate thing, a fragility of convalescence, but of true convalescence, with the promise in it of strength.

How far her last hours with Ranald had contributed to this, she could not be sure. There was something about it all, Aunt Phemie deeply felt, which was more than a personal relationship, which in some vague indefinable way was fundamental and lasting. Yet it was, at the moment anyhow, indissolubly linked with Ranald.

Recent broken weather had delayed the harvest. Now as Aunt Phemie left the cartshed, where she had stabled her car, it began to rain in earnest, and for three days the wind blew and rain showers slashed and tore along the ripe grain fields. Much of the heavier growth was flattened, and old Will, smoking his pipe by a sheltered gable of the steading, thought stoically of scything and extra labour. It so often happened. Ay, that's the way it went. Aunt Phemie could never quite achieve this stoical acceptance; was still inclined to be pursued by the thought: If only it had kept off for a week or two! or had come in some moderation! But no, it must slash away and flatten as if at the very heart of nature waste had no meaning. Yet she understood Will's attitude too; and indeed found in it a strange enduring power. She was satisfied that the men of the land never cursed the weather; just as, she felt sure, real seamen never cursed the sea. There was something in this acceptance of the elements that had in it the strength of a grey rock. This was how real men endured.

But Nan secretly looked upon the rain storm in quite a different way. She could not be kept in, and sometimes in the lee of a hedge or an elm tree she would glance around to make sure she could not be seen and then, the wet slash on her face, would laugh and suck the rain drops from her cold lips.

A flying wildness, a soddenness in the beaten earth, a freshness, a brawling of gushets, a positive spate in the miniature greenbanked burn that wound its crooked way down from the high dam, a dripping lushness of wild flowers, a crush of green stems, clover leaves and silvered rain drops, glistening berries of the wild rose—ah lovely! lovely! She broke a hip with her thumb nail, scooped out the white hairy seeds, and chewed the red skin. Like tasting her childhood, living over again. Crushed red and rain drops in her mouth, and a cold nose. When she began to shiver she went home. Aunt Phemie scolded her and she put an arm round Aunt Phemie's waist, and Aunt Phemie told her she would have less of her blarney, and they had tea. But Nan did not now talk much about Ranald, hardly any at all. Aunt Phemie always knew, however, when she was upstairs writing.

When it looked as if the storm was going to batter everything, leaving the flattened grain as rot for a second growth to penetrate, the atmosphere cleared miraculously, and the sky. The wind blew from the opposite direction, was dry and light, and searched out the dampest places with a remarkable and happy persistence. This scented wind went to Nan's head a little, at times to her feet. The flattened grain under the rain had affected her occasionally with an extreme sense of dismay (not unalloyed, however, with a secret marvelling at so prodigal a waste), but now when the dry wind had done its work, the grain lay as if finally dead.

But when the mowing started on the low fields it was remarkable how the men "worked away with it"; soon in their rows the stooks arose and, beyond a lengthy stubble in places, the harvest was in truth being "won".

The work in the harvest field fascinated Nan. It aroused in her some obscure atavistic instincts which at moments held a thrill as sharp and clean as frost. Her body felt extraordinarily light, as if every clot and congestion and poison had been purged by her illness. It grew easily tired but only needed a minute's rest for recovery; and inside her head, thought and impulse moved with the fine ease of the wind. The wind—the wind came to her from immense distances, wherein time and space were never confused yet were divided by no more than a momentary emphasis. Men and women were reaping actual fields now and in remote times. As in a dream, time itself became distance backward in space; but being awake, she had the sensation of time as distinct from space. The wind in her face and hair was now and then, for a tranced moment, a sheer laughing intoxication. She shook her head, opened her mouth, and said "Ah-h-h."

When some of the women from the farm cottages turned out, Nan joined them. The Agricultural Executive Committee had compelled so extensive a cultivation of grain that there was insufficient labour to deal with the harvesting in anything like reasonable time. Aunt Phemie had had several consultations with the grieve about this, but he was inclined to go canny, to suggest that they would manage, said that he had "spoken" some help from the high crofts, and generally did not seem to favour a strong application to the distant "prisoners-of-war camp". They discussed it right through to the "leading" of the stooks from the fields. "It's not everyone can build a stack," said the grieve, who held the old notion that finely built and roofed stacks were a farm's crowning glory. "We can work so long as there's daylight in it," he concluded.

Aunt Phemie kept an eye on Nan who really wasn't much use. She hadn't the pith, and the skin on her hands was too tender, but she was desperately willing. The second night she slept for ten solid hours. She awoke stiff and comically happy. But nothing would finally repress her. For all the time she had one consuming notion of her own: she wanted to drive the tractor.

She made advances to the tractor lad. He was twenty, shy, open-faced, with a swaying lithe body, Will's youngest son and a grand worker. She talked to him about engines, about a high-powered American car which she had driven in London for a time for an American officer. She sat in the driver's iron seat of the tractor, and finally drove it a short distance with George standing on behind.

Before Nan's enthusiasm when the tractor was silent, George

admitted, "Och, she's not bad. But if you saw the red International Diesel, with caterpillars—you drive her with two handles and she'll turn on a sixpence."

"No!"

"Yes," said George. "They got one—under the American lease-lend, they say—at Balgruan. I had a go at her. She'll do anything."

When Nan came into the lamp-lit kitchen she said, "Aunt Phemie, I nearly kissed George."

Aunt Phemie turned from the frying pan, a knife in her hand. "Nan Gordon, you'll please keep your hands off my men. I saw you trying to vamp that fine lad. You ought to be ashamed of yourself."

"Do you think he would have misunderstood me?" asked Nan with a mixture of regret and wonder. "He's a nice boy. His skin is golden with the sun."

"You leave his skin alone," said Aunt Phemie, turning to her work.

"Aunt Phemie … ! But I suppose I must," added Nan, sadly. "It seems an awful waste. What a gorgeous day it's been! I'm drenched with it." She lay back in her chair and stuck her legs out. "Do you know, a moment comes now and then when I know life is divine. It's like a stolen moment—or is it a lost one, lost from somewhere? To-morrow I'm going to have a wee vamp at the grieve."

"You're not ettling to kiss *him,* are you?"

"No…. But it's an idea!" Nan shook with laughter.

She found, however, that she had to do very little vamping of the grieve the following afternoon. They were working a top field whose boundary fence on the east side ran right up to the western tip of the Dark Wood. The field heaved and rolled in great smooth billows and the wind had flattened the grain badly in one part and it was impossible for the mower to cut it unless it were first struck up or straightened with a fork. This was exacting and tiresome work and the grieve needed all the assistance he could get if the tractor were not to be delayed in its continuous and ever-narrowing round of the twenty-acre field. So for the evening spell Nan was given her chance on the tractor, with Will mounted on the binder behind. Nan let the clutch in and, as she moved off, the grieve, standing some distance in front, watched her coming as he leaned on his fork, put out a hand and waved her a few inches in towards the standing corn, checked her, watched, and nodded. She had it! He stood aside and gave her a smile as she roared magnificently past with a smart salute for him as her commanding officer. I have got the exact distance of the off wheel from the grain, she thought; I can hold that till all the cows come home! A hoarse yell above the roar of the exhaust, a backward glimpse of a wildly gesticulating Will, and she stood on the neutral lever with her heart in her mouth and the engine vibration quivering to her thigh. As Will climbed down she leashed the lever and joined him. "An ould domned bit o' wire," Will was muttering as he tugged it clear, but no actual damage had been done to the cutting teeth. "I'm thinking you're a lucky one," he said with a slow smile as he threw the rusty loop of fencing wire from him. (Afterwards she told Aunt Phemie that she also could have kissed him.) Mounted again, she now realised why George seemed to be looking back most of the time he was pulling the binder. Plainly one had to stop pretty smartly if things went wrong and it was difficult to hear an ordinary cry above the roar of the engine. At the off bottom corner she did a loop into the open field, bumping over a couple of sheaves—bad! bad! she cried to herself, ashamed to look round at Will—and then swung in for the up gradient. Now she wanted to help the engine, to give it more juice, but the throttle was open, and for a few moments she waited with a curiously helpless feeling. What happened gave her a profound thrill, for it was exactly as if the engine came alive on its own. Its growl deepened, its power increased, all its internal horses put their heads down, took the full weight on their collars and walked into and up that gradient with their song of unconquerable strength. The great spiked wheels dipped into an old rabbit burrow, rode a grey stone, lurched and steadied, went remorselessly on. She turned to Will. He nodded but upward, with a tilt of his head that threw the humour into the air. You're doing fine! His face was weathered and antique, the ginger moustache might have been growing in more than one place, but his eyes were living and looking at her and laughing. Round came the wooden arms, the flyers, swishing the standing grain over the cutting teeth, and the teeth cut it, and up flowed the cut grain, and the inner hands of the machine gathered and tied it, and round came a fork and shot the bound sheaf clean into the open field. Oh it was wonderful! wonderful! The grain went down and was reaped in a continuous golden wave, like the wave a great ship sends from her bow. You could grow dizzy looking at it. It was marvellous! Oh, it was splendid, splendid, and she patted the driving wheel and gripped it hard and looked back, and beheld the golden wave going down and Will like some old earth god aloft on his chariot. Inside her a song sang to the earth, and to the sky as she went riding into it over the last crest.

And now here she was, throttled back, bearing down on George, glad to have remembered his instruction that you could shove the throttle home going downhill. She gave him a wave, shaking her lifted hand in a hurrah! and George, smiling, gave her a sideways nod. There was something shy in his frankness that touched her heart, for she had feared lest deep in him he might resent her taking his place on the seat of mystery. But there was nothing of that, and with a warm stirring of gratitude she respected these men for it, and would do what she could for them, until the last mortal sheaf was reaped. And now here was the grieve, the undemonstrative man, watching her as she came. He stood aside as she passed and gave her a nod of approval. She had completed her first circuit. She looked round at Will. He tilted his head. You're doing fine!

They struck a bad patch and Nan was glad when the grieve decided to shove in a new set of cutting teeth, for she had been getting a crick in her neck and a certain soreness in other muscles. She watched the grieve hammering away, then strolled up to where George was working on a tangled whorl like the unruly hair on the crown of a boy's head. The second and third horsemen—Davie and Alan, douce married men—were also busy hitting up the tumbled stalks. She chatted away gaily to

George about his engine and the crick in her neck, stretching her blue-trousered legs, rubbing her neck and laughing. "You'll know more about it in the morning!" promised Alan, who had a compact bony face and an elemental humour in his eyes. She brought Davie into the talk also, and when George said "They're waving on you," she turned away like a truant schoolgirl and went hurriedly down the field.

Two pictures of that evening were to remain with her. As the shadows had lengthened the wind had dropped, and now with the sun gone and the first smother of darkening come upon the land, the full harvest moon rose over a low ridge of hill. It was golden and immense, august and slow; it was the ancient harvest moon of many rites; it came up like the fire-warmed face of an old sky god, and looked upon the earth. It's incredible! Nan whispered to herself. But she knew it was not incredible. As she took the steep incline, she turned to watch the binder and caught the tilt of Will's head as it drew her attention to the moon. She nodded back and smiled. Plainly he thought the sight of the moon would please her! Conversation on the high seas! She felt a melting in her breast. The engine roared. She rode right over the crest, the moon far on her right, with already its glisten on the Dark Wood. "Dear God!" she cried, for no other words would come of themselves to carry her emotion. She cried them aloud, and the engine drowned them, and she was grateful to the engine for its conspiracy. For nothing like this was ever drowned; and always the harvest moon rose in its season.

The second picture seemed as old as the moon. The amount of standing grain was rapidly dwindling and most of the flattened patches had been cut, so there was little to do for the four men with the forks. As she swung in for the top stretch in the deep twilight, already irradiated with the moon's green light, she saw George leaning in over the grain listening, poised like a primitive hunter, still as a heron. Davie and Alan were waiting, their forks in their hands. As she came roaring along a rabbit bolted from the standing grain. Two forks clashed, then George was in hot pursuit. The rabbit doubled, for it could not run fast over the strong sharp stubble. George struck twice and missed. Davie and

Alan swayed in their mirth. She heard Will's shout and brought the tractor back into proper line. She did not see George kill the rabbit, but she felt the killing in her heart.

She felt it as a sharp pain, but somehow it did not touch the picture of the men themselves, eager, full of friendliness and laughter, hunting in the deep twilight. And this twilight under that great moon darkened their figures so that they were here and now, as sharp as the pain in her heart, and yet distant in time's landscape, far back and bewitched, and known to her. It was at once the gloaming of her childhood and of herself as a woman in remote times. Looking back at the binder, she glimpsed Will's face and it seemed more than ever like an earth god's; the flyers came round and the golden grain went down in a wave; the iron fork like a great serpent's tongue shot the bound sheaf clear; and she fancied that in the antique face on its chariot there dwelt a smile of understanding and beneficence.

Suddenly she saw Aunt Phemie standing talking to the grieve, who waved her from the grain in a comprehensive gesture. She saluted as she passed, finished her line, and swung round and down to the flat space to which the grieve had pointed. George appeared, ran the engine for a little, and fixed it for the night.

As the engine stopped, the silence of the evening came full upon her. Aunt Phemie's voice had a note in it that was somehow of her familiar essence, found again after a long time.

The men took their own short cut to the cottages and the women cried good night to them, Nan waving her hand aloft. Will lifted an arm like an old flail in special salute to his partner.

Nan took Aunt Phemie's arm and chatted away about the work, but there was a quietness in her voice and a wonder. As they came down through the thistledown field, she paused and looked abroad upon the valley.

"Oh, Aunt Phemie," she said, "how lovely is the world!"

5

Three nights later, with the reaping finished and a blatter of rain about the stooks, Nan came into the lamplit kitchen with a letter and a periodical in her hand. She had bathed and now moved in a leisurely way, the field labour still sluggish in her body. Aunt Phemie had found at last the leaflet of instructions for her petrol iron which had been giving her some trouble.

"They're wanting me back," said Nan, stretching herself in her chair and dropping the magazine and letter on the floor.

Aunt Phemie looked up. "Are they?"

Nan nodded. "Uhm. Marion says the arty maiden they have isn't worth her feed. Besides, she says, she giggles. Marion is really very nice about it. They can't keep my job for me indefinitely. Could I give a date—and so on."

"And what do you think?"

"I'll go, of course. It's my job. I thought of saying in ten days or so. You'll need all the help you can for the leading."

"You know you haven't to think of that?"

"Haven't I? You would almost think by the way you speak that it wasn't my harvest."

"I don't, my dear. The oftener you're in this home the happier it will be for me. Never forget that—and then I won't have to say it again."

"Please, Aunt Phemie, don't make me soft. Oh, dash it!" she said and swiftly wiped her eyes and smiled. "I had a letter from Ranald. It's—a nice letter."

"So well it might!"

Nan jumped up, put her hand to the small of her back, said "I do believe it's lumbago!" thrust both arms round Aunt Phemie, kissed the top of her head, and walked round the kitchen looking at things. "I'll come back here. I'll double back like a hare if they're after me."

"That's the ticket!" said Aunt Phemie. "There's nothing like having a good bolt-hole. And when you desert me entirely I'll know you're happy."

"You know I'll never desert you till the last going down of the sun."

"That's sweet of you."

"A trifle grandiloquent mayhap," Nan admitted judiciously,

"but terribly exact. Just terribly." She sat down abruptly. "So I'll make it a week Monday, shall I?"

"Very well. If you feel you must go so soon?"

"You know I must."

"Yes, I know, my dear. You have your own way to make. I understand."

"About Ranald—I feel I haven't been very helpful to him. I lost my head a bit. I feel I know better now." She was a trifle awkward and shy. She did not look at Aunt Phemie, who said nothing.

"Aunt Phemie?"

"Yes?" said Aunt Phemie.

"You don't think a great deal of Ranald, do you?"

Aunt Phemie thoughtfully regarded the leaflet in her hand and placed it on her knee. She smiled, "I'm not the one principally concerned, am I?"

"I'll tell you what you think," said Nan quietly without answering her smile. "You think he's hard and unfeeling and matter-of-fact. Not like a lover."

"I see you understand how old-fashioned I am, pure early-Victorian."

Nan shook her head. "I know you see … It's really a terrible thing that's happening, Aunt Phemie. A person like Ranald could talk to the men there, to the farm workers, and find out about everything, and have a scheme for putting things right, but he does not somehow care for the men themselves. I'm not putting it well——"

"You are, my dear. Ranald would be bored here, with our folk. He would have no-one to talk to. Yet he could spend his whole life applying the political theory in his head to us folk and our farms."

"He would mean it for your good."

"And for the good of all the world. I know."

"And it *would* be for the good of all the world."

"Yes. And therefore those who are against that good—must be removed."

"I see you know," said Nan, calmly. "But what other way is there?"

"I doubt if that's what's worrying you," said Aunt Phemie.

Nan looked at her in a calm objective way, and Aunt Phemie saw that she could be unyielding and tough. "What is?"

"It's the something that's missing," replied Aunt Phemie.

"You mean an emotion like kindness or love?"

"Well?"

"When you allow the emotions to interfere with work that has got to be done you merely create an unholy mess."

"True."

"So where are you?"

"We're just both sitting here—knowing there's something missing. That is our irreducible fact."

"But it's illogical. And if we clearly saw the necessity for what has to be done, then we would no longer feel bothered about—about the something missing."

"You mean we should be freed from it?"

"Well, shouldn't we?"

"You may now be begging the question. However, it is too deep a thing to be clever about. I am just not sure about all this, Nan. In history, at all times, there were those who thought they were eternally right. In every kind of religion, for example. And people were removed, often horribly. And we think now that those who removed them weren't so very right. At least we should know by this time that roasting an unbeliever was a poor way of proving or establishing anything."

"I see your point. But surely we must first of all understand things with a scientific clearness. It's awful being muddled. And terribly dangerous. I admit I was getting to that stage when, if I heard any of our great war leaders talking loudly of 'freedom', it used to make me feel utterly hopeless. I understood Ranald then. It drew me close to him."

"Because Ranald knows what freedom really means?"

"Yes."

"He told me about it," said Aunt Phemie simply. "And theoretically I think I understood. But in reality, I doubt if we would ever agree."

"Why?"

"Because you cannot—at least we cannot yet—treat the human mind as you do things on a glass slide in a laboratory. We just cannot test it in that scientific way. The real science subjects are based on mathematics. Psychology isn't."

"But psychology is a science."

"In the sense that we know some things about the mind, yes. But the laws of the mind are different in kind from the laws of matter or mathematics. That two and two make four will hold for all time possibly. But Ranald's idea of necessity in human affairs cannot be proved to hold like that."

"But he thinks it can."

"When a thing can be proved in that way, it is no longer denied by sane people. Anyway, all I know about psychoanalysis or anything psychic at all is that the experts themselves disagree on quite fundamental things or theories. And if they disagree, who is to tell me what necessity is for my mind? A consciousness of necessity! Whose consciousness? and whose necessity?"

"But surely it is clear that if you are conscious of necessity you are then free to make the best job you can of it, so that you can get the maximum freedom from it."

"Of course. Hitler said to the German people: It is necessary for me to have supreme power in order that I may give you all you want and make you the greatest people in the world. They obviously believed him and were thus freed from the necessity of having anything to do with politics. Any who questioned his consciousness of necessity were disposed of in scientific ways which we now know."

"But we knew Hitler was wrong from the beginning."

"Yes. We had different ideas from him of what constituted necessity and freedom in human affairs. But we had exactly the same ideas concerning explosives and two and two making four."

"Did you argue like that with Ranald?"

"No. But I have been haunted by it since."

"I wish you had. He can explain everything. I do not say that lightly or foolishly. But there is a whole philosophy, covering history and necessity, covering every conceivable kind of argument, which—just—does have the answers."

"I know. He could flatten me out. I was even nervous of talking to him. I felt his certainty in him. But that does not alter me. No dictator will ever convince me, for example, that it is desirable to attain freedom from freedom of discussion or criticism. Nor do I think that he will finally prove his point by shooting me for opening my mouth."

Nan looked at her for a long moment, a smile dawning in her face. "Would you like your cigarette holder?"

"You're a young monkey," said Aunt Phemie; "that's what you are."

"You can have no idea of the amount of good this is doing me," said Nan.

"Well, you have had enough good for one night. And it's time we both were in bed. I'll only add this, that it's not his philosophy I am questioning: it's the application of it. And that's what is so terribly important to us as women."

"Why us as women?"

"Because when men get theories in the head, they go mad."

Nan's smile sank deep. "And what happens when women get theories in the head?"

"They go doubly mad."

Nan laughed softly. "This sounds so beautifully illogical—and true! It warms me." She looked around the kitchen. "I feel we are like two women sitting at the bottom of the well of the world."

"With the something that is missing in our hearts."

"Yes!" said Nan with a brilliant flash from her eyes. "And we cannot climb up to give it."

Aunt Phemie smiled. "Perhaps that's it. Perhaps," she added with a deepening humour, "it may be that we are not illogical at all but quite scientific. For what can be complete—if something is missing?"

"Q.E.D. Quod erat demonstrandum." Nan swayed. "How we loved the important sound of it at school—and laughed, shutting the book with a slap!"

"And it isn't enough," said Aunt Phemie, "to say: we'll leave the something out meantime. Emotion is part of us, by far the greater part indeed. That, anyhow, is how it seems to me."

"And if you leave it out—leave out kindness and love, say—believing it's only for a little time, you may end by leaving it out altogether."

"Something else, the opposite emotion, takes its place. Perhaps it's dialectical."

"Lovely!" exclaimed Nan.

"Instead of kindness, malice. Instead of love, hate. But the awful thing seems to be that once folk like—like Know-all—I can't help thinking about him—once people like that say you have got to hate and destroy in order that you may create——"Aunt Phemie shook her head. "I may be a sentimental woman, my dear. And I am not now thinking of Christianity, or com-munism, or anarchism, or capitalism, or any system at all. But if I said to Know-all: All right, let us hate and destroy in order that we may create love and kindness and tolerance, what would he think?"

"He would think you had a smell," said Nan, her face hardening.

Aunt Phemie nodded. "Hate feeds on itself. He now wants power, in order to show you how he would deal with the old virtues—that soft dangerous muck. Am I right?"

"About him—yes. But you terribly misunderstand, in other ways," said Nan with a glisten of pain in her eyes. "Ranald is not like that. You don't know him. You only saw him for a little while. He must have seemed unreal to you. But he is very real. We had lovely times together. Gay and full of fun. There's something you have got to get through—to reach him. I can't explain it to you."

"My dear, I wasn't thinking of Ranald," said Aunt Phemie gently. "I was thinking of what has happened to the world—and may happen again even more terribly. Like a foolish woman I ask: How *could* it happen? What was the something that did it? And I know it could only have been something in the mind of man."

"We're at the bottom of the well again," said Nan with a twisted smile.

"It did happen," repeated Aunt Phemie fatally. Then she stirred with a smile. "Your clever friends would think us not a little vague and sentimental. So let us be sensible and go to bed."

6

Aunt Phemie was worried. If her idea had been, however indirectly, through whatever kind of talk, to lead Nan away from Ranald, or at least to set her on her own feet so that time and judgement would be given a chance, she now realised she had to dismiss it. It was clear that Nan had made up her mind. She was going back to London to be with Ranald, probably to live with him. And in some profound sort of way her mind had matured. For Aunt Phemie now definitely to go against her in this would not do any good, and it might do harm. It would do harm. In a lost moment Nan might again need someone with her in the well at the bottom of the world!

Aunt Phemie smiled a trifle grimly as she drove on. When she found out all there was to find out from the police, she would write Ranald. She parked her car in the station square and went down to the police station. A constable, writing at a desk, believed that the inspector was in. Presently he opened a door and Inspector Geddes, when he was informed by Mrs. Robertson that she wished to speak to him, asked her to sit down.

His face was curiously bare and expressionless, his water-blue eyes steady and without any feeling. Without his hat he looked like a church elder and spoke in a slow quiet voice.

"I have called to see you about my niece, Nan Gordon, who has been staying with me." Aunt Phemie paused for a moment, but as he had nothing to say, she continued, "I understood that you might have wanted to see her. She had not been well, as I gather the doctor told you. She has really had a very bad time, following a nervous breakdown in London. I was wondering whether you needed anything from her?"

"To what exactly are you referring?" he asked without any stress, his eyes on her face.

"Well, it was in connection with the discovery of the body in the mountains. She had nothing to do with it, but I just wondered if—if anything more was needed?"

"Would she like to make a statement?"

"Oh no," said Aunt Phemie. "That, frankly, is just what I was hoping she would not have to do. I should not like her to get troubled again. I was hoping the doctor had made that clear."

"He did," said the inspector.

"Then—then I hope that's all right. She is due to go back to London soon. I was in town and I thought I would just come and tell you."

"I see." He sat quite still. "She knows Mr. Adam McAlpine?"

"She met him, by chance, at the Altfey burn. That's really all."

"She saw the body?"

"I think she saw something, but she was very confused about it. Earlier, she had overheard some of the farm workers giving gruesome details of the murder of old Farquhar. That upset her badly. She had been through the London blitz, and came home, as I say, in a very nervous condition, for a quiet rest. It was too much for her. You can understand that?"

He gave a small nod and remained thoughtful. "The body had been drowned. The doctor's report and the Procurator-Fiscal's investigation were satisfactory. As far as your niece is concerned I see no particular reason for further action. She is well enough now?"

"She is getting on, thank you. In fact I have had her out helping with the harvest." Aunt Phemie's tone had lightened and she smiled.

"You know Adam McAlpine very well yourself?"

"No," said Aunt Phemie at once. "I don't know him well. But I was talking to him in town one day." She stirred and her brows gathered very slightly. "As you can understand, Inspector, I have been very troubled about my niece. I just felt it was too bad that she should have had that set-back. I wanted to find out all I could. I did not want any more trouble, if I could help it." Her manner now was frank and forthright.

"Did you find out anything?"

"No. I admit he's a bit difficult to bring to the point, but I satisfied myself that his meeting with my niece had been accidental and that on the whole he did his best to help her. It was all clear enough."

"You found him difficult?"

"I felt he didn't like to be questioned. I don't think he meant anything by it, but—well——" She smiled.

He nodded quite distinctly. "I had some difficulty with him—over another matter." He looked at her.

"Had you? I ran him out to collect his painting materials which he had left at the shepherd's cottage. That helped our talk."

"You know what happened out there?"

"I had heard about it—actually from our postman."

"Only from the postman?"

"Yes." She held his eyes.

"Mr. McAlpine didn't say anything about it?" he asked.

"Yes, he did. It was a bit of a shock to me. We had a young man staying with us, but he said nothing."

"Nothing at all?"

"No."

"Do you think Mr. Ranald Surrey was the man who—shoved McAlpine into the river?"

"I'll tell you all I know, Inspector. Mr. Surrey said nothing to us, but he was marked on the face. He said when he came in that he had simply had a fall. That was the day it happened. Now I don't know what Mr. McAlpine said to you. But I gathered from him that he and Mr. Surrey had had a difference of opinion at the falls pool. Mr. Surrey said nothing of that to us."

"Why?"

"I suppose because he didn't want to upset my niece. He and she were—well, more than friends in London. In fact it was I who asked him to come up, thinking that his presence for a few days would help her. Now I had told him how my niece had had her set-back, about her meeting with Mr. McAlpine and the discovery of the body. So the conclusion I came to was that Mr. Surrey had met Mr. McAlpine at the falls pool and began to question him about his conduct. And that would have been enough to start anything!"

Inspector Geddes leaned back and nodded more than once, slowly. A smile made his face suddenly human. "That was just the final confirmation I wanted. As Mr. McAlpine has made no charge against anyone, we had nothing to act on. I suspected the girl in the case, but this makes it all clear. I see."

"I am glad if I have been of any help." She paused. "And I don't know if Mr. Surrey did actually knock Mr. McAlpine into the river."

"What makes you think that?"

"Mr. McAlpine said to me that he fell in—that he stepped back over the ledge or something like that."

Inspector Geddes smiled very dryly. "Apparently he volunteered—some such information—to the Fiscal, for he wouldn't tell me much. I concluded that that was his vanity. Presumably he would not like to admit that Mr. Surrey had been capable of assisting him over the ledge."

Aunt Phemie said nothing, for the inspector had contrived a considerable condensation of venom and satisfaction in his last sentence. Clearly he was pleased with Ranald.

"There was a time," he went on, moved further to speech, "when we thought we might have had to question you all at Greenbank. But as we knew exactly when Mr. Surrey had arrived, it was clear that there could be no possible bearing on the Farquhar case. Actually there never was much doubt, I may say, particularly after the body of Gordon MacMaster had been examined—and the clothing and boots."

"He—did do it?"

"We think there can be no doubt about it. The evidence he left at the cottage was very clear. As it happened it had been raining the night before and there's a lot of mud about the cottage. The story was written in the gutters, the mud. And he left behind one or two personal things, including his bonnet. Then we knew his history. When he got crossed he was very excitable. There was something a little weak—here." The inspector almost touched his forehead. "Occasionally he got a craving for drink. It was a sad case; a legacy of the last war."

"Dreadful," murmured Aunt Phemie.

"Yes. Gordon MacMaster was old Farquhar's special friend. He spent an occasional night there. But the old man was a bit tight with money."

"Did you find the money?"

"We found the deposit receipt, as you may know. But no notes. Our theory now is that when Gordie came properly to himself, he would throw the money from him or stuff it in a hole. He was not a bad fellow. He must have crossed the burn above the falls; that would be on his direct way to the mountains. When he realised what he had done, he would be making off, away from every living place. The deposit receipt was dropped or thrown in the burn, carried down, and cast up on the stones, where it got caught. Actually we don't know if there was any more paper money. We think it likely, but we don't know. Farquhar may have had a hidey-hole for it. We have searched his cottage upside down. But when old men go like that about money—they're queer."

There was silence for a little while. The inspector had accepted Mrs. Robertson as a responsible citizen, and now she got an entirely different impression of him. The dull blue of his eyes, though still without any lively expression, had yet a certain weariness, almost sadness, as if he did not sleep well or had trouble at home. She also got the impression that though his movements were slow, he would arrive there, like fate.

"It affected us all very much," said Aunt Phemie. "My niece felt that a shadow—the death and destruction she had come through—had followed her. You can understand that. And it seemed terrible in our quiet countryside."

He smiled a trifle sardonically. "If you knew the number of cases of stolen goods—motor cars and bicycles and house-breakings—that we have on hand, you might be surprised. Not to mention violence and fire-raising. If we have another war, it's not the police we'll be needing next time but a Gestapo."

"You think so?"

"I know."

Aunt Phemie could not speak for a moment. "It's very terrible."

"Ay, it's a bad look-out for the world. Men lie now as naturally as they drink. It's a case of: Can I get off with it?"

"Not all men surely?"

"Perhaps not. But enough." Then he added, "What did you think of Adam McAlpine?" as though this question underlay all his talk.

"Well," replied Aunt Phemie, gathering her wits, "I thought he was peculiar, abrupt, but I must say I thought he was honest. He did not strike me as the sort of man who would scheme out anything."

"You think not?"

"I should say definitely not. He might get carried away, on the spur of the moment, but I think—I think—that deep in him there is—is something—I rather like." Her eyes gleamed as with an unexpected discovery. "Of course I'm only talking from a single impression."

"I'm afraid he certainly did not like *us*."

"No," said Aunt Phemie. "I suppose he wouldn't."

"Why do you suppose so?" The cool question came rather quickly.

"Because," answered Aunt Phemie, "I think he is the kind who will have a hatred of any authority. It may have something to do with his upbringing. I simply don't know."

"Well," said Inspector Geddes, "he'll have to learn to understand and obey authority or one of these days it is going to be the worse for him. I have the notion that he knew more about Gordon MacMaster's movements on the fatal day than he cared to let on."

"Not really?" Her eyes were on the inspector's face.

"I'm not saying it had anything to do with the murder itself. I don't think it had. But we know he was up there painting—at the falls—very early in the morning. He saw someone. He said afterwards it was the shepherd. But it seemed queer to me that he should on that occasion have been there so early."

Aunt Phemie had turned her face to the window. She knew the inspector was waiting, but the words that formed in her mind, of their own accord and with a staggering effect of irony, were:

Perhaps he wanted to see the early light of the world being sucked under! She actually said, "All I know about painters is that they are interested in light at all times of the day."

"Are they?"

His laconic tone drew her eyes. "I understand so."

"My information is to the effect that if an artist was painting in an afternoon light, he would not also be wanting to paint onto the same picture in a morning light."

She nodded thoughtfully. She just could not begin to explain that an artist might want to get the intimate feel of his subject in all lights. For one rather cold and terrible moment she glimpsed what seemed an eternal antithesis between Authority and the Artist.

"And then when he reported that he had found the body. ... However," and the inspector squared his shoulders, "the shepherd had seen your niece in his company and that made a difference. If it hadn't been that he was more amenable with the Fiscal, he mightn't be in London yet."

"Is he gone then?"

"Yes."

Aunt Phemie broke the silence. "It's been very good of you, Inspector, to have helped me like this. I hesitated coming but— I should not hesitate again."

"That's all right, Mrs. Robertson. Perhaps you have helped to clear my mind, too."

They shook hands and Aunt Phemie left. As she drove home, she was satisfied she could now write Ranald and invite him up again and include in her letter some innocuous statement about having met Adam McAlpine. That would be bound to ease his mind. *Surely it would?* she asked of herself far inwardly, with a sharp recurrence of the old hopeless distress.

7

Rain comes; but the weather glass goes down so quickly that it will start going up again very soon. Thunder in the warm September air; heavy clouds. It clears by midday and here's a drying wind. On the lower fields the grain was stacked, but now as Aunt Phemie and Nan wandered up by the top field which Nan had helped to cut, the stooks, having bowed their heads just perceptibly under the rain, had forgotten to lift them. "They are dead ripe," said Aunt Phemie, pausing to straighten a couple of drunken sheaves.

Nan regarded the whole field, the long rows of stooks wandering up and over those swelling breasts of land where she had driven the tractor. "I feel they are largely mine," she said.

"You think you own them now?" suggested Aunt Phemie with a speculative smile.

"No," replied Nan. "I feel I know them. There is something between us."

Aunt Phemie laughed lightly as she lifted the small canvas satchel containing their picnic tea. It was Sunday and the fields were quiet.

"I have a real grievance," Nan continued. "I should have been at the leading of this field, and now to-morrow I'm off. There's something all wrong about that."

"Despite your blisters?"

"Despite my blisters," replied Nan involuntarily looking at her hands for she had kept forking sheaves to the floats with an undefeatable persistence. She continued on her way, with a glance for the Dark Wood over on the right. Aunt Phemie followed, her eyes for a moment holding a detached appreciation of the carriage of Nan's head and the easy movement of her body. Whatever else might come to that body, health had for the time being come to dwell there anyway. Aunt Phemie could reasonably take some satisfaction to herself for that. They were all under heaven, under rain and storm and sun, but the stooks did contrive to appear. One could have hope.

"Where now?" asked Aunt Phemie, as Nan bore slightly to the left.

Nan turned her head over her shoulder. "You would never guess my secret intention." She contemplated Aunt Phemie with a veiled amusement then strode on with a laugh.

"Nan Gordon, if you think you are going to drag me——"

"No preaching, please. Besides, where do you think I am going to drag you?" She stopped.

Aunt Phemie looked at her steadily. "Well, where?"

Nan suddenly took the satchel from her. "It's my turn." In the slight confusion, she said, "I want to put a circle sunwise round the shadow. That will keep you quite safe till I come back."

"You're quite daft," said Aunt Phemie, "completely daft."

"To-day you are in my hands," said Nan, "blisters an' all. You promised."

Aunt Phemie sighed. Nan took her arm for a pace or two and shook her. "The stooks have gone to my head," she whispered, "but don't tell anyone." She broke away and walked on.

They crossed the moor slowly because Nan, in the exuberance of her health, found an insatiable interest in everything that grew or ran or flew. By the time they reached the burn, panting, she mimicked old Will's voice: "I'm fair sweatin'." She blew on her jumper at the neck and shook it, sending air currents down her breast, and fanned herself with her arms, and then finding that she was really waving her arms, she shouted "Hurrah!"

Aunt Phemie sat down. "I'm fair longing for my tea."

Nan swooped on her and snatched the satchel away; as quickly she sat by Aunt Phemie, her hands decorously in her lap. "I'm going to tell you a story. Do you see that pool there, just there, with the bubbles coming in behind the boulder in a jingaring." She nodded to the bubbles and looked sideways at Aunt Phemie.

"I observe them," remarked Aunt Phemie.

"Thank you," said Nan. "Observe them closely, and on dark days and in diverse places they will perform for you, sometimes with the grace of a minuet, sometimes with the whirl and breakaway of an eightsome reel. I have come to the conclusion after much thought—and not inconsiderable experience—that they represent the treasure we lay up for ourselves on earth."

"And heaven?"

"I don't know about heaven," replied Nan in the same courteous manner, "but with this treasure in my hands I am prepared, in the vulgar parlance of our day, to take a chance on God."

"You would present Him with his own creation?"

"From my heart," concluded Nan. "Now I was about to tell you a story. Once upon a time I was bathing in that pool and some of the bubbles sailed away laughing, for the pool and myself made a great commotion, shouting and splashing together. Then I climbed out and sunned myself dry on the rock. Then I dressed and sat me down, and in the same moment a man appeared before me. As he had not been visible anywhere on the moor, I was forced to conclude that he had been lying just over there watching me in the pool."

"You did not tell me this?"

"No," answered Nan. "I was disturbed at that time. The man was Adam. He is no more to me now than the first Adam. But then he disturbed me. There was something in him that I knew. I know it still. But I could never go with him on his road. I cannot tell you why. Perhaps I am afraid of going too far; something warns me. I think the thing that warns me is life, but I am not sure. A woman's life and the stooks and the harvest. But I am not sure, Aunt Phemie."

"You just feel you know?"

"Yes, I feel I know."

"Was he unpleasant?" asked Aunt Phemie.

"Oh no." And then Nan told how they went up as far as the little falls and parted on that day. Her tone became simpler as she described how they met again and set out for the peat hags and black lochans in the lost boggy place between one mountain and another, but now there was an inflection of strangeness as in the voice of one telling a disturbing dream. The personal nature of this was warm in her cheeks and visible in her lashes, for sometimes her eyes regarded her fingers as they tilted up the starry purple florets on a stalk of heather before lifting swiftly and glistening-bright to the mountains again.

"Why did he want to go there?" asked Aunt Phemie following the slow barren curve of the strath.

"He said he wanted to take me to the source. Not only the

source of the burn. I don't know," replied Nan. After a little she went on, "He had a peculiar kind of humour. I can see the expression in his eyes when he said, 'I'll show you what we come out of.' But it was not nasty. It was exciting, yet I didn't want it. Yet I was curious. I thought: This once, just this once, in order to see."

Aunt Phemie nodded.

"So I went." Nan paused. "But there was also something else. But I am not too sure about it now, because I find it difficult to know what actually happened or what I dreamed afterwards. Talk about primeval creatures of the slime!" She smiled wanly. "Horrible, oh horrible!" She shook her head. "Isn't it awful that the mind can be like that? That it can make things like that, give eyes to peat-hags and lift gaping jaws and slither and roll over? And not only that, but the something behind it, that *does* it. I can't explain. It's worse than the horrors we know now, the unthinkable war horrors that men can commit. They daze us. We get sort of glutted. But you have to be nearly mad—perhaps quite mad for long moments—to know what—what *does* it."

"My dear," murmured Aunt Phemie.

"Let me get it over," said Nan. "I had the awful feeling that he knew something *more*. He said it was the sort of place that a murderer would make for; not the businesslike murderer that we know to-day, but the one who would waken to a feeling of guilt. The old-fashioned murderer. It was an elaborate kind of joke for Adam, but there was something in it that—that worked me up. Though of course I showed nothing. I tried not to anyway. And then we sat down. He began to look at me and make love with his looks and his words. And then he put his hands on me, not—not roughly—but—but I went mad, screaming and tearing away... I don't blame him. I asked for it. He could not know that I was trying to—to conquer the shadow! He caught me and held me. We staggered and I believe I would have gone in. The hump in the water. He pulled, and the face came up, sideways first ..." Nan's head bowed, her eyes shut, and her hands closed into two tight fists.

Aunt Phemie sat staring at the mountains in a deep anguish. Presently she looked at Nan to find her smiling.

"Merely a small twinge," said Nan.

But Aunt Phemie could not match her change of mood and looked about for the tea satchel.

Nan shook her head. "No," she said. "This is my day. And first of all we're going to bathe. I'm going into that pool there, and you're going into the one below. We need one each for freedom——"

"Me!"

"Now, listen. Please, Aunt Phemie. Do it. The pool will take it away. Then we'll be washed and cleansed and in our right skins. I'm not asking you lightly. Please."

"But we have nothing to dry ourselves with even."

"My dear, look!" And Nan exhibited with a gesture the sky and the sun. "Oh, Aunt Phemie, Aunt Phemie!" and she brought her open hands against her breasts, and smiled, and jumped up.

When they had bathed and drunk their tea and were going down the burnside, Aunt Phemie admitted that a certain lightness had come upon her, for she saw at the same time that not only a lightness but a strength had come upon Nan, and inwardly she marvelled at a something of wisdom which that blithe body out of its terrors had contrived to distil, and again she was aware, as in the cornfield, of hope stirring in the mysterious essence of the world.

Nan told about the hawk, quite naturally now, freed from any stress or mannerism, and they inspected the falls pool in the gorge; but Aunt Phemie said nothing of what had happened there. They left the pool and came back until Nan paused by a path going up slantwise through the birches. It was hardly more than a sheep track. "I have wondered where that goes," she said.

"You'll have to go on wondering," replied Aunt Phemie.

"I have the feeling it goes up towards Farquhar's cottage."

As Aunt Phemie had had the same feeling, she said lightly, "In that case it's too steep for me."

"You know it's not," said Nan. "Come on. Let's go."

"Nan Gordon——"

"It's my day. And you know it's not morbid. I want to go."

"Now look——"

"Please, Aunt Phemie. Come with me. Come on. Do."

It was a long climb and once when they rested Nan said, "I'll tell you a queer thing. You know when I was talking about these horrors. The odd bit is that it's yourself, the thing you know as *yourself* that's horrified. You hate these things and want to escape from them. They are not you, not the real you. Yet I suppose they must be, for if you imagine them where can they come from but yourself?"

"I have always found that difficult," answered Aunt Phemie, "and no amount of dividing up the mind into ids and super-egos and censors ever quite convinced me. So I gave it up!"

"I don't care what they say. It's not just developing a conscience. The horror is beyond that, and the I that escapes it is the—is the whole being or soul. It's so easy to have theories about it. But the experience itself has an absoluteness about it … I don't know." Nan looked about her and saw that autumn had touched the birches since she had been in the gorge last. "I suppose theories are necessary," she said.

Aunt Phemie laughed as she glanced at Nan and saw her eyes on the yellow streaks painted here and there upon the green leaves. The gorge in the September stillness of the afternoon hung in a tranced beauty.

When they came upon the cottage they involuntarily stood at a little distance from it. It was a long building on a very slight slope, the upper part being the dwelling-house, the lower part the byre. The dwelling-house had a tarred felt roof; the byre was thatched, with weeds growing out of the old straw. The door of the byre stood open, but the entrance to the dwelling-house had been boarded up; the new nailed planks were like scars. The two small windows were dark and blind. They had expected an air of death and desertion but not this ominous stillness, this feeling that the acts of the horrid drama had been left invisibly behind. Nan went slowly forward. Aunt Phemie glanced about her but could not raise her voice to call Nan. She tried to be sensible and glance around, but her eyes on their own were searching ahead for the police inspector's story in the mud. Some hens' feathers about her feet and the deep cloven imprints of hoofs in the grass startled her into realising that, of course, there must have been animal life about the place. She wondered who had taken the living things away and thought of the police. Nan was standing at a little distance from the door of the cottage and Aunt Phemie could see she was hesitating about going to the kitchen window to look in. As she went and took Nan's arm she said quietly, "Come, let us go." Nan regarded her with a curious, remote smile. "Wait," she said and left Aunt Phemie, going down towards the byre. She passed the open door slowly, like a curious schoolgirl, and, with a look over her shoulder at Aunt Phemie, disappeared round the lower end of the cottage. Aunt Phemie started after her, then stopped. A touch of panic or anger made her want to shout to Nan to come back. She stood, feeling a horrible nakedness in their intrusion, and glanced about her. This was awful. She waited, suddenly aware that she was guarding the eyes of the windows from Nan. But after a time she could wait no longer and started down towards the byre. A light-voiced "Hullo!" swung her back. Nan had gone right round the building and was now coming to meet her. Aunt Phemie's expression did not soften. "Let us go," she said, turning away, and they left the cottage, walking in silence.

They went over the rise, saw the moor stretching away below them, the Dark Wood, the fields of Aunt Phemie's farm, and the whole broad familiar valley. The sun had set beyond the mountains; its great afterglow was hazed and silver-molten, with red on massive cloud banks in the south. Nan looked at it all but did not speak. Aunt Phemie took the slanting path down the slope, and presently left it to follow a narrow track amid tall bracken. As Nan contemplated Aunt Phemie's purposeful back, she smiled to herself in a truant way. As they neared the bottom, she asked, "You're not annoyed with me, are you, Aunt Phemie?"

"No," replied Aunt Phemie calmly and without turning round, "but I didn't like it."

"I didn't like it either," said Nan, "but I'm glad I did it."

As they came out of the bracken on a last few yards of green slope, Aunt Phemie stopped.

"You see," said Nan coming beside her, "I had to be freed from it."

Aunt Phemie looked at her, at the shy searching humour in the eyes, and said, "You're just a monkey!"

Nan caught her arm affectionately. "Let us sit down. I'm tired."

They sat down. "You'll forgive me, my dear," said Aunt Phemie. "I hadn't thought of it like that. I suppose I felt I should have kept you from it."

"Oh, Aunt Phemie," said Nan, "you make me feel a fraud. You're so good to me. Do you know what I did, what I wanted to do?"

Aunt Phemie looked at her.

"You may think it childish, but try to understand, too. Will you?"

"Proceed," said Aunt Phemie.

"All these figures of men stalking about, and murder. Did you feel them," she asked in a quieter voice, "about the old cottage?"

"Well?" Aunt Phemie waited.

"I put," said Nan, "a sun-circle round the cottage. I thought that might help."

"Perhaps it will," said Aunt Phemie.

"I know what you are thinking. You are thinking: So long as it will help me." Nan nodded. "But I also said a few words. I won't tell you what. Words of peace—for those gone and for those to come. That's all."

"That was very lovely of you, my dear," said Aunt Phemie, moved.

"What more can we do?" asked Nan.

"If only we could all do that."

"I know," said Nan, "and oh! if only we could be free to talk like this, naturally; not to see the sneering face."

There was silence for a little and then Aunt Phemie felt, from a glimpse of Nan's expression which had gone still and serious, that all this play was leading to something more definite.

"I am going back to London. I have made up my mind, Aunt Phemie. I am going to help Ranald all I can. I shall give him all that's in me. But I shall never betray—this world—all this, that's in me and you. That's, maybe, all I have to give."

Aunt Phemie could not speak.

"Perhaps you don't agree with me," said Nan. "Maybe I understand that, too. But it's what I have got to do. And this time—I'll not break easily." She smiled.

"You feel that's your duty? What you can do for yourself and the world?" asked Aunt Phemie quietly.

Nan glanced at her and then picked about the grass with her fingers. "You are forgetting what we found at the bottom of the well of the world."

Aunt Phemie looked at her.

Nan met the look for a moment with bright glancing eyes. "Love," she murmured.

Aunt Phemie sat quite still, staring over the moor. Then she nodded. Nan, with a quick look, saw that tears had come into her eyes; in her own profound way, Aunt Phemie had at last understood and agreed.

As they went on, Nan said, "We'll go back through the Dark Wood; it's on our way home anyway."

Aunt Phemie, through a sudden deeper meaning in the simple words, smiled to her. In a moment Nan was delighted and caught her arm. But some little distance from the wood, Nan stopped dramatically. "Listen!" she said, breathless in the vivid moment. A bird was singing in the Dark Wood.